the dolls

the dolls

KIKI SULLIVAN

BALZER + BRAY

An Imprint of HarperCollins*Publishers*

Balzer + Bray is an imprint of HarperCollins Publishers.

The Dolls

Library of Congress Cataloging-in-Publication Data
Sullivan, Kiki.
    The dolls / Kiki Sullivan. — First edition.
        pages   cm
    Summary: "Eveny Cheval returns to Louisiana after growing up in
New York and discovers she's a voodoo queen" — Provided by publisher.
    ISBN 978-0-06-228148-7 (paperback)
    [1. Voodoo—Fiction. 2. Friendship—Fiction. 3. Louisiana—Fic-
tion.]   I. Title.
PZ7.S9524Do   2014   2013047968
[Fic]—dc23   CIP
                                                                AC

Typography by Torborg Davern
14 15 16 17 18   LP/RRDH   10 9 8 7 6 5 4 3 2 1
❖
First Edition

TO JAMES, CHLOE, EDDIE, AND COLTON:

I CAN'T WAIT TO SEE WHO YOU GROW UP TO BE

I

When I open my eyes and blink into the milky morning sunlight, there's no longer snow on the ground outside the car. Instead of the brown-gray tableau of a New York winter, endless cypress trees line the road, their branches heavy with Spanish moss and their green leaves catching the first rays of dawn.

As I struggle upright from a deep slouch in the passenger seat, it takes me a second to remember exactly where we are: Louisiana—or en route to Louisiana, anyhow. I'd fallen asleep just before midnight some eight hundred miles into our drive. Now, just after six a.m., thick white fog swirls around us, making it seem like we've been swallowed whole by a silent, drooping forest.

"Good morning," I croak, unwinding a tangle of red hair from my watchband.

"Morning, sleepyhead," Aunt Bea replies without turning. She's focused intently on the road ahead as if expecting cross traffic, though the woods appear entirely deserted. "Did you sleep okay?"

I glance at my watch. "I guess I did," I say. "How are you feeling?" She's been awake for at least a day, running on coffee and Red Bull.

"I'm hanging in," Aunt Bea says, her face taut with exhaustion. "We'll be there soon."

"Cool." I try to smile, but it comes out as a grimace. I still don't understand why we're doing this.

Three days ago, my life was normal: winter break was almost over, and I was getting ready to celebrate my birthday and start the second semester of junior year. Then Aunt Bea—my legal guardian since I was three—announced over coffee and Cheerios that we were moving back to Carrefour, Louisiana, the town we left fourteen years ago right after my mom killed herself.

"I miss Brooklyn already," I murmur as I look out the window again.

"Give Carrefour a chance, Eveny. Believe me when I say you'll fit in fine."

"You don't know that." The thing is, I've always felt a half step different from everyone else, more at home in gardens and with plants than with real people. Still, I managed to develop a small, tight-knit group of friends back in New York. Starting over feels daunting.

"Carrefour isn't exactly new to you," Aunt Bea says, reading my mind. "People will know who you are."

"That's what I'm afraid of: being the girl whose mom offed herself by driving into a tree."

"Oh, Eveny," Aunt Bea sighs, "no one's going to judge you for that. If anything, they'll feel bad for you."

"I definitely don't need anyone's pity." After all, my memories of my mom are all good ones—up until the day it all ended.

"You know, it's okay to let people in," Aunt Bea says after a pause. "Your mom being gone is still hard for me too. But you deserve to know who she really was. I think being in Carrefour, where people knew her, will be a good thing."

She looks miserable, so I force a smile and say, "Moving back will be good for you too."

Aunt Bea's been dreaming for years about opening her own bakery, but in New York she could never afford to do it. In Carrefour, she'll be leasing a kitchen space downtown and is already making plans to open within the next week and a half. As frustrated as I am about this move, it will be positive for her, at least. And that's something.

I take a deep breath and add, "If you think this is the right thing, I'm on board." I spend the next hour of the drive trying to convince myself the words are true.

It's 8:46 in the morning and I'm texting with my best friend Meredith when Aunt Bea announces, in a voice that sounds oddly choked, that we're almost there.

I look up in surprise as we approach an impenetrable-looking iron gate. On either side, as far as I can see, a stone wall ten feet tall extends into the swampy forest. Above the gate is a rusted sign that says *Carrefour, Louisiana: Residents Only* in swirling script.

"Residents only?" I ask. "How are we going to get in?"

"We're residents, Eveny." Aunt Bea shifts the car into park and steps out into the foggy morning. She rummages in her purse for a moment before pulling out an antique-looking bronze key. She inserts it into an ornate keyhole and hurries back to the car just as the gate begins to creak loudly open.

"What the . . . ?" I say, my voice trailing off as she gets in and begins driving through. I turn around and watch as the gate closes slowly behind us, its hinges squealing in protest. "What *was* that?"

"My key to Carrefour," she says, like it's the most obvious thing in the world. "Every family has one. It's the only way in or out."

"Weird," I murmur. We continue through a swampy area that gets darker and darker as more tangled branches stretch overhead. Mist is rising from the shallow water surrounding the road, and as we break through a clearing, my confusion deepens. I thought I'd recognize Carrefour right away, but this place doesn't look at all familiar.

The town that lives in my memories is southern, Gothic, and filled with old mansions and stately, moss-draped cypress trees. But what's rolling by my window is a lot plainer than that, making me wonder if I've imagined everything. Bland row houses line the paved streets, and kids play in a few of the yards. I see a yellow car jacked up on bricks in front of one of the homes and a cluster of plump, middle-aged women wearing dresses and wide-brimmed hats sitting on a front porch of another. A tangle of little boys kicks a soccer ball lazily around the end of a street, and two girls ride rusted bikes in circles at the end of a cul-de-sac.

"This is Carrefour?" I ask.

"*Technically*, yes," Aunt Bea responds. "But you didn't spend much time out here in the Périphérie."

The name rings a vague bell, but I can't place it. Behind the row houses, I glimpse marshy wetlands, gnarled cypresses, and a pale green film on the surface of what appears to be a stagnant creek. Spanish moss hangs from hickory branches that arch over the road like a canopy. Above them, the sky swirls with the dark clouds of a coming storm.

I look out the window again, feeling a little sad. "I just don't remember the town looking like this." Not that I'm judging. I loved the cluttered disarray of Brooklyn. But I'd always thought of Carrefour as so opulent—and so wealthy.

"This was always the . . . less privileged area of Carrefour," Aunt Bea says, her brow creasing. "But it seems like it's gotten a whole lot worse since we left."

"Because of the bad economy?" I guess as the road leads us past the last dilapidated house and into a deep, misty forest.

"Maybe," she says slowly. "But I'd be willing to bet central Carrefour is doing just fine."

As we round another bend and emerge from the woods, sunlight suddenly streams in from all directions. In under a half mile, we've driven into an entirely different world.

Just beyond the final creeping cypress tree of the Périphérie sits the edge of the most perfect-looking town I've ever seen. As we begin making our way through a neighborhood, I see immaculately manicured lawns, houses with picket fences and matching shutters, and gardens blooming in brilliant color even though it's January. "It's like one big country club," I say.

I stare out the window as Aunt Bea takes a left, turning into what appears to be Carrefour's downtown area. On the corner there's an ice cream parlor flanked by a café with an old-fashioned *Enjoy a Coke* sign out front, and beside it a little French bistro called Maxine's. A half dozen shops that look like they belong in an Atlantic seaside resort town—not middle-of-nowhere Louisiana—extend down the left side of the street.

"That's where my bakery will be," Aunt Bea says, pointing to a sliver of storefront next door to a boutique called Lulu's. "It used to be a little walk-up hamburger stand when your mom and I were kids."

Perfect canopies of blue and white stripes shade the sidewalks of the main street—which is actually called Main Street—and the store windows are all cloaked in curtains of sea-foam green and pale yellow. The buildings are a uniform clapboard white, and the people strolling along look like they've been plucked from Martha's Vineyard and dropped here in their shirtdresses, khakis, and button-down shirts.

"They know it's winter, right?" I ask as I watch two women emerge from the market with a wicker picnic basket. "And that they're not actually on their way to a clambake?"

Aunt Bea laughs. "Roll down the windows. It won't feel like winter here."

I give her a skeptical look, but by the time my window is halfway down, I realize that it must be in the low seventies outside. "But it's January," I say.

"It's Carrefour," she says without explaining.

"Does everything here look like a postcard?" I ask, wriggling out of the sweatshirt I've been wearing since we left New York.

"Wait until you see our house," she says, and, suddenly, I feel uneasy. The last clear memory I have of this town is standing in our front hallway with my mother's two best friends, Ms. St. Pierre and Ms. Marceau, as the police chief arrived to tell me the news. *Honey, your mama killed herself,* he'd drawled. *Drove right into a tree.* I'd screamed and screamed until I passed out.

"There's your school." Bea cuts into my thoughts as we pass a sprawling brick building with an ornate sign that reads *Pointe Laveau Academy* in Victorian script, just like the entrance gate. The parking lot is full of expensive sports cars, and two impossibly thin girls in white oxfords, maroon plaid skirts, and knee socks walk across the lawn, deep in conversation.

"Isn't there a public school in town?" My skin itches just thinking about wearing a uniform, never mind fitting in with a bunch of rich kids.

"There is," Aunt Bea answers lightly, "but your great-grandmother founded Pointe Laveau Academy, and it's where your grandma, your mom, and I went."

I'm about to argue, but then I look out the window and realize the sun has slipped behind the clouds, casting long, eerie shadows over the cemetery we're about to pass on the edge of town. Suddenly, a vivid memory hits me like a punch to the gut.

It's my mother's funeral, and I'm standing among soaring white tombs, my eyes sore from crying. A man with sandy hair and dark sunglasses slips from the shadows and bends to speak to me, his voice low, his words fast. "You must listen to me, Eveny, I don't have much time." He's a stranger, but there's something familiar about him. "They're coming for you. You have to be ready." He melts back into the shadows before I can ask what he means. . . .

I gasp and push the image away as I try to catch my breath.

Aunt Bea looks at me sharply. "What's wrong?"

"Nothing," I say. "Just a weird memory." I hesitate. "Of Mom's funeral."

"Honey, you were only three then," Aunt Bea says gently. I don't think I'm imagining the concern on her face. "What are you remembering?"

I feel silly, because how can I recall someone I've never

met, someone who left before I was even born, someone I've only seen one picture of in my life?

"I think my father was—" I start to say, but the words get caught in my throat as I notice a shirtless guy jogging around the outer rim of the cemetery, his head bent, his caramel-colored skin glistening with sweat. He looks up as we pass, and for an instant, our eyes meet, and it feels like the world slows on its axis. Then, just as quickly, we're moving past him toward the south side of the graveyard.

"Who was that?" I ask, spinning around in my seat to look out the back window. The guy has stopped running and is standing in the middle of the road, staring after us. His muscular chest rises and falls as he catches his breath.

"Who?" Aunt Bea asks, glancing in the rearview.

"That guy running around the cemetery," I say. "He was about my age."

"Honey, we've been gone fourteen years," she points out gently. "He would have been a toddler last time we were here."

"Oh, right." My heart sinks a little.

I turn back around as the road winds up the middle of three small hills that sit on the south side of the cemetery. Ahead of us, at the top of the slope, looms a huge white house, a mansion really. As we follow the drive around to the front, I take in the Gothic columns, the enormous *Gone with the Wind* porch, the steps leading down to a sprawling, immaculately maintained lawn. A thin veil of fog swirls around the property.

"This is . . . ours?" I ask. But I already know the answer. I remember my mother teaching me how to ride a tricycle in the driveway; I remember doing lopsided cartwheels in the yard; I remember being happy here. How had I managed to mostly block this place out? And more importantly, why have we been living in a tiny Brooklyn apartment when we own a place like this?

"Actually," Aunt Bea says, "it's yours." When I turn to look at her, she's already watching me closely. "Welcome home, Eveny."

2

I'm still standing outside the passenger door of the car, staring up at my house—my *mansion* —when I feel a warm hand on my arm. Startled, I spin around and see an old man peering at me.

"Eveny," he says in a low, rumbly voice. His dark brown skin is a sharp contrast to his snow-white hair. He must be at least seventy-five, but his wide gray eyes are startlingly clear.

"Where did you come from?" I ask, my heart still pounding.

He beams at me. "From the garden. I didn't mean to scare you, dear. Do you remember me? I'm Boniface. Boniface Baptiste."

"Boniface? Geez, of course," I say. He was the house's caretaker when I was little. He was around all the time, and he even used to babysit me sometimes when my mother and Aunt Bea ran errands together. "You still work here?"

"I live just out back in the caretaker's cottage. I've been looking after the Cheval mansion for practically as long as I can remember. Come on," he says, gently placing a hand on my back and leading me toward the house. "Let me show you around."

Aunt Bea has already vanished somewhere, so it's just me as Boniface talks slowly about how he took the sheets off the furniture, shook the dust out of the curtains, and scrubbed the beautiful hardwood floors before we arrived.

"I miss your mama all the time," he says abruptly as we come to the front door. "You're the spitting image of her, you know. Same red hair, same green eyes, same lovely smile."

He opens the huge black front door for me, and I feel a pang the moment I step over the threshold. I stand frozen in the front hallway as I'm hit with a barrage of hazy memories. But it's not until I look to my right and see a set of closed double doors painted a somber red that I feel the breath knocked out of me. "That's the parlor," I say softly.

"You remember it?"

"I don't know. . . ." I'm confused. I don't recall ever being inside the room, but something about it lurks in a far corner of my mind. Suddenly, my heart is racing and my lungs are constricting. I reach for the big bronze door handle, but Boniface steps in front of me.

"It's locked, I'm afraid. Haven't seen the key in years." He's already walking away by the time I can breathe again.

"What is it with this town and keys?" I mutter.

"Just wait until you see your bedroom," Boniface calls over his shoulder. "I took the liberty of decorating a bit. I wanted you to feel at home here," he's saying as I catch up to him on the wide wooden stairway.

Upstairs, Boniface pushes open the door at the end of the hall and motions for me to step inside. The bedroom, which last held my little twin bed and the big armchair where my mother read me stories at night, has been transformed.

The walls have been painted sky blue—my favorite color—and are lined with colorful photos of flowers. There are framed shots of lilies in a field, lavender in a garden, sunflowers in a white pitcher on a farm table, and cornflowers in a vase. Pushed up against the right wall is a teak sleigh bed with a fluffy white comforter. Above it, a beautiful wreath of dried poppies and peonies hangs from the wall. To my left is a huge picture window framed by gauzy white curtains.

"It's perfect," I breathe. In fact, it's nearly as large as our entire apartment in Brooklyn.

"Your aunt called and told me all about your interest in botany." Boniface is smiling at me. "Well I'll let you get settled, then."

As he leaves, I feel myself beginning to warm to the place. But then I make the mistake of wandering toward the window, which is arched and beautiful and diffuses the rays of soft morning light. I'd forgotten that it overlooks the cemetery we passed earlier, and as I gaze out now at the sprawling, fog-shrouded field of ornate crypts, I feel a chill go through me.

Even when I back away and try to focus again on my great room, my veins feel like they're filled with ice.

I'm sitting on the deck just after sunset, trying to figure out how it's seventy degrees here in the dead of winter, when my phone rings.

It's Meredith, who launches into an off-key rendition of "Happy Birthday" as soon as I say hello. "So how's podunk Louisiana?" she asks when she's done assaulting my eardrums.

"Well, it's not New York. And this whole town is surrounded by a big wall, so it's like we're completely trapped." I feel a million miles away from my best friend as I hear laughter and honking horns in the background. The sounds of the city sure beat the silence out here in the middle of nowhere. Aunt Bea and Boniface have gone into town to pick up some things for the new bakery, and I feel like I'm the only person left on earth. I absentmindedly flick on and off the flashlight I'd grabbed from inside, watching the deck alternately illuminate and plunge into darkness.

"You won't believe how crazy the wedding was today without you," Meredith says.

"The Michaelsons?" I ask, trying not to sound as sad as I feel. "Or the Harrises?" For the last year and a half, Mer and I have worked for Blossom and Bloom, a florist in our neighborhood. The owner, Pauline, always said I had a sixth sense about which flowers fit which brides. Working for her is one of the things I'll miss most.

"The Michaelsons," Meredith replies. "It was just me and Pauline because David called in sick. We ran out of lisianthus and had to figure out what to sub in."

"What'd you use? Texas bluebonnets?" I lived for those emergencies, the ones where you ran out of the blooms you were intending to use, so you had to find something else, something that fit both the bride's vision and your own sense of the couple.

"We only had purple statice."

"I'm sure that worked great," I lie. Purple statice is a filler, so the substitution would have changed the whole feel of the bouquets. I'm so dorky—I'm the only person in the world who would care about something like that.

"Anyway, what did you say about there being a wall around the town?" Meredith asks, and I'm relieved for the change of subject because it momentarily stops me from thinking about the life I left behind.

I quickly recap what Aunt Bea told me about the gate. Then I tell her about the weather, the cemetery just beyond the garden wall, and the strange, swirling mist.

"No offense," Meredith says when I'm done, "but Carrefour sounds crazypants."

I'm surprised to realize I feel a bit defensive. "It's not so bad."

"Whatever you say. Anyways, what're you doing for your birthday?"

"Nothing yet." In fact, I'm beginning to wonder if Aunt

Bea has even remembered, because it's just after eight p.m., and she hasn't wished me a happy birthday. No cake. No ice cream. No singing. Nothing.

"Maybe Bea's planning to surprise you."

"Maybe." I turn the flashlight off and tap it absently against my knee.

I'm about to tell Meredith about the intimidating-looking Pointe Laveau Academy when something darts across the backyard. I blink into the darkness and sit up, my heart pounding. Meredith launches into a story about how Jon Dashiell hit on Holly Henderson right in front of her boy-friend, but I'm not listening. "Shhhh," I finally manage.

"Did you just shush me?"

"I think I heard a noise," I whisper. "There's definitely something in my backyard."

"Kind of like how you always thought you saw some guy lurking in the shadows here in Brooklyn?" she asks, laughing.

"No," I mutter, feeling stupid. Three months ago, I'd begun to notice a slender man with white-blond hair loiter-ing behind me wherever I went. I'd be walking home from school, and I'd catch a glimpse of him in the shadows, or I'd be window-shopping in SoHo with Meredith and see his reflection in a glass storefront. When I finally told Meredith about it, she'd laughed for a full minute. Like she's doing now.

But I tune her out as I strain to see across the darkness. The moon is half full, so it's casting light over my mother's rose garden, which Boniface has so carefully maintained.

Beyond that lies her vegetable garden, lush with greens, toma-
toes, and herbs. It backs up against the cemetery wall edging
our property. That's where I see a shadow slinking along now.

I squint, then draw in a sharp breath as I realize it's
human-shaped. I blink a few times and can just make out the
faint silhouette of a person methodically picking something
from one of the plants near the wall.

"Hey!" I drop my phone and call out. "Hey you! Stop!" I'm
dashing across the backyard in defense of my mom's beloved
garden before I realize how stupid I'm being. How do I know
it's not some creepy guy waiting to rob our house—or worse?

Suddenly, there's a thud, and the person goes down hard.

"Damn it!" comes a curse in the darkness, and I'm hugely
relieved to realize the voice is female. I almost trip over her,
and as I beam my flashlight down, I see a girl about my age
with wild, sun-kissed blond waves. She's in a white cotton
dress, and her feet are bare.

"What do you think you're doing?" I demand.

"Who in the hell are you?" the girl shoots back in a thick
southern accent.

"I *live* here. This is my yard. What are *you* doing in it?"

She looks perplexed. "But this is the Cheval mansion."

"Yeah, so? I'm Eveny Cheval."

The girl stares at me like I've just told her I'm the President
of the United States. "Huh?" she manages.

"I just moved in," I say, growing more confident. "And I
want to know what you're doing on my property."

"Uh, picking herbs," she says, adding defensively, "My friends and I pick stuff here all the time. It's no big deal."

"What do you need herbs for?"

"Recipes and stuff," she mumbles.

She's obviously lying. "What, is Boniface growing pot out here?"

The girl laughs and unfolds her left hand. "Not that I know of," she says. I peer at her palm. Indeed, I see only lavender, thyme, and lemongrass.

"Told you so," she says. She sticks out her right hand to shake mine. "I'm Glory Jones."

Her grasp is warm and firm, and she grins at me as I help her up. "So you must be starting school in Carrefour?" she asks as she brushes the earth off her dress. When I nod, she asks, "Pointe Laveau?"

"Not that I have much of a choice."

Glory shrugs. "It's not so bad. You get used to the uniforms. Plus, it's fun to accessorize." She jiggles her armful of bracelets and bangles.

It still sounds like torture to me, but I find myself smiling anyhow. "You go there too?"

"Yeah. Maybe we'll have some classes together. Do you know what you have for first period yet?"

I shake my head. "I actually don't start until next week."

"How come?"

"I think the days off are my consolation prize for my aunt dragging me halfway across the country on my seventeenth birthday."

"You're seventeen?" she asks in a small voice. "When? Today?"

"Yes . . . ," I say slowly.

"Oh." Glory gives me an uneasy smile. "Well, it was nice to meet you, Eveny." She's already backing up. "I've got to go meet my friend Arelia now. I guess I'll see you at school next week. And, um, happy birthday."

I stare after her as she hurries away. I'm still trying to figure out what just happened when she pauses and turns to face me. "Listen, Eveny," she says solemnly, "be careful." And then she's up and over the back wall.

I blink into the darkness, then shake my head. Glory Jones was weird. But I like weird.

By the time Aunt Bea arrives home a couple of hours later, I've called Meredith back twice, but her phone's going straight to voice mail. I try not to feel hurt that she's out celebrating my birthday without me.

Aunt Bea brings me a chocolate cake from the market in town, and although it tastes a little like cardboard, I'm grateful for the effort. "I wanted to bake you something special," she tells me, "but my pans and mixing bowls haven't arrived yet. I promise, I'll make you whatever you want next week."

She finds a single, dusty candle in a drawer, and she and Boniface sing "Happy Birthday" to me as she sets the cake down atop the little table on the back porch. Boniface flips a switch inside the house, and the garden is illuminated by a hundred little fairy lights overhead. I take a deep breath and prepare to make a wish, but a gust of wind sweeps in and snuffs the flame for me. I shiver, even though it's not cold outside.

"Happy birthday, sweet girl," Aunt Bea whispers into my hair. She walks away without another word, leaving Boniface and me to eat our cake in silence.

That night, I lie awake in bed for hours. The wind howls angrily outside my window, and I swear I can hear sirens in the distance. Finally, with Glory Jones's odd words of caution ringing in my ears, I drift off to sleep.

I rarely dream, but the images that assault me tonight are as clear as the vision I had of my mother's funeral. First, I see the hallway outside my bedroom door, then the stairway leading to the front hall. As I begin making my way down the steps, I'm hit with the sudden, powerful scent of rusted iron in the air, and that's when I see it: blood beginning to pour out from beneath the closed parlor doors, pooling thick and nearly black on the hardwood floor.

I gasp and begin to run back up the stairs, but the crimson ocean is rising fast, and soon I can feel it, hot and sticky, licking at my ankles and then my legs. "No!" I cry out. The faster I retreat up the stairs, the faster the tide advances until there's nowhere else for me to go. The whole house is filling with blood. . . .

I wake with a jolt, screaming. Aunt Bea rushes into my room and turns on the light. "What happened?"

"A nightmare," I gasp as I try to catch my breath. My legs still feel wet and sticky. "There was so much blood. . . ."

"It was only a dream." She strokes my back, and my heartbeat begins to return to normal.

After she's gone, I stare at the ceiling for a long time. It's not until the first rays of dawn begin to filter through my windows that I finally drift off into a dreamless sleep.

3

torms pound the bayou all week, making it impossible to venture out on one of the old bikes from the shed in the backyard. Like many people who grew up in New York City, I never learned to drive, and Aunt Bea is too busy setting up her bakery to teach me now. She's making several trips a day into town to prep her kitchen space, in hopes of opening sometime next week. I keep offering to help, but she insists this is something she has to do on her own.

Now I have nothing to do but explore the house while the rain comes down in a steady, driving rhythm. I try to imagine my mom walking these same halls when she was my age, but I can only visualize her as she was when she died: twenty-eight years old, already worn down by life, the premature lines around her eyes suggesting the weight she must have felt on her shoulders before she killed herself.

I wander from room to room, trying to piece together my family's past as lightning illuminates the cloud-spackled sky. In the living room, I see black-and-white photos of a woman in a flapper outfit—my great-great-grandmother, perhaps— and of two teenagers listening to an old-time radio in what looks like the early 1960s.

In one of the photos on the wall alongside the staircase, Boniface is holding my mom and Aunt Bea as little girls, one on either shoulder, as he grins at the camera. He doesn't look much younger than he does now, although the photo must have been taken thirty-five years ago.

I continue up the stairs to a big piece of glossy, polished wood hanging from the wall. The words carved into it are so ornate that I have to squint to make them out.

> *For each ray of light, there's a stroke of dark.*
> *For each possibility, one has gone.*
> *For each action, a reaction.*
> *Ever in balance, the world spins on.*

Weird, I think. It sounds almost like a warning. Or maybe I'm just taking it that way because I can't shake my creepy dream.

I spend the next several hours searching every picture in the house for an image of my dad, the piece of my family history I understand the least. I've only ever seen one photo of him: a faded picture where he's standing in my mother's rose garden, holding one of her purple Rose of Life blooms and grinning at the camera. Aunt Bea hates his guts, though she's made a point of telling me that his leaving right before I was born had nothing to do with me. "He just wasn't the man we all thought he was," she always says.

By Wednesday evening, the only place in the house I haven't explored is the room off the front hall with the blood-red doors, the one from my nightmare.

"I'm still looking for the key," Boniface keeps telling me.

There's a sharp knock on the front door at two thirty Thursday afternoon, just as I'm in the middle of texting with Meredith about a bag she's debating buying at Michael Kors.

I bet it's the UPS man with my Pointe Laveau uniform, I text as I get up to answer the door.

I can't believe you have to wear a uniform, she texts back. *CRAPTASTIC!!!!!!*

I want to be insulted, but I completely agree. Plaid and a white oxford shirt are not exactly the fashion statement of the year.

But when I swing the door open, it's not the UPS man at all. It's a guy my age with brown hair, muddy hazel eyes, and a deep tan.

"Eveny?" he asks, staring at me like he's seen a ghost.

"Yes . . ." I'm wondering why he seems to know me. He's in a black suit with a pale blue shirt and a dark gray tie; he looks like he's on the way to a prom.

"It's Drew Grady." His baritone has an appealing southern twang to it. "Don't you remember me?" He grins, and suddenly, I do.

"We used to play together," I say. His mom was friends with my mom, and they'd sometimes get together to chat while we chased each other around the playground on Main Street. "I used to dump sand in your pants."

"Every time our moms' backs were turned," he says with a laugh.

"So what are you doing here?"

"My mom heard you and your aunt had moved back. I didn't believe it, but I was walking by and saw all the curtains open."

"Dressed kind of formally for a walk, aren't you?" I ask. From the way he's shifting around, and the fact that the suit doesn't quite fit in the shoulders, I'd bet that he's more of a Levi's kind of guy. He looks itchy.

His face registers surprise, as if he's just remembered what he's wearing. "Oh, right. Well, I'm on my way to a funeral."

"Geez, I'm sorry. Whose funeral is it?"

He looks down. "A girl at Pointe Laveau Academy. Same year as us."

"Really? That's so sad."

Drew shrugs and clears his throat. "Well, um, it was good to see you, Eveny. I'll come back at a better time."

"Wait!" I call as he starts to walk away. "Can I come with you?"

"Um . . . ," he begins.

"It's just that I've been stuck here all week." I realize how odd my request sounds, but I'm desperate to go *anywhere*. "I'm completely bored."

"You want to go to a stranger's funeral with me?" Drew asks.

Sure, it's probably not the most appropriate thing to do, but I'm going to go crazy if I don't get out of the house. "Please?" I venture.

"Yeah, okay, it'll be nice to have some company," Drew says after a moment.

I ask him to hang on for a second then race upstairs to throw on a gray dress and a black sweater, which are the most somber pieces I spot in a scan of my closet. I shoot Meredith a text to tell her I'm going out and will talk to her later, but she doesn't reply.

When I get back downstairs, Drew points to my ballet flats. "You're going to want something other than those. It's really muddy after all the rain this week."

I settle for the battered motorcycle boots that saw me through last winter's snowstorms in New York, and although I feel stupid wearing them with a flouncy dress, Drew gives me a thumbs-up. "You look real pretty," he says, his cheeks turning a cute color of pink.

I leave a note for Aunt Bea, then hurry out the door. "So what happened to the girl who died?" I ask as we trudge through my backyard.

"I can't believe you didn't hear," he says. "She committed suicide. The way she did it was awful, actually." He points to a spot in the cemetery wall where a few bricks are missing, and he offers me a hand to help boost me up and over. I land with a wet thud, and mud flies up around me, staining my dress.

"Why, what did she do?" I ask as he splashes over the wall too. I'm trying not to think of my mom and her suicide.

"Apparently she drank a bottle of vodka, then stabbed herself in the chest. Right through the heart."

"Through the *heart*?"

Drew looks down at the soggy ground as we begin walking again. "The medical examiner told the paper she was probably dead within seconds. But what a horrible way to go."

I shudder. "The police are sure that she did it to herself, that it wasn't murder or something?"

Drew looks at me sharply. "Of course not. Things like that don't happen in Carrefour." His tone is final. "Anyway, I heard the police found a suicide note. There's a rumor that it was some kind of a satanic ritual or something."

"You've got to be kidding me."

Drew shrugs. "Let's just say that this is a place where things sometimes happen without an explanation. Strange things."

"Oh, great," I mutter. *What has Aunt Bea gotten me into by moving us here?*

The ceremony has just begun as we approach, and we're careful to tread quietly. People still turn and stare, though, and I'm not sure whether it's because I'm the new girl in town or because sloshing into the middle of a funeral is plain rude.

"Sorry I made you late," I whisper to Drew as the minister begins to read from the Bible in a monotone voice.

"Don't apologize." He reaches for my hand and squeezes. "I'm glad you came."

He lets go, and I can feel my heart thudding. I don't exactly have a ton of experience in the boy department. Back in Brooklyn, Meredith was usually the one at the center of attention while I played wingwoman, which was fine by me.

My mind wanders as I scan the crowd, wondering which people here will be my classmates at Pointe Laveau.

And that's when I see them.

Across the group of mourners, two impossibly beautiful girls are staring right at me. One is a gorgeous honey blonde with perfectly tanned skin, ridiculously long legs, and huge blue eyes. The other, who's even more stunning, has glistening cocoa skin, a model's body, and mounds of wildly gorgeous ebony curls that surround her like a halo. Both are dressed in clothes that are obviously designer and expensive; the blonde is in a black lace minidress plus open-toed stilettos and loads of pearls, while the dark-haired girl is wearing a formfitting leather sheath, fishnet stockings, and leather spike-heeled boots that come up over her knees. Both have nearly identical black stones with jagged edges hanging from long chains around their necks. They're surrounded by three guys and two other girls, all of whom are also gorgeous, but not as much so as the two in the middle.

The dark-haired girl's eyes burn into mine, and I look quickly away, embarrassed to have been caught gawking. There's something vaguely familiar about them that I can't quite put my finger on. "Who are *they*?" I whisper to Drew.

"Everyone calls them the Dolls," he says, and I sense disgust in his tone. "The whole group of them. They all go to Pointe Laveau too."

"Oh." My heart sinks. I hoped to make a fresh start here; I'd even hoped that coming from New York City might make me seem a little edgy. But with girls like that at Pointe Laveau, my dream is fading fast. In the cool department, I obviously don't hold a candle to them.

"I call that one Medusa," Drew adds in a whisper. He nods slightly toward the girl with the cocoa skin and the killer curls, the one who's still staring at me.

"Because of her hair?" I vaguely remember the story of Medusa from Greek mythology; she was a monster with serpents growing out of her head.

"Sure, that's one reason."

I'm trying to puzzle out what he means as the minister asks everyone to bow their heads and pray. As he begins to read from the Bible, I sneak a look back at the Dolls and am unsettled to see the Medusa girl still staring at me. She holds my gaze for a moment then reaches into her purse and whispers to it. Something moves inside, and I clap my hand over my mouth when I realize it's a fat black snake, which is weaving back and forth, its eyes fixed on her face. I take a big step back, nearly tripping over Drew's foot.

"Drew!" I whisper urgently, pointing shakily in the direction of her purse. "She has a snake!"

"Like I said," he replies with a laugh. "Not just her hair."

I shoot him a look; I don't see anything funny about this. "Who in their right mind would bring a snake to a funeral?"

"Who says she's in her right mind?"

My heart is still pounding when I notice something else; although Medusa and her blond friend have finally looked away, and most of her group appears to be paying attention to the ceremony, one of the guys is staring directly at me, an indecipherable expression on his face.

Suddenly, I recognize him: it's the gorgeous jogger I caught a glimpse of the day we moved to Carrefour, and he's even hotter than I'd originally thought. He has smooth caramel skin, close-cropped dark hair, and pale blue eyes, and judging from what I saw that day out the car window, he has a hot body hidden under his crisp charcoal suit. I can feel the heat rising to my cheeks, but I'm finding it impossible to look away.

The minister puts the Bible down then and begins to speak. "It is with great sadness today that we lay to rest one of this town's daughters, only seventeen years old. She was a member of our church, and I knew her as a kind, good-hearted young woman. I pray that the Lord is welcoming Glory Anne Jones into his kingdom."

My heart skips a beat, and I momentarily forget all about

the hot jogger. "Wait, it's *Glory Jones* who died?"

Drew looks surprised. "You knew her?"

"N-not really," I stammer. "We just met once. She was picking herbs in my yard on Saturday night and I interrupted her. She seemed . . . nice. Happy. Not like she was planning to kill herself."

"Wait, you saw her Saturday night?" Drew asks. "What time?"

"Maybe eight, eight thirty."

"Eveny," he says, his voice hollow, "that was the night she died. You may have been the last person to see her alive."

4

The rest of the ceremony goes by in a blur. I'm reeling as the minister drones on about how much Glory will be missed, and leads the group in a closing prayer. All I can think is, *The only new person I've met so far in Carrefour is dead.*

After the funeral, I'm still deep in thought and staring at the tomb where Glory has just been interred when I hear Drew say, "Brace yourself." I look up to see the group of four stunning girls and three perfect guys approaching. I open my mouth to say hi, but the girl in the middle, the one with the Medusa curls, speaks first.

"You're new," she says bluntly. "And very underdressed." Up close, she's even more stunning. Her dark skin is flawless, and her eyes are a startling violet. I glance uneasily at her big black bag.

"You have a snake," I reply and immediately feel like a fool.

After a tense silence, she surprises me by laughing. "You're very observant, new girl," she says, her silken voice dripping with sarcasm. "What's your name?"

I take a deep breath. I'm not ready to be marked as the poor little daughter of the suicidal lady just yet, so I shoot back, "What's *yours*?"

She looks caught off guard. Behind her, I see the guy with the blue eyes hide a smile. "You must be the only person in a hundred-mile radius who doesn't know," she says.

"I must be," I reply, trying to sound a lot more confident than I feel.

When she replies, her words are clipped and cold. "Have it your way. I'm Peregrine Marceau, and this is Chloe St. Pierre." She jerks a thumb at the Barbie doll girl beside her and adds, "Obviously."

"Wait, I know you. I mean I *knew* you," I clarify.

"What are you talking about?" asks the blonde. Her tone is aggressive, but I have a feeling she's trying to sound tougher than she is to match up to her friend.

"We played together when we were kids," I say. Their mothers were my mother's best friends, the two women who accompanied the police chief the night he told me my mother was dead. And their families are, if I remember right, the two other founding families of Carrefour.

"What on *earth* are you babbling about?" Peregrine asks in a bored voice.

"I'm Eveny Cheval," I say.

The girls' eyes widen, and behind them, I hear the gorgeous guy draw a deep breath.

"Eveny *Cheval*?" Chloe repeats in a whisper. She touches the black stone hanging from her neck and looks at Peregrine. "Sandrine Cheval's daughter?"

"That's me," I say weakly. It's just like I thought; everyone knows I'm the girl with the dead mom. The two girls behind Chloe and Peregrine are whispering furiously and shooting me strange looks. The guys are standing silent, but all of them are gazing at me too.

"Eveny," Peregrine says after a moment. "Why yes, of course." She pauses then shoots me a dazzling and undoubtedly fake smile. "Our mothers will be thrilled we ran into you. They'll want to see you immediately."

With that, she whirls on her stiletto heel and whisks away.

"Well, welcome home," says Chloe, giving me an odd look before following Peregrine. The other two girls skitter after them, while the three guys take turns sizing me up as I stand self-consciously glued to the spot. The first guy, who has floppy hair and hazel eyes, waits only a moment before running after the others and grabbing Chloe's hand. The second, who's smarmily handsome in a Clark Gable kind of way, shoots me a knowing look before turning. But the blue-eyed guy stands as rooted to the ground as I am before Peregrine calls for him. He looks back once with a confused expression on his face before following after the rest of the Dolls.

"Well, that was bizarre." I feel strangely breathless after they're gone.

Beside me, Drew snorts. "Welcome to Carrefour."

We walk back to the house in silence as I think about the perplexing reaction of the girls I remember vaguely from childhood. I'd expected a weird welcome, since I'm sure everyone in town knows the tragic story of my mom, but they'd stared as if I were a movie star—or a murderer. There must be something I'm not getting.

"You want to sit outside for a bit?" I ask once we've climbed over my back wall. Drew agrees, so I dash inside to grab two Cokes from the refrigerator before leading him out to the garden. Boniface is there trimming rosebushes and humming to himself, but when he sees us, he says hello, winks at me, then makes himself scarce.

"Well, that's about the welcome home I'd expect from that group," Drew says once we're alone.

"I thought they might judge me for what happened to my mom," I say as we sit down on the edge of one of the rose planters. "But that felt like an overreaction, right?"

"They're just weird. It's not about your mom's death as much as it's about them thinking they're better than everyone. They're only giving you a hard time because you're new here and they can."

"Well, they sound delightful," I reply. "This school year should be great."

Drew laughs. "Hey, Carrefour's not all bad. Wait until you

come out for a day in the Périphérie." He pauses. "In fact, how about Sunday? There's a crawfish boil at my buddy's place."

He launches into an elaborate explanation about how it's a big Louisiana tradition, and although it's early in the season for fresh crawfish, he has a friend who flash-freezes them each year so he can host big blowout parties in the winter. "There's corn, potatoes, onions, sausages, hot sauce . . ." He keeps going, but I tune out when he begins listing beers.

I find myself thinking instead about the cute guy from the funeral and feel immediately foolish when I interrupt Drew's story to ask, "Who was that guy, anyway?"

Drew stops mid-sentence and looks at me. "What guy?"

I swallow hard. "Sorry," I say. "Just the one from the funeral who was looking at me funny."

"Eveny, they were *all* looking at you funny."

"But I mean the one with the blue eyes," I mumble.

"The light-skinned black dude?" Drew asks.

I hesitate, not quite liking the face he makes as he says it.

Drew rolls his eyes. "Oh, that's Caleb Shaw," he continues. "He's, like, a genius at school or something. I heard he got a perfect score on his PSAT in the fall, but he's a little . . . odd."

"Meaning what?"

"I don't know. Like he's always leaving town for a few days at a time. Most people in Carrefour only leave once or twice a year, if at all. But it's like Caleb thinks Carrefour isn't good enough for him." I think Drew's being critical until he adds, "Though I kind of admire the guy for realizing there's more out there than what this town has to offer."

"Do you know where he goes?"

"Nah. He kind of keeps to himself." He gives me a look as he adds, "Every girl in Carrefour is in love with him. Don't tell me you are too."

"Of course not," I say quickly. "I don't even know him."

"Well, I'm sure you'll have a crush on him soon enough, just like everyone else." He studies me for a moment. "So you want to know about the others too?"

"Sure." I'm embarrassed that he apparently thinks I just want to hear about Caleb, although that's exactly what I want.

"The guy with the dark hair who looks like a model is Pascal Auteuil," he begins. "Rich as sin, and the biggest man-whore in town. Rumor is he's even slept with a few teachers."

"Ew," I say, wrinkling my nose.

"The other dude's Justin Cooper. Never heard of him a year ago, but now he's always there, following Chloe around like a lost puppy. In case you hadn't guessed, pretty much every guy in town lusts after her and Peregrine."

"Do . . . you feel that way about them too?" I hate that I sound jealous, because I'm not exactly. I just don't want to hear that Drew is also under the snake girl's spell.

Drew's eyes bore into mine as he says, "No. I appreciate it when a girl is kind and down-to-earth." He pauses and adds, "Like you."

I look away, flustered. "So who are the other two?"

"They're impossible to tell apart—not that you really have

to. I've never seen them separated from each other—or from Peregrine and Chloe. Out in the Périphérie, we call them the Clones, but their real names are Margaux and Arelia."

"Arelia?" It takes me a moment to realize why the name rings a bell. "Wait, that's who Glory said she was going to meet the night she died."

"She did?" Drew blinks a few times. "Did she say anything else?"

"Not really." I shudder. "I still don't understand it. She seemed like she was in a good mood. We talked about school. She was picking herbs. Why would she be doing that if she was on her way to stab herself through the heart?"

He hesitates. "I have no idea. But Glory, she was a cool girl. Not like the rest of the Dolls." He checks his watch and stands up. "Listen, I'd better be going. But how about Sunday? The Périphérie's always a good time. I promise, you'll have fun."

I tell him I'm in, and he says he'll pick me up at five thirty. But as I walk him out of the garden toward the front yard and we hug good-bye, I'm only thinking about Glory and what she could have been doing the night she died. And despite myself, I'm also thinking of the guy with the brilliant blue eyes, the intriguing Caleb Shaw.

That night, I dream again of the parlor off the front hall. I'm walking down the stairs, but when I look at my feet, I'm surprised to find that I'm floating. In a panic, I grab for the railing, but my hand goes right through it. I'm being carried toward the parlor, powerless to stop.

I smell blood in the air, and there's the scent of roses and fire too. As I float across the front hallway, the parlor doors creak open, and blood oozes out. I hear crying from inside the room and as I move through the doorway, I see a little girl standing off to the left, her back to me, the bottom of her nightgown soaked in blood. There's something beside her on the ground, and I strain to see, but it's hidden in the shadows.

That's when the girl turns. Her hands are stained with blood, and her face is streaked with tears. My whole body goes cold as I recognize her immediately.

It's me, as a child.

"*Please help*," she whimpers.

I wake up with a start. It takes me an hour to fall asleep again, and the smell of blood and death are still with me when morning comes.

5

By the time I finally drag myself out of bed the next morning, Aunt Bea is gone. She's left a note saying she went out early to receive a big shipment of bakery supplies, scribbling on the bottom, *Only five days to go until the opening!*

I pour myself a bowl of cereal and settle at the kitchen table with my laptop, determined to find out more about Glory's death. I Google her name, but nothing appears. I try *suicide + Carrefour*, thinking that maybe Glory's name wasn't printed in the paper because she was a minor. But I strike out there too.

I backspace again and this time, I type in *Carrefour newspaper*. But when I press enter, I'm only hit with a long list of meaningless options that have nothing to do with this place.

I'm still staring at the screen, trying to decide what to

search for next, when I hear Boniface's voice from the back garden. I look out the window and see him talking to two women wearing expensive-looking black dresses and heels that make their legs look miles long. I recognize them immediately—not just from my foggy memories, but also because they look exactly like their daughters.

Annabelle Marceau and Scarlett St. Pierre. I haven't seen them since the night they accompanied the police chief to deliver the news that changed my life. *Honey, your mama killed herself. Drove right into a tree.*

Boniface's eyes meet mine through the windowpane, and as he approaches the back door, I see him grimacing.

"Eveny, we have a couple of visitors," he says. He lingers uncertainly for a moment before walking back toward the garden.

"Ms. St. Pierre, right?" I say, smiling at the one whose honey-blond hair cascades over her shoulders just like Chloe's. "And Ms. Marceau?" I ask, glancing at the one who looks like a slightly older version of Peregrine, but with short, spiky black hair.

"I *knew* she'd remember us, Annabelle," trills the blonde. "And I'll be damned if you are not just the *spitting* image of your mother!"

"Thanks," I say awkwardly. "Want to come in?"

"Don't mind if we do," Peregrine's mother says, already sweeping past me like she owns the place. "It's been ages since we've been inside this house, hasn't it?"

Chloe's mother hands me a white cardboard box wrapped in an intricately tied purple ribbon. "This is for you, sugar," she says. "It's a coffee cake."

"We baked it for you last night," Peregrine's mother adds. "A little welcome-home treat!"

They stand there smiling at me for so long that the silence grows uncomfortable. "Would you like a cup of coffee?" I finally ask, trying to be polite. I turn and walk toward the kitchen, and they click-clack after me in their impossibly high heels.

"Have a seat," I say, gesturing to the kitchen table. I pull out a filter, line the coffeemaker with it, and scoop in several tablespoons of Folgers.

"Don't you have any chicory coffee?" Chloe's mother asks.

"Just the Folgers," I tell her as I add water, push the start button, and grab three mugs from the cabinet. "This cake looks delicious," I tell them.

"Oh, it is!" Chloe's mother bubbles. "It has rosemary to ward off evil, cloves to help foster friendship—with our daughters, of course—huckleberry to help you remember your dreams, and just a pinch of cinnamon to help promote good taste, because, let's face it, you're in Carrefour now."

"Okay . . . ," I say slowly.

"Of course it's nothing like the cakes your aunt bakes," Peregrine's mother adds. "We can't *wait* to have her little bakery open! What's she calling it?"

"Sandrine's Bakeshop. After my mom."

"How lovely. I remember your mama and your aunt baking up a storm when we were your age." She gets a faraway look in her eye and adds, "We miss her so much, Eveny, we really do."

"Yeah. Me too." I pour three cups of coffee and ask if they want cream and sugar. They decline.

"So, Eveny," Peregrine's mother says a moment later as I hand steaming mugs to them. "All those years you were gone, did your aunt tell you much about Carrefour?"

I shake my head.

The women exchange looks. "I see," Peregrine's mother says. "So she hasn't explained any of the . . . customs of the town or anything?"

"Customs?" I ask blankly.

"Oh, Annabelle, stop putting Eveny on the spot," Chloe's mother says quickly. She turns to me. "I think what Annabelle is wondering is whether you'd heard of the Mardi Gras Ball. It's coming up in about a month you know."

"Sorry, doesn't ring a bell. My aunt and I didn't spend a lot of time talking about this place. I think it reminded her of my mom."

"Your aunt never was a big fan of Carrefour," Chloe's mother says with a sigh. "But we'll change that yet, right Eveny?" She claps her hands in a way that reminds me of a preschool teacher trying to coax a child into singing along.

"Sure," I say. I glance down at my computer. "Listen, while I have you here, do you know the website for the local paper?"

"The local paper?" Peregrine's mother asks.

"Yeah. I was trying to read more about what happened to Glory Jones."

"Why on earth would you want to do that?" she asks.

"Well, I met her the night she died, actually."

Chloe's mother goes suddenly pale, and Peregrine's mother freezes. "Did you?" she asks.

"She just didn't seem suicidal to me," I continue. "I thought maybe if I read about what happened, it might make more sense. But I can't seem to find anything about it on the internet."

Peregrine's mother takes a second to recover before speaking. "Of course not. We're not on the internet, dear."

"What's not on the internet? The whole town?" When she nods, I add, "But that doesn't make any sense."

"We like our seclusion from the world, Eveny," Chloe's mother says. "It's one of the wonderful things about living in Carrefour. We don't air our dirty laundry. We don't get unwanted visitors. Everyone knows everyone, and nothing bad ever happens."

I shake my head in disbelief. "What about Glory dying? What about my mother dying?"

"Those were both very unfortunate incidents," Peregrine's mother says, looking out the window.

"Try your cake, sugar," Chloe's mother urges.

I clear my throat and take a bite, even though I'm not hungry. "Delicious," I say politely. And actually, it is—it tastes a bit like the lemon cake they served in the Polish deli below our apartment in Brooklyn, but with a spicy, herbal twist.

"Really, Eveny, there's no reason to go looking into poor Glory's death," Peregrine's mother says after I've taken a second bite. "It's a tragedy, but it's all very straightforward."

But the more they brush off my questions, the more I'm convinced they're hiding something. "My friend Drew said there was a rumor about something satanic going on."

Both women laugh. "Satanic?" Peregrine's mother asks. "That's a new one."

"In any case, enough talk about death!" Chloe's mother says brightly. "Let's talk about you! I understand you're interested in botany?"

"Yeah." I nod. "I always have been. I was in charge of our community garden back in Brooklyn, and I worked for about a year and a half for a wedding florist."

"Your mother would have been so proud," Chloe's mother says. "She was very passionate about flowers and herbs." She glances at Peregrine's mother and adds, "We all are. Annabelle, me, our daughters . . . I think you'll find that this is a wonderful place to live if you're interested in gardening."

"Great," I say, forcing a smile. I can't exactly imagine their supermodel daughters in muddy jeans and canvas gloves, digging in the dirt. "Must be nice to have good weather year-round."

The mothers eat their cake and drink their coffee quickly as they chatter about all the social gatherings I can get involved with now that I'm back. Apparently, I just haven't *lived* until I've attended the annual Mardi Gras Ball.

"You are *so* lucky, Eveny," Peregrine's mother says as she finishes the last of her coffee cake. "It's *the* social event of the year. It'll be a wonderful welcome home for you!"

"Thanks for the coffee, sugar," Chloe's mom says. She stands up and brings her mug and plate to the sink.

Peregrine's mom hands her dishes to me. "We're sure we'll be seeing a lot more of you."

"You must promise us, Eveny, that you'll spend some time with our daughters," Chloe's mom says. "They're *ever* so delighted that you're back, and they can't wait to get to know you."

I want to tell her that based on the way Peregrine and Chloe were looking me up and down at the funeral like I was yesterday's garbage, I'm not expecting a call from them anytime soon.

"Sure, I'd love to hang out," I say, forcing a smile as I walk them to the door.

"Make sure you eat that cake, now!" Chloe's mother says brightly. They both air-kiss me on their way out, and a moment later, they're vanishing down my long driveway in a sleek silver Bentley coupe.

Later that afternoon, I'm wobbling down Main Street on a 1970s cruiser that Boniface found for me in the storage shed. Its red paint is chipped in places, and I've managed to convince myself that the rust stains and loud rattling noise aren't all that obvious until people start to turn and stare at me. I'm relieved when I spot my aunt's bakery, which now has a purple sign above the front door that says *Sandrine's Bakeshop*.

"Aunt Bea?" I call out as I head inside, where the air is soft with cinnamon and chocolate. She's painted the walls pale pink and decorated them with a dozen ornate French-style mirrors in various shapes and sizes. As I step up to the polished silver counter and the big glass case, I think how proud my mom would have been to have her name on a place like this.

"Eveny? That you?" I hear my aunt's voice from the back, and a moment later she emerges wearing a flour-streaked blue apron over jeans.

"Aunt Bea, the bakery's beautiful!" I tell her. "I can't believe you put this together in a week."

"I hoped you'd like it." She smiles at me. "Want to try one of my chocolate lavender cupcakes? I have some cooling."

"Maybe later. I just had some lemon herb cake."

She looks confused. "Where did that come from?"

"Peregrine's and Chloe's mothers dropped by to welcome us to town."

I expect her to be pleased, but instead her face darkens. "What did they say?"

"That their daughters are positively *thrilled* to have me back." I roll my eyes. "Doubtful."

"I suspect you'll have more in common with them than

you imagine," she says. "Now, would you mind helping me frost some cupcakes? I want to take them home for Boniface to thank him for all his hard work."

She brings me a tray of unfrosted cakes and a pastry bag, setting them on a table in front of the bakery window. "I'll be in the back if you need me."

I spend the next few minutes piping caramel cream onto little pillows of chocolate. As I work, my head is swirling with a thousand questions about my mom, prompted by my brief visit with her two best friends. I've Googled her before, hoping to find some information about her death, but not even an obituary popped up. Just like with Glory.

"Hey, Aunt Bea?" I ask when I'm finished, setting the tray of frosted cupcakes on the counter in the back. "Does Carrefour have a newspaper?"

"Sure, it's a weekly one. Why?"

"I'm trying to understand what happened with Glory Jones. I don't get what would make someone who seemed so happy kill herself."

She studies me briefly before saying, "Try the library. Mrs. Potter, who runs the place, prides herself on keeping perfect town records. Or at least she used to when I was growing up here." She walks me to the door and points down the street. "It's just past the theater, on the left side."

"Thanks," I say, but she puts a hand on my shoulder to stop me.

"I know you're going to look up your mom's death as well,"

she says. "Just don't read too much into it. Things in this town are never quite what they appear."

She heads back inside without explaining more. I'm still puzzling over her words as I make my way up Main Street toward the library.

"Can I help you, dear?" asks the old woman behind the front desk as I walk in.

"Do you keep archives from the local paper here?"

She peers at me over her glasses. "I haven't seen you around before. Are you from the Périphérie?"

I'm not sure what that has to do with newspaper archives, but I reply politely, "No, ma'am. I live on the other side of the cemetery. I just moved back to town."

Her eyes widen. "You're Sandrine Cheval's daughter, aren't you?" she breathes. "Well, I'll be damned."

"You knew my mom?"

"Honey, everyone knew your mom." She seems to gather her composure as she gestures for me to follow her. "How nice to see you back in Carrefour."

She leads me down a hallway to a small room, explaining as we go that it's a bit old-fashioned but that they still keep the archives on microfiche. "I find that the tried and true way is often the best way," she says confidently. "Now, what can I help you find?"

"Actually, I was wondering whether I could see this week's paper. And"—I pause, a little embarrassed—"if you have the paper from the week my mom died, I'd like to read that too."

"You don't want to go reading something like that, honey."

"But I do," I say, not sure why I'm explaining myself to a stranger. "So if you could bring me the articles, that would be great."

She purses her lips and leaves, returning less than a minute later with three slides.

"Here's this week's paper, which I just put on microfiche yesterday, and the . . . older ones. You just move them under the glass there," she says, gesturing to a microscope-like device on a desk, "and they'll show up on the screen." I thank her and she walks out, muttering to herself as she shuts the door behind her. I use the knob on the side of the machine to focus the lens and begin reading the article from the front page of the most recent *Carrefour Weekly Chronicle*, titled "Local Girl Stabs Self."

According to the paper, Glory was a well-liked, straight-A student who lived in Carrefour her whole life. Her mom is quoted as saying, "There was absolutely no indication that something like this could happen." Peregrine and Chloe are both quoted too, with Peregrine describing Glory as, "a true, trustworthy friend," and Chloe saying—apparently through sobs, according to the reporter—that she'll always blame herself for not protecting her friend.

Protecting her? Seems like a bizarre way to talk about a suicide.

Glory's body, the paper says, was found in a wooded area along Cyprès Avenue on the north side of town by a possum hunter from the Périphérie who was trolling the woods before dawn. The police were called right away, but it was too late. The medical examiner estimated the time of death between 11:00 p.m. and 1:00 a.m. the night before.

Just a few hours after I'd met her.

"It's definitely a suicide, although the manner of death was highly unusual," the chief of police, Randall Sangerman, told the paper. "No prints on the body or on the knife, except for her own. Our department sends its deepest sympathies to her parents."

I search the rest of the newspaper, but there's nothing else about Glory, nothing that puts me any closer to understanding why she'd take her own life.

Confused, I pull out the slide and insert the first one from fourteen years ago, the one from the day after my mother's death. I take a steadying breath, adjust the viewfinder, and begin to read.

Sandrine Cheval, 28, died when her car slammed into a tree along the bayou on Route 786, on the outskirts of the Périphérie, near the town wall. "Death occurred when a shard from the windshield sliced open the carotid artery in her neck," the medical examiner told the reporter. *"Ms. Cheval likely died almost instantaneously."* The newspaper promises more information in its next issue.

I sit back, the breath knocked out of me. I've never heard the detail about her neck being cut open. It makes me profoundly sad, and I sit there for a moment wondering what could have been going through her mind in those final seconds before she died so horrifically.

I clear my throat before loading and focusing the next slide. The front-page headline screams, "Carrefour Mom's Death Ruled a Suicide." The police chief at the time told the paper, *"Based on the lack of brake marks on the road, the speed at which she was traveling, the fact that Ms. Cheval had to have turned the wheel very sharply at the last minute, and the lack of any intoxicants in her system, we've concluded that Ms. Cheval's death wasn't an accident but rather a self-inflicted incident."* The article concludes by saying that Sandrine Cheval is survived by a younger sister, Beatrice, and a daughter, Eveny, age three.

I look at the screen for a long time through eyes blurred with tears. I've heard bits and pieces about my mother's car crash from Aunt Bea, but it never seems to add up. Seeing it in black and white makes it even more confusing. My mother was happy and loving, with a whole life in front of her. Why would someone like that deliberately drive her car into a tree?

I switch the screen off, and stand up. It's irrational to search for answers that don't exist.

I shake my head, grab the microfiche slides, and walk out to the librarian's desk.

"Did you find what you were looking for?" she asks.

"Not exactly," I tell her. "But thanks for your help." Her eyes look sad, and I can feel her watching me as I walk out the front door.

I'm in a fog, puzzling over the new details of my mom's death, as I head back out onto Main Street. I'm so caught up in my thoughts that I don't notice the guy rounding the corner of the library building until I run straight into him.

"Oh my gosh, I'm so sorry!" I exclaim. "I wasn't looking. . . ." I'm about to ask if he's okay, but my breath catches as I look up and realize that the solid, muscular chest I've just collided with belongs to the guy from the cemetery, the guy with the blue eyes. Caleb Shaw.

"It was my fault too." He reaches out with both hands to steady me. "You okay?"

His voice is deep and warm, just like I imagined it would be. I blush as I look down and realize the hairs on my arms are all standing on end. "Uh-huh," I finally say.

He looks unconvinced. "You sure?"

"Uh-huh," I manage to repeat. *Brilliant conversational skills, Eveny.*

He stares at me for a minute, and at the same time we both realize that his hands are still on my arms, holding me upright. He pulls away like he's been burned. "Well, I'm just headed into the library to check out a few books," he says.

"Yeah, reading's cool," I mumble. I immediately want to smack myself. *Reading's cool?*

I can see a smile tugging at the corner of his perfect mouth. "Sure," he says.

"Cool," I manage to say very uncoolly.

"Right. So see you later then?"

"Later," I squeak.

He gives me a long, searching look and then vanishes through the library door.

I stand there frozen in place for a moment before shaking myself out of it.

"*Reading's cool*?" I say aloud. "Who *says* that?"

I can feel my cheeks flaming in embarrassment the whole way home.

6

"*I* don't even know if it's a date," I tell Meredith on Sunday evening as I put makeup on in the bathroom mirror. I'm wearing a long-sleeved black T-shirt, my old leather jacket, and a pair of skinny jeans, which I'm hoping are appropriate for the crawfish boil Drew's taking me to tonight. At Meredith's insistence, I've swapped my Converse for a pair of cowboy boots.

"But you said this Drew guy's cute?" she prompts. I have her on speakerphone, and the way her voice fills my room, as if she's right here with me, makes me miss my old life in New York so much it hurts.

"Very," I tell her. I put the tube of mascara down and concentrate on dusting some blush on my cheeks.

"So do you like him?" she asks.

"I don't know," I tell her. "The thing is, there's this other guy. . . ."

Meredith is silent as I tell her about Caleb and the way our eyes met across the cemetery on Thursday. I refrain from telling her about our spectacularly dorky encounter Friday outside the library.

"Girl, for all you know this Caleb guy is gay. He could have been staring at Drew," Meredith points out. "Go for the guy who's already into you. How cool will you be if you start at a new school already having a boyfriend?"

I shrug before realizing she can't see me. "I don't even know if he's interested. Besides, the girls I was telling you about don't seem to like him."

"Well, they sound like snobby little rhymes-with-witches," Meredith sniffs. "So who cares?"

"I guess you're right. But they're from my past too. Everything feels totally complicated here."

"Or maybe you've just been reading too many angsty novels," Meredith says. "You don't need to have every step planned out. Just do this crawfish boil, have a good time, go with it, and make out with the Drew guy if you want to."

I swallow hard. I wish it were that easy. I wish I weren't thinking about Caleb. I wish I hadn't spent the last twenty-four hours daydreaming about being pressed up against the solid chest I'd collided with outside the library.

The doorbell rings, snapping me out of it. "That's him. I've got to go."

"Have fun!" she replies. She makes some kissy-kissy sounds, then I hear the phone click and she's gone.

"Eveny!" Aunt Bea's voice wafts up from the front hallway. "Drew's at the door!"

"I'll be right down!" I take one last look in the mirror, spiral my fingers through a few errant curls, and head for the stairs.

On the drive over to the crawfish boil in Drew's pickup truck, I once again note that the Périphérie is practically the polar opposite of central Carrefour. In my part of town, every building sports a fresh coat of paint, every neighborhood looks like it could have been lifted from *Better Homes and Gardens*, and every person strolling by looks like they've been styled for a photo shoot.

But as soon as we make it through the thick tangle of trees that surrounds the center of town, it's like we've driven into a new universe.

"It's so different out here," I say, hoping that I don't sound like a snob.

Drew looks amused. "Poor, you mean."

"No, that's not what I meant," I say quickly. "It actually seems like it has character."

"I think you mean decay."

"Not at all. It's just odd that there'd be such a big divide between the two sides of town."

Drew raises an eyebrow. "You have a lot to learn about this place."

"Even the weather is different," I add. Indeed, outside

Drew's pickup, clouds swirl against a dark, ominous sky, and it feels like the temperature has dropped twenty degrees since we emerged from the trees. I shiver and roll my window up.

"I heard once that the temperature variation between the two areas has something to do with water vapor from the bayou," Drew replies. "I'm no meteorologist, but it never made much sense to me."

We arrive at Drew's friend Teddy's house a few minutes after six. Most of the guys are wearing sweatshirts and jeans, and about half of them are in maroon and beige letter jackets that I assume are from Carrefour Secondary. Most of the girls are in cowboy hats and jeans or denim miniskirts. The only piece of my outfit that fits with this crowd are the cowboy boots Meredith insisted I wear.

There's a bonfire blazing in the middle of the yard with a few dozen people clustered around it, talking, laughing, and occasionally sloshing their drinks out of red Solo cups. On the side of the house, two huge pots at least three feet high and three feet across are simmering on big propane burners, sending giant puffs of steam shooting skyward.

"What are those?" I ask, pointing at the pots.

"That's where they cook the crawfish."

Just then, a guy with green eyes, freckles, and a cleft chin, all shaded by a giant cowboy hat, materializes next to us. "It ain't crawfish season yet, but we got a whole load of those daddies in the freezer from last year's catch, and we got to use them up before we can start getting 'em fresh again. That's why I'm calling this my Clean Out the Freezer Crawfish Boil." He sticks out his hand and adds, "You must be Eveny. Real pretty name. I'm Teddy. Welcome to Freezer Night."

I laugh, shake his hand, and thank him for inviting me.

"Thank this guy," he says, clapping Drew on the back. "He's been raving about you since you got back into town. We've all been dying to meet you. So this is your first crawfish boil?"

"It is." I can't help but grin at him. He's a ball of happy energy.

"Sweet! So what'll you have? We got beer, or there's something my girl Sara over there made called Swamp Punch. No idea what's in it."

"I'll stick with the beer."

"Smart girl," he says with a wink. "I'll be right back. You want a beer too?" he asks Drew.

"Just one. I gotta get this girl home safe."

"He seems nice," I say to Drew as we watch Teddy bound off toward the back deck, which is lined with three rusted-looking kegs. "He goes to Pointe Laveau too?" I'm already imagining a new life where I hang out with the down-to-earth people from the Périphérie even if I go to school at Snob Central.

"Nah," Drew says, kicking the dirt and looking down. "Pointe Laveau is kinda reserved for *your kind*."

"Excuse me?"

"The people who live in the privileged part of town. People with money. Out here, none of us can afford the tuition, so every year six merit-based scholarships per grade are awarded to Périphérie kids. I guess it's some kind of philanthropic gesture."

I'm quiet for a moment. "Just so you know, my aunt Bea and I weren't rich when we lived in New York."

"Eveny, you live in a mansion. Your family founded this town. You're probably one of the richest people in Louisiana."

I don't know what to say.

Finally, Drew sighs. "Maybe your aunt was trying to raise you with some values. Most of those spoiled rich kids don't have any."

I swallow the urge to defend the Dolls. In a strange way, I feel as much a part of them as this life out here, because even if we're polar opposites now, we share a past. I don't know whether I'm rich or poor, refined or casual, city or country. But I have the uneasy feeling that living in two worlds isn't going to be easy for long.

The crawfish boil turns out to be a blast.

Even though I worried I wouldn't belong, everyone is being really nice. Drew leads me around the sprawling yard, his hand lightly resting on the small of my back, and he introduces me to so many people that I start forgetting names. There's a raucous game of cornhole—which apparently involves throwing beanbags into a board with holes cut out—going on near the bayou, and in the yard another group is playing beer pong. There's country music blasting from speakers on the back deck, which has turned into a dance floor.

Everyone shrieks with excitement when Teddy announces the crawfish are ready to boil, and Drew excuses himself to go help. I stand alone and clap along with everyone as Drew, Teddy, and two other guys dump huge cases of crawfish into the boiling pots, which are already simmering with red potatoes, corn, and spices like garlic powder, onion powder, and cayenne pepper. The air smells sweet and spicy, and I find myself getting hungrier and hungrier.

"Thirty minutes till we eat!" Teddy announces. "Y'all better work up your appetites!"

The crowd cheers, and the dancing on the deck gets more frenzied. When Drew comes to find me a minute later, his cheeks are flushed and he's grinning. "Man, I love a good crawfish boil," he says. "Want to go take a quick walk down the bayou while we wait for the food?"

"Sure." His enthusiasm is contagious, and I find myself smiling too.

We grab a flashlight from the deck and stroll toward the back of the yard, where it dissolves into a mess of dying cypress trees, brown Spanish moss, and darkness. When Drew grabs my hand, I don't pull away.

It only takes a few minutes for the noise of the party to vanish behind us. Out here, the night is thick, and the buzz of mosquitoes is a steady soundtrack.

"So," he says after we sit down in the grass, "do you remember the time you and your mom came out to visit us and my mom made her special gumbo?"

I shake my head sadly. "I wish I did. I think maybe I blocked out most of my memories of being a kid here."

"But you remember your mom?"

"Yeah. I still think about her a lot." I pause. "She died a long time ago, though. Sometimes I wonder if there's something wrong with me for not moving on."

"Eveny! That's crazy! She was your mother. Of course you're still thinking about her."

I look out in the blackness. There's rustling in the trees and splashing in the water, and although I don't know what's out there, I realize I feel safe with Drew.

"She's just on my mind a lot more since we've moved back. I think—" I hesitate. "I think I still can't wrap my head around the idea that she took her own life."

Drew studies me for a long time and then pulls me into a hug. "I'm so sorry you went through all that, Eveny."

I'm relieved that he understands and grateful when he abruptly changes the subject, chattering about a science project he's working on until we're called to eat.

As we stroll back to Teddy's house, he tells me all about his band, which is called Little Brother and plays something called bayou fusion rock music.

"Bayou fusion rock?" I repeat.

He laughs and says it's their own form of banjo-driven rock 'n' roll. "Like if the Eagles, the Avett Brothers, and a New Orleans jazz band got together and had a music baby. I play the guitar," he adds. "Teddy's our drummer; he thinks we'll get a record deal if we can just get in front of the right people."

"Is that what you want to do with your life, go into music?" I ask.

"Who wouldn't want to be a rock star, right? But I'm not a total idiot; I know those things don't always work out. I'm going to go to college too, so I have a backup plan."

"Where do you want to go?"

"LSU," he says instantly. "No doubt. But I'll have to get a scholarship or take out a bunch of student loans. It's not like my parents have the money for something like that anymore."

"Anymore?"

He shakes his head. "Let's not talk money right now. Too much of a downer. So how about you? Planning to go to college?"

"Yeah, NYU," I answer without hesitation.

"You want to go back to New York?" he asks in surprise.

"No offense, but this isn't home. New York is."

"Well," Drew says, "we'll see about that. This town has a funny way of sinking its teeth into you."

Ten minutes later, I'm standing in Teddy's backyard again, watching as the guys pull giant metal strainers out of the huge pots, shake them dry, and dump them on long picnic tables covered in newspaper. A sea of what look like miniature lobsters pours out alongside hundreds of potatoes and ears of bright yellow corn that have been cut into thirds.

"Dig in!" Drew shouts at me across the yard as he carries

one of the strainers toward the back deck, where Teddy's already hosing them off.

I laugh as the crowd descends on the tables, piling big handfuls of crawfish, corn, and potatoes onto Styrofoam plates. Drew arrives at my side a moment later and leads me over to scoop up my own dinner, then we retreat to a quiet corner of the yard, where we sit down, leaning our backs against a big oak tree. Drew teaches me how to eat the crawfish, which is kind of a gross process: you twist them in half, suck the heads, and then squeeze the tails to get the meat out.

"You're a natural," Drew marvels after I've decapitated my fourth crawfish.

"Maybe I belong here after all."

"I guess we'll see," he says, suddenly serious. "You've got some potato on your face." He reaches over to gently brush a speck off my chin, and from the way he pauses and looks at me, I have the uneasy feeling he's going to make a move. But then he pulls back and looks down. "Glad you liked everything," he says. "I'd better get you home once we're done eating before your aunt skins me alive."

7

I'm nervous the next morning as I get ready for my first day at Pointe Laveau. Even with Aunt Bea's tailoring, my uniform looks terrible. My white oxford shirt is boxy, my maroon plaid skirt comes down just past my knees, and my white socks and black oxfords make me look suspiciously like a seventy-five-year-old orthopedic patient.

"You sure these are the shoes we have to wear?" I ask Aunt Bea as I round the corner into the kitchen.

"That's what the school guidebook said," she tells me apologetically. "For what it's worth, I think you look cute in a retro kind of way."

I text a photo of my uniform to Meredith, hoping she'll make me feel better, but she doesn't reply. It takes me a few minutes to remember that Louisiana is an hour behind New York, so she's probably already at school with her phone off.

At breakfast, Aunt Bea seems even more nervous than I do. She spills her coffee, knocks over her juice, and drops her toast on the floor twice.

"You're going to have a great first day!" she tells me with a smile that looks as fake as it probably is.

"You're acting a little weird," I say. "Everything okay with the bakery?" Her grand opening party is scheduled for Wednesday night, and the closer it gets, the more scatterbrained she's becoming.

"It's you I'm concerned about; I remember how tough first days are. But you're going to do great."

"Sure I am," I reply drily. "What could possibly go wrong in a school full of beautiful rich people?"

"Stop worrying," she says, but she's chewing her lip the way she always does when she's uneasy. I'm relieved when she drops me off in front of the school twenty minutes later because her nerves are rubbing off on me.

Pointe Laveau Academy must have been built right around the same time as my house, because it has the same kind of dramatic, neo-Gothic construction. The main building has narrow, arched windows, steep gables, and a bell tower, and the outlying buildings, which are clustered around a green space I can barely see from the street, are flatter versions of the same design. The complex looks like a cross between a church and an old prison. I shudder as I walk up the front steps and lose the sunlight.

Just before I enter the building, my phone dings with a

text message. It's from Drew.

Sorry, he says, *but I won't be at school. Woke up sick this morning. Hope you didn't get my germs. Have a good first day!*

My heart sinks. He's my only friend here, and now I'll have to brave my debut alone. I text him back, *Aw, feel better!,* then I switch my phone to silent and head inside to start my new life.

"Eveny Cheval," the pudgy school secretary says flatly as I enter the front office, which is decked out in regal-looking furniture with eggplant-colored cushions.

I nod, wondering how she knew it was me.

"We never get new students here," she remarks, answering the question I haven't asked. She fluffs her bleached-blond curls and purses her bright pink lips at me. "Except scholarship kids from out in the Périphérie once in a while. But I know all of them in advance."

"Oh, do you live out there, in the Périphérie?" I ask, trying to be polite.

"Are you being smart with me?" She glares back.

"What? No, of course not."

"Well, last time I checked, I wasn't sitting on a mountain of gold coins in a mansion like you people," she says. "But I'm certainly not from out *there.*" I just stare at her, wondering how I've managed to piss off the first person I've encountered. "Now go on," she says, handing over my class schedule. "Your books are in your locker."

I take a deep breath and head into the main hallway,

which is teeming with students. The first thing I notice is that although all the girls are wearing the same uniform I am, every single one of them is pulling it off way better. None of them are in clunky loafers; they seem to be wearing everything from ballet flats to cowboy boots to strappy heels. My heart sinks as I realize the first impression I make here will be one of dorkiness.

The guys are all wearing pressed khakis and pale purple oxford shirts with the initials of the school emblazoned on their left breast pockets. They, too, seem to have skipped anything resembling an official dress code. I spot a few purple and gold letter jackets, but most of the guys are dressed in pieces that smack a bit more of individuality—leather bombers, a few blazers, a handful of hoodies.

Everyone is streaming by in a hurry, and nearly all of them are shooting me curious glances, but no one stops to help. I look down at the schedule again. It says on the top that I've been assigned to locker 445.

Yet I have no idea where locker 445 might be, or how I'll find my first class. I look around, hoping I'll spot Peregrine or Chloe or another one of the Dolls, because at least they're not complete strangers.

That's when I notice that the hallway is draped in black crepe ribbons. Signs that say *We love you, Glory* and *We'll miss you, Glory* are taped on walls, and I spot a few photographs on a pin board nearby, framed in black. I step closer and see Glory Jones's face smiling out at me.

"You look lost." A voice comes from the right, startling me, and I turn to see a slender girl with a heart-shaped face, big brown eyes, and thick dark hair. She's wearing a purple tissue-weight cardigan and faded purple Converse high-tops with her uniform, almost as if she's trying to look anti-glamorous. I like her instantly.

"Yeah. It's my first day, and I have no idea how to get to my locker," I admit. "Or my first class. And I'm beginning to feel like an idiot."

"It was super rude of Mrs. Perkins to send you off without telling you where to go. I'd blame it on all that tacky hair bleach going to her head, but around here, if you're not one of the chosen ones, you can forget about anyone giving a crap about you."

"The chosen ones?"

She laughs, although it sounds a bit like a snort. "You'll see." She squints at my schedule and says, "All right, let's get you to your locker." We begin walking, and she adds, "By the way, I'm Liv."

"Eveny," I reply.

She reads my schedule as we dodge other students in the hall. "Cool, we have physics together sixth period," she says. "Other than that, our classes don't match up. But I'll show you where your first period is."

We reach a row of lockers, and she points to one near the middle. "Here we are. Locker 445."

I look at the slip of paper, which tells me the combination

is 16-7-13. I turn the dials, and the door pops open, revealing a neat stack of books—and a name scratched into the inside panel: *Glory Jones*. I freeze.

"This was Glory Jones's locker?" I ask.

Liv peers inside and sees the curvy letters too. "Can't believe they'd reassign it so soon. Then again, Glory was one of the nice ones. She'd probably want you to have it."

I grab my textbooks for English and trig, my first two classes. But what I'm thinking is that, nice or not, Glory would probably prefer to still be here, using her own locker.

The bell rings. "Here we go again," Liv mutters. She points down the hall and says, "Your English class is that way. Fifth door on the right. Mrs. Shriver. You'll be fine."

I take a deep breath, clutch my books to my chest, and begin walking, relieved that I've now met at least one potential friend who's not dead.

The second bell rings a millisecond before I walk into English, which makes me officially late.

I feel two dozen pairs of eyes on me as I hand Mrs. Shriver my schedule and mumble that I'm new here.

"Oh yes, Eveny Cheval," she says. "We were expecting you. You can take that empty seat in the last row."

"No." I hear a languid voice from the back, and I turn to see Peregrine, decked out in thick eyeliner, dark lipstick, and a lacy black silk camisole under her standard-issue oxford shirt. The same stone necklace I noticed at the funeral dangles in her cleavage, and she's wearing a close-fitting black quilted leather vest. "Eveny will sit right here." She gestures daintily to an empty chair beside her.

I hesitate, wondering if she's just being nice to me because her mother said she had to, but she snaps her fingers, gestures to the seat, and says, "We don't have all day, Eveny. Chop chop."

"Go on, take the seat, dear," Mrs. Shriver says, seeming to recover a bit as I move down the aisle toward Peregrine.

"Nice shoes," Peregrine says, raising an eyebrow at me after I sit. "Did you borrow them from a nursing home?"

"The dress code said we had to wear black loafers and knee socks," I say, glancing down. She's wearing strappy black platform stiletto sandals on her bare, perfectly pedicured feet. I feel ridiculous.

"Eveny, you'll soon learn that *we* don't have to do anything," she says. She turns away without elaborating.

As Mrs. Shriver begins to talk about *The Great Gatsby*, which I read last year in my American Lit class, I spot Chloe sitting beside Peregrine, wearing a dark fur stole. She's paired her oxford with a set of Chanel pearls featuring a diamond-encrusted, interlocking double *C*. Her high-heeled Mary Janes are studded with what look like diamonds, and her hair is artfully mussed.

"Yoo-hoo, Eveny!" she says, waving at me pleasantly. "Welcome!"

I wave back to Chloe vaguely as I realize that no one

seems to be paying any attention to Mrs. Shriver. A cluster of skater-looking guys in the back of the room have pushed their desks together and are playing games on their iPhones. I recognize Arelia and Margaux sitting just behind Peregrine and Chloe, dressed in matching leopard-print cardigans and sky-high heels. There are a few guys wearing purple and gold letter jackets near the center of the room and three cheerleaders who, even in their short-skirted uniforms, look frumpy compared to the Dolls.

I glance down and realize suddenly that Peregrine's big, studded designer tote, which is lying half open on the floor beside her desk, appears to be moving. I let out a strangled gasp as her snake pokes its head out and blinks its beady eyes at me. Mrs. Shriver's monotone monologue about Daisy Buchanan and Nick Carraway screeches to a halt.

"Is there a problem, Ms. Cheval?" Mrs. Shriver asks.

"Uh, no." I'm pretty sure I've now turned as red as my skirt. "Sorry."

"Oh, relax, Eveny," Peregrine says in a bored voice, examining her nails. "It's just Audowido." She looks up at Mrs. Shriver and says, "Don't worry. Everything's under control. You can resume your lecture."

Mrs. Shriver shrugs and begins droning again. I turn to Peregrine. "You bring the *snake* to *school*?"

She looks at me blankly. "Of course." She pauses and adds, "His name is Audowido, by the way. Addressing him simply as 'the snake' is so impersonal. He really dislikes it."

"Oh," I say helplessly.

"I accept your apology," Peregrine says.

I spend the remainder of the class sneaking occasional glances at Audowido, who just keeps staring at me with his unblinking little eyes.

The rest of the morning goes by uneventfully—and thankfully without any other reptilian appearances. There's no one I know in my fourth-period economics class, so when the bell rings and everyone begins flowing toward the cafeteria, I let myself get swept up by the current. The whole way there, I'm hoping I won't have to eat alone.

It's Liv I want to run into, but I see Peregrine and Chloe first, mostly because they're impossible to miss. Not only are they undoubtedly the most gorgeous girls in school, but they're being trailed by a crowd of adoring-looking guys as they sweep into the cafeteria in a cloud of expensive perfume.

"Eveny!" Peregrine exclaims, whisking over to where I'm standing in the caf line, trying to decide between the fried chicken and the gumbo. "What on earth are you doing?"

The cafeteria seems to grind to a halt. Everyone is staring at us, and I can hear a few whispered voices asking who I am and what I'm doing talking with the Dolls.

"Getting ready to order lunch?" I venture.

Both girls laugh like I've said something hilarious. "Oh, nonsense, Eveny," Chloe says. "You'll eat with us in the Hickories, of course."

I open my mouth to reply, but Peregrine beats me to it. "Seating in the Hickories is by invitation only," she says. "And we have a very exclusive list. Obviously you'll want to join us."

It's admittedly nice to have someone asking me to hang out with them, but not for the wrong reasons. The last thing I need is their pity. "Look, just because your moms knew my mom doesn't mean you have to invite me to eat with you," I say stiffly. "I'm fine on my own."

"Oh yes, you look like you're already an *enormous* social success." She gazes around pointedly to underscore the fact that I'm all by myself. "Well?" she prompts. "Are you coming, or are you expecting an engraved invitation?"

"Fine. I'll come find you after I order," I mutter.

"Eveny," Chloe says slowly, looking at me like I'm a mental patient, "we don't *order* our food here. Our lunch is *catered*. Come on."

Confused, I follow them up the grassy knoll behind the school, where I spot Arelia and Margaux spreading out a huge blanket in the shade of an enormous, swooping hickory tree. The grassy patch is surrounded by a dozen smaller hickories, all dripping with sun-dappled Spanish moss. I notice Pascal lounging against one and Justin standing beneath another. He gazes adoringly at Chloe as we approach. "Hey, baby doll," he drawls, stepping out to wrap his arms around her.

She kisses him chastely and steps back to Peregrine's side.

"Gin and tonic?" Arelia asks eagerly as she smoothes a corner of the blanket. It's cashmere, I notice. "Or would you prefer champagne today?"

I'm expecting Peregrine and Chloe to laugh like this is some kind of inside joke. But Peregrine chirps, "G and T," and Chloe says, "Same for me."

Arelia turns to me next, looking confused. I stare right back, trying to figure out how they're planning to drink alcohol out in the open on school property.

"Arelia?" Peregrine begins. "Aren't you going to ask Eveny what she'd like?"

"Seriously?" Arelia says. When Peregrine nods, she turns and says in a tight voice, "Eveny, would you like a gin and tonic too?"

"Uh," I say. Chloe nods encouragingly, so I add, "Sure, okay. Thanks."

Arelia makes me a drink, muttering to herself, as Justin wanders over and drapes himself over Chloe's shoulders like a scarf.

"I missed you today," he says, nuzzling her ear.

"Honestly, Justin, I just saw you three hours ago," Chloe replies with a roll of her eyes, but her expression is delighted.

Five minutes later, we're all seated on the soft blanket, holding crystal tumblers full of ice, liquor, lime wedges, and what look like tiny purple verbena flowers. "Cheers to old friends returning," Peregrine says, holding up her glass in a toast. We all raise our glasses, and everyone turns to look at me.

"And to happy reunions?" I say.

"Hear, hear!" Chloe says cheerfully as Justin plays with her hair. We clink glasses, and I watch as everyone takes a long sip of their drinks. I sniff mine suspiciously. Call me crazy, but it doesn't seem like the first day at a new school is the time to start with a liquor habit.

Fortunately, no one seems to notice I'm not drinking. I watch as Chloe wriggles free of Justin to whisper something to Peregrine. Pascal leers at them while licking his lips, and Justin watches Chloe's every movement like his life depends on it. I'm so intrigued by the fact that Margaux and Arelia are unpacking a full lunch of tea sandwiches and salads from a giant picnic basket that I don't notice anyone else approaching the Hickories until a shadow falls over us. I look up and my heart nearly stops.

It's Caleb Shaw, and in his Pointe Laveau uniform, with a charcoal gray hoodie and navy Chuck Taylors, he's even more gorgeous than he was outside the library.

"Oh," is the first thing he says when he realizes I'm sitting there. I could swear that there's some sort of accusation in his eyes as he stares at me.

"Um," I reply, feeling my cheeks heat up.

"Titillating conversation, kids," Peregrine says, looking amused.

I try to think of something to say, but his gaze is turning my brain to mush.

"I think I'm going to eat in the caf today," Caleb says, refocusing on the group.

"Don't be ridiculous, Caleb," Peregrine says. "Or are you just being pissy because you didn't get to go away this weekend?"

"No, I think being pissy is your thing, not mine."

Peregrine rolls her eyes, but she's smiling.

"You eat with us *every* day," Chloe says. "You're not going to be rude to Eveny, are you?"

He glances at me uncertainly.

"Of course not." But he avoids looking at me as he settles on the far end of the blanket.

Peregrine must notice the same thing, because she's looking back and forth between us with a small smile on her face. "Well, then," she says finally, looking at Chloe.

I cast sidelong glances at Caleb while Arelia and Margaux quickly pile sandwich quarters and spoonfuls of macaroni salad onto gold-rimmed bone china plates and hand them out.

I'm the last to receive my food, which Arelia shoves at me. I take a bite of an egg salad sandwich, which is soft and delicious, as the others take big swigs of their cocktails.

"So, how do you concentrate in the afternoon if you drink these at lunch?" I ask after a moment, holding up my drink.

"We don't have to *concentrate,* silly!" Chloe trills. "Besides, that's what the verbena flower is for. It enhances concentration."

I look at her in confusion. When I was a kid, my mom used to make up funny bedtime stories about herbs and their magical powers—which is probably one of the things that got me so interested in botany—so I'm no stranger to superstition.

But do these girls truly believe that the verbena is having some sort of effect on them? I recall the strange words of Chloe's mom as she handed me the coffee cake last week, and I realize that maybe the answer is yes.

I watch in silence as they continue to sip and eat. Even in the humidity of midday, everyone's hair is perfect, and the girls' makeup hasn't budged. I'm sure that I, on the other hand, look like I've stuck my finger in a light socket, frizzing my hair and insta-melting the foundation off my face. Yet no one has said anything biting about the way I look, although I'm expecting Peregrine to be full of snide remarks.

Margaux spoons second helpings of macaroni salad on Pascal's plate as the conversation turns to the Mardi Gras Ball.

"It's the pinnacle of Carrefour social events," Pascal says, settling down next to me as he digs into his salad. He reaches over after a moment and runs a finger up my spine, which makes me shiver. "Maybe you can be my date."

"Maybe," I say noncommittally, trying to figure out why an impeccably dressed, smarmily handsome guy like Pascal would have any interest in a human frizzball like me. Perhaps because I'm new?

As if she's reading my mind, Peregrine smirks and says, "Pascal, maybe *you* can refrain from attempting to bang the new girl for at least a few days."

I feel eyes on me again, and this time when I look up, Caleb holds my gaze for a long moment before looking away.

Pascal eventually scoots over to flirt with Margaux, and I

see Arelia beginning to gather up the dirty dishes on her own. No one makes a move to help, so I stand, grab a few empty plates and glasses, and make my way over to the picnic basket. I'm about to ask where we wash them—I'm still confused that they eat on china and sip from crystal in the middle of school—but Arelia silences me with a dirty look.

"Just so you know," she says under her breath as Peregrine and Chloe chatter behind us, "it took Margaux and me *years* to become Dolls. So don't make the mistake of assuming that just because you're a Cheval, every door in the world is going to open for you. You still have to work your way up."

"I'm not assuming anything," I reply. I have no idea what she's talking about.

As Arelia snatches the dishes from my hand, I see Caleb stand, hitch his backpack onto his shoulder, and nod good-bye to everyone. As he begins to trudge down the hill, I grab my bag too and quickly thank Peregrine and Chloe for the invitation to eat with them.

"Where are you going in such a hurry, Eveny?" Peregrine asks knowingly.

"Just to class."

"Nothing to do with the cute boy you're chasing after?" Peregrine singsongs. I can hear them laughing as I dash down the hill to catch up with Caleb.

"Hey," I say, pulling up beside him.

He turns and looks oddly nonplussed to see me. "Oh. Hey."

"So," I begin awkwardly, "I'm Eveny."

"I know." For a moment he looks straight ahead, and I have the feeling he's not going to say anything else. But then, as if he's conceding something, he adds, "The girl who thinks reading is cool."

"Well, it is," I say defensively, which makes him laugh.

But his smile is gone as quickly as it appeared, replaced with an expression that looks inexplicably frustrated. "I'm Caleb," he says.

"I know," I reply. A loaded silence stretches between us. I can't figure out why I'm feeling uneasy, or why he's acting almost standoffish. "So, what class are you headed to?" I ask.

"American history."

"Oh, me too!" But he doesn't say a word, and we sink back into silence.

This time, it's Caleb who breaks it. "So you moved from New York?" His tone is reluctant, like he doesn't want to be talking to me at all.

"Yeah, really suddenly. It was right before my birthday last week, and my aunt was just like, 'Hey, we're moving back to Louisiana.' I didn't even have time to prepare for it, you know? I mean, one second, I live in New York, the next second, I'm in the passenger seat of a car headed a thousand miles away. . . ."

I realize I'm babbling. I clamp my mouth shut, embarrassed.

"I've always wanted to go," Caleb says a few seconds later, as if I haven't just sounded like a rambling idiot. "To New York,

I mean. It looks like it would be a pretty cool place. Millions of people. More restaurants than you could visit in a lifetime. Something for everyone."

I'm hit with a pang of longing. "You'd love it there."

"You miss it, I take it?"

"I do. It's home."

Caleb doesn't reply right away. Finally, he turns to look at me. "I thought you'd be back in Carrefour sooner, to be honest."

The change of topic catches me off guard. "What do you mean? You knew who I was before I got here?"

He half smiles at me but doesn't elaborate. "Anyway, happy birthday," he adds after a pause. "Seventeen's the big one."

"Well, not as big as eighteen," I say.

"Not around here."

8

*C*aleb sits across the classroom and doesn't acknowledge me once during the entire fifty-minute period. When the bell rings, he strides out without looking back, and by the time I make it into the hallway, he's completely gone. I hate that this leaves me feeling so disappointed.

I'm relieved to find Liv, the girl from this morning, saving a seat for me in physics, my last class.

"How was your first day?" she asks as I sit down beside her.

"Honestly? Kind of weird."

"That's pretty much every day at Pointe Laveau. I found that out last year when I transferred from Carrefour Secondary. You might as well know I'm from the Périphérie."

"Cool. My friend Drew lives there too. Actually, I was just out there last night with him for a crawfish boil."

"Drew Grady? How do you know him?"

"Our moms were friends when we were kids."

She stares at me oddly as the bell rings. The middle-aged, bespectacled Mr. Cronin welcomes me to class and launches into a lecture about action and reaction. When he finishes and assigns us to review chapters six and seven with a partner, Liv and I resume our conversation.

"I'm sorry, you said you went to the Périphérie last night?" Liv asks.

"Right," I say. I don't get why she's reacting like I've told her I went to Mars.

"But you live on this side of town, don't you?"

"Yes," I say slowly.

"It's just that usually people from this side of town don't spend much time on the other side of the bayou." She shakes her head. "Anyway, Drew's a cool guy. Did he tell you about his band?"

"I think I heard the term 'bayou fusion rock' fifty times last night."

She smiles. "He's a little obsessed. He kind of considers music his ticket out of this town. I've got to say, I think he's kind of onto something."

"His band's good?"

"They're awesome. I'm planning to go to school for music production someday, and I think it would be pretty cool to work with a group like that." She pauses. "Anyway, I know how you must feel, being new and all. I started at the beginning of sophomore year, and it was like no one wanted anything to do with me. Newcomers aren't exactly welcomed with open arms."

"I'm noticing that," I tell her. "So how did you wind up here?"

"The kid with the scholarship before me flunked out. When the spot was offered to me, my dad wouldn't even listen." Her tone is bitter, but only a little. "Switching to this school, it's like crossing a line. People expect you to be different, so it's harder to hang out with everyone back home. But I don't fit at Pointe Laveau because I'm from the Périphérie."

"People really judge you for that?" I ask.

She looks at me like I'm nuts. "Dude, it's the *poor* side of town. That means everything in this place." She pauses. "So what brought you to Carrefour anyhow? We never get new people."

"I'm not exactly new." I tell her what happened with my mother and moving away.

"Your mom's the one who committed suicide? Man, I'm sorry. I remember hearing about that." She looks genuinely sad.

When the bell rings at the end of class, everyone scrambles to grab their bags and dash for the door. Liv walks out with me and hands me a slip of paper with her phone number.

"It's nice to have someone new here," she says. "Other than my best friend Max, who I'll introduce you to tomorrow, and Drew, who's cool, this whole school is really lame."

"What about Peregrine and Chloe and their friends?" I ask carefully.

Liv snorts. "If you're into staring at yourself in the mirror, getting wasted, and maxing out your mother's credit cards, then yeah, they're awesome."

As if on cue, the Dolls round the corner in a cluster. "Eveny!" Peregrine exclaims, stopping in front of us and ignoring Liv entirely. The whole clique draws to a halt behind her. "How was your first day, darling?" Then, without waiting for an answer, she rolls on. "Listen, Chloe and I have a surprise for you! We're getting you a haircut and a makeover on Thursday after school. We've already scheduled an appointment for you at Cristof's Salon."

"But—" I begin to protest, weakly reaching up to touch my tangled mass of red curls. Much as it would be nice to look a little better than I do now, I think I have a grand total of about seventeen dollars in my bank account at the moment. I'm guessing Cristof's services cost more than that. "I'm not sure I can afford it."

"Don't be ridiculous. It's our treat," Peregrine cuts me off. "We won't take no for an answer. Consider it a happy birthday and welcome-back-to-town gift."

Before I can reply, the Dolls are already walking away. Arelia casts me a dirty look over her shoulder, and then they turn the corner and are gone.

When I look back at Liv, she's staring at me suspiciously. "You're friends with *them*?"

"My mom was friends with their moms," I try to explain.

"That doesn't answer why they seem to think you're their new BFF."

"I know," I say helplessly. "I don't understand it either."

"Right," she says. "Well, I'll see you tomorrow." As she walks away, I know a wall has gone up between us. I wonder if the Dolls have done something cruel to Liv, and suddenly, I feel guilty. But even though all the logic in me tells me I should steer clear, I'm feeling more and more drawn to them by the day. It's like they hold the key to who I once was—and who I'm supposed to be.

Everyone else is roaring out of the parking lot in their expensive cars, but Aunt Bea left a voice mail saying that she's tied up with something at the bakery and can't reach Boniface to ask him to get me, so I'm stuck walking home. I don't mind, actually. I used to walk all the time in New York; it was a chance to be alone with my thoughts, even in a sea of people.

But fifteen minutes later, the sun disappears completely, the humidity becomes oppressive, and the clouds turn black. I quicken my pace, but I'm only halfway around the cemetery when there's a deep, earthshaking rumble and the skies open up.

I curse and begin running toward my house, but the rain is coming down in driving torrents, soaking me to the core, and the road is getting muddier by the second. Lightning is flashing everywhere, sending electricity crackling through the air. The wind is holding me back, and I look up nervously at all the arching oak and cypress trees over the road; any of them could be a lightning rod in a storm. It would be just my luck to have survived my first day of school only to get electrocuted on the way home.

As I trip and fall over a branch in the road, sending mud splattering all over my uniform, I notice a black Jeep Cherokee with a faded surfboard strapped to the top pulling up on my left.

"Get in!" yells the driver through the open window. It takes me a moment of wiping the rain out of my eyes to realize it's Caleb. I scramble ungracefully to my feet, slosh through a puddle, yank the door open, and tumble inside.

"Sorry about your seat," I say as my drenched skirt squishes loudly against the vinyl.

"It'll dry," Caleb replies. As soon as I shut the door behind me, he guns the engine and continues up the road without another word.

"Thanks for stopping," I say. I smooth my hair a little but suspect it doesn't help. "So you live out in this direction too?" I have to raise my voice to be heard over the roar of the downpour.

He nods, and for a moment I'm afraid he's not going to answer. Then he says, "Other side of the cemetery from your place."

"How do you know where I live?"

"Eveny, everyone knows. Your family is as legendary in

this town as Chloe's and Peregrine's." He doesn't elaborate, nor does he look at me.

"So," I say, bridging the silence. "I heard you aced your PSATs." And then, because I apparently have some sort of disease that makes me blurt out idiotic things in front of handsome, enigmatic guys, I hear myself add, "Rock on."

I can see him hiding a smile. "No big deal," he says gruffly. But then he adds, "Does that mean you've been checking up on me?"

"What? No. Of course not." I can feel my cheeks turning red. "But I did notice that you surf." Outside, there's a huge roll of thunder, and lightning crackles across the sky.

"How do you know that?"

I point upward. "There's a board strapped to the roof."

He laughs. "Right. Yeah, I take my board out whenever I get a chance. Or I used to, anyhow. I won't be going much anymore." A muscle in his jaw twitches as his expression hardens.

He probably wants me to shut up, but it's not every day you meet a hot surfer who also happens to be a mysterious PSAT-acing genius, and I'm desperate to know more about him. "So, surfing, huh? I thought we were pretty landlocked here," I say.

"We are." For the first time since I've met him, his face relaxes a little. "I actually drive to a beach in the Florida panhandle called Sailfish Island, which is about four and a half hours away." A faraway look crosses his eyes for a moment as he adds, "You wouldn't believe the way the sunrise looks over the Gulf from the east side of the island."

"Sounds beautiful," I say, embarrassed that I'm suddenly picturing myself with Caleb on a beach watching the sun come up. Stupid overactive imagination. "So you think you'll get out there again soon?"

Everything in his face immediately shuts down. "Things are different now. It's a long story." He stares straight ahead, and I have the strangest feeling he's suddenly mad at me.

I try to make casual conversation as Caleb turns onto the road leading up the hill toward my house, but his only replies are one-word answers.

By the time he pulls up my driveway and sweeps the Jeep around in front of the house, the silence and tension in the car are so thick I can feel them.

"Well," I say awkwardly, grabbing my sopping backpack from the floor, "thank you again."

When he doesn't reply, I get out into the rain, which is pounding down so hard that I barely hear him say, "Rock on, Eveny," in that perfect, deep voice of his, just before I slam the door closed.

And then, before I have the chance to react, he's already pulling away.

9

The storms have passed by that evening, but the humidity lingers in the air, making it hard to breathe. Drew is still out sick, and I try calling him a few times but it goes straight to voice mail. I remind him he's invited to Aunt Bea's bakery opening on Wednesday night, but he texts back that he's not sure he'll feel well enough to be there.

I eat lunch Tuesday and Wednesday inside the caf with Liv and her friend Max, a scrawny, smart guy who wears thick hipster glasses and announces right away that he's gay. "Just so you don't accidentally develop a crush on me," he adds quite seriously. "It's been known to happen." He tells me that he's from central Carrefour instead of the Périphérie, but that he's always been kind of different from the other kids at Pointe Laveau, so he has that in common with Liv.

"You may have noticed," he says stiffly, "that unless you get a blessing from Peregrine and Chloe, you might as well not exist around here."

Liv chomps angrily on her burger and says, "Eveny *hasn't* noticed, considering the Dolls are, like, totally fixated on her."

And as bizarre as it seems, she's right. Peregrine and Chloe beam at me in English class, wave hello to me in the halls, and seem bewildered when I say I'll be eating in the caf instead of the Hickories.

"But no one *ever* turns down an invitation to eat with us," Chloe tells me Wednesday, looking truly baffled as she wanders away from me and heads outside.

The thing is, even though I know it's supposed to be some kind of huge deal to be invited into the Dolls' inner circle, I'd prefer to eat with people I like. And I like Liv and Max. They remind me of my friends back in New York, but more than that, they're *normal*. The Dolls, on the other hand, seem like they're from Planet Glamour. I look out the window at their tree-shaded spot overlooking the school, and I see both Peregrine and Chloe gazing at me coolly, as if they can read my mind.

"Told you that you couldn't just automatically become one of us," Arelia trills as she passes me in the hall on the way to fifth period.

"I never said I wanted to," I reply sweetly, although she's already disappearing around the corner with Margaux. But I feel a little annoyed that she apparently thinks I've been banished from the Hickories for not being cool enough.

Caleb Shaw is the one flaw in my plan, because if I exile myself from the glamazons in the Hickories, I'll be writing myself out of his life too. He doesn't even look at me in American history, the one class we share, though I have the weirdest feeling he's aware of my every move. He shifts in his seat each time I shift in mine, and sometimes I swear I can feel his eyes on me even though he's always gazing off into space when I turn around.

Boniface picks me up after school on Wednesday and drives me the short distance to Aunt Bea's bakery for the opening.

"Any luck finding the key for the parlor doors?" I ask him on the way. I still can't shake the nightmares I've had twice now, and I've begun to think that the only way to convince myself they're just dreams is to get inside the room.

"Not yet, Eveny," he says, and the uneasy feeling sticks with me as we drive the rest of the way to Main Street in silence.

Aunt Bea is rushing around like a flour-covered maniac when we get there, and the bakery smells heavenly. The plan for the opening night party is that she'll have miniature versions of a dozen of her signature pastries circulated by two waiters. Because the shop is so tiny, the celebration will spill out onto the street, so Boniface heads outside to set up a few high-top tables and tablecloths while I go into the back to help frost miniature cakes.

"Did you invite any of your new friends?" Aunt Bea asks

hopefully as she hands me a pastry-decorating bag filled with lemon-thyme icing for the olive oil cakes.

"A few," I tell her as I carefully pipe the pale yellow icing. "I texted Drew, but he's been out sick. There's a girl Liv at school who might make it, and maybe this guy Max too."

The timer goes off on one of her ovens, and she turns to remove a baking sheet full of chocolate mint meringues. "And how about Peregrine and Chloe?"

"I didn't ask them."

"They might come with their mothers," Aunt Bea says lightly. "I felt like I needed to invite them since they were such close friends of your mom's."

"Makes sense."

Aunt Bea peers at me curiously. "You aren't getting along with them?"

"I'm not *not* getting along with them," I hedge. "They've actually been pretty nice to me. It's just that they're so . . . different." She waits for me to continue, and after a moment, I add, "I guess I don't really get why they want to be friends with me. They're completely opposite from me in every way."

Aunt Bea turns away and begins to frost a big tray full of chocolate lavender cakes. "Tradition means a lot in this town," she says.

"Everyone keeps saying that," I say, "but I have to be friends with them just because my great-great-grandma liked their great-great-grandma?"

"It's more than that. But I'm glad you're a little skeptical.

It's important that you remember who you are and how I raised you."

Three hours later, the bakery and sidewalk out front are filled with at least a hundred people. Everyone seems to know Aunt Bea and Boniface, and I watch with pride as they circulate among the crowd.

Along with the chocolate lavender cakes, the lemon-thyme olive oil cakes, and the chocolate mint meringues, Aunt Bea has also prepared butter sage cookies, rosemary popcorn balls, pear and bay leaf tarts, and several other herb-based confections. "I wanted to honor my sister, Sandrine, whom many of you knew," Aunt Bea says in an impromptu speech on the front step just past six thirty. "She loved flowers and herbs, so we'll specialize in just that: baked goods with an herbal or floral twist. I hope you enjoy tonight's party, and please do come see me again soon."

The crowd applauds and goes back to chowing down. I feel proud of Aunt Bea and especially connected to my mother as I jump behind the counter and help the two harried waiters fill up champagne flutes. Liv and Max make a brief appearance and thank me politely for inviting them, but they disappear soon after, Liv mumbling that this isn't exactly her crowd. I don't have time to feel bad, though, because Peregrine, Chloe, and the other Dolls sweep in a few minutes later.

"So sorry we're late, sweetie," Peregrine says as she glides over to me. She's wearing a floor-length leather coat, a leather miniskirt, a sheer silk blouse, and leather stiletto heels that lace up to her knees. Her stone necklace catches the pale light of the bakery and shimmers against her dark skin. "But it's dreadfully tacky to arrive on time, don't you think?"

I open my mouth to reply, but Chloe beats me to it. "We really did mean to be here earlier," she says. "But Pascal couldn't decide on a pair of shoes."

He looks offended. "I have over a hundred," he says. "And I wanted to look just right."

"You look nice," I say. And aside from his smarmy expression, he does. He's in a tailored black suit with an eggplant-colored shirt that's unbuttoned at the collar. The expensive-looking tasseled leather loafers he's wearing complete the look.

"They're Italian," he says, gesturing to his shoes. "Custom made."

Chloe looks like she's channeling vintage Carrie Bradshaw in a frilly pale pink tutu made from a hundred layers of tulle. Her legs look long and tanned, and she's wearing camel-colored stiletto ankle boots, a tight, military-style camel leather jacket, and an intricately beaded white tank top to complete the look. Like Peregrine, she's wearing her black stone necklace. Justin, in designer jeans and a suit jacket with a lime green pocket square, is draped on her arm like an accessory. "This place is gorgeous, Eveny," he tells me before asking if that was Max and Liv he saw just a few minutes ago. He looks weirdly disappointed when I tell him they've already gone.

Arelia and Margaux are there too, wearing nearly matching little black dresses.

"Where's Caleb?" I whisper to Chloe as the others move toward the bakery counter to grab drinks.

"Ah, so you *do* like him," she says knowingly. "Peregrine was right."

"No." I can feel myself turning red. "I mean, I barely know him. I just thought he was always with you guys."

"Not always," she says. "He goes away a lot."

"Surfing, right?"

She looks surprised. "I see you've talked to him." When I nod, she looks troubled. "Just so you know, he kind of broke Peregrine's heart last year."

I feel like she's dumped a bucket of water over my head. "He and Peregrine dated?"

But then Chloe leans closer and says, "Don't tell Peregrine I told you, but I don't know if I'd call it dating exactly. She was in love with him forever, and they finally went out on a few dates, but nothing ever happened."

"Do you know why?"

"I just don't think he was that into her."

"Come on. That's impossible."

"No, Caleb's different. I think that's what drove Peregrine nuts: the idea that he wasn't automatically attracted to her like every other guy in the world." The corner of Chloe's mouth twitches, and I have the feeling that she was at least a little bit glad to see someone reject Peregrine. "Anyway, she hasn't dated anyone since then."

"But she's surrounded by guys every time I see her."

KIKI SULLIVAN 97

"I didn't say she doesn't make out or have fun with them. She just doesn't let them in anymore."

"So she still likes Caleb?" I wonder if being interested in him makes me a traitor to the girl who's inexplicably trying to befriend me. Not that I owe Peregrine anything.

"They're just good friends now. But I think she's still pissed that she couldn't have him. Anyway, I'd be careful, that's all."

She lingers for a moment like she wants to say more, but then she drifts away. Shortly thereafter, she and the Dolls leave without saying good-bye.

It's not until the party is winding down and the last few stragglers are finishing their champagne that I spot him. Or at least I think I do. He's standing outside the bakery window, dressed in jeans and a tight gray T-shirt. But his face is obscured by the shadows, so I'm not one hundred percent sure.

I hurry out the front door of the bakery. "Caleb?" I call. But the street is empty, and I feel foolish. I've reached a real low point if I'm conjuring imaginary images of the guy I'm developing a very real crush on.

"Ready to head home?" Aunt Bea comes up behind me and puts a hand on my shoulder. "I'm beat. I can do all the cleanup tomorrow morning."

"Sounds good," I reply. "Mom would be really proud of you, Aunt Bea."

She gives me a hug. "She'd be proud of you too, honey," she says. "In so very many ways."

I'm wound up from the party and confused about Peregrine and Caleb's dating history and Chloe's warning, so it takes me until almost two in the morning to drift off into an uneasy sleep.

For the first time in almost a week, the strange nightmare returns. I'm floating down the stairs again, and just like before, the hallway begins to fill with blood. But now there are voices too, coming from behind the closed doors.

> *For each ray of light, there's a stroke of dark.*
> *For each possibility, one has gone.*
> *For each action, a reaction.*
> *Ever in balance, the world spins on.*

The voices fade away as I float into the parlor, which I now notice has walls lined with broad crystal mirrors. When I blink into the darkness, I can just barely make out the shape of the toddler version of myself standing in blood, crying.

"Eveny!" I call to her, but she can't hear me. She falls to her knees in the darkness, still sobbing. "Eveny!" I cry out again, and this time she turns, her face and hands streaked with blood. . . .

I awaken with a start, drenched in sweat. The visions are getting more and more vivid; this one was like watching a movie on a high-def screen. I've never dreamed like this before. *What the hell is going on here?*

I try to go back to sleep, but it's impossible. After a while, I glance at my clock and see that it's 2:36 a.m. I flick my bedside light on and get up. Maybe I'll feel better if I can get into the parlor and reassure myself that the dreams aren't real.

I rifle through my bag until I find a couple of paper clips in a side pocket, then I quickly bend one so that it's a single long piece of metal and the other so that it's folded over once on itself: a picklock, like Mer taught me to make last summer when I was locked out of my apartment. I shove both make-shift tools into the pocket of my sweatpants, grab a flashlight, and head out my bedroom door.

I creep down the stairs, keeping my flashlight aimed low. In the front hall, I bend to inspect the floor just outside the parlor. This is the spot where the blood always pools in my nightmare, but of course it looks completely normal now. *It's just a dream, you dork*, I tell myself. But then I touch the ground to get my balance as I stand up, and for the quickest of instants, I catch a flash of crimson staining the beautiful hardwood.

"You're seeing things," I tell myself aloud. But when I reach tentatively for the floor again, the dark stain reappears the moment my index finger makes contact. I hold it there this time long enough to notice two tiny, child-sized footprints in the faded stain. I stand up, and the floor returns to looking normal.

"What the . . . ?" I whisper. I reach for the thick brass handle of the parlor door, but I pull away as soon as my fingers make contact. It's burning hot. I try again, holding on tighter as I tug hard, and when I yank my hand back, my palm is a scalded red.

My hand shaking, I pull the paper clip tools from my pocket and prepare to insert the longer one into the lock on the door. But the second metal touches metal, I'm struck with a jolt of electricity so sharp that I'm thrown backward.

Completely weirded out, I scramble to my feet and place my palm against the wood of the door, trying to steady myself. But the instant my skin makes contact, I'm hit with a vivid image.

There's blood everywhere, and suddenly, a shadow in the corner of the parlor catches my eye. Before I have a chance to call out or see who it is, the figure slips out the door in silence. . . .

I yank my hand away. "This can't be happening."

I take a deep breath and reach for the door once more, tentatively, but nothing happens. I pull away and try again, but when my finger connects with the door, there's nothing unusual about it, no uninvited images of blood and shadows.

Slowly, I back away. Am I losing my mind?

But when I look down at my right palm, it's still red, throbbing, and painful—proof that I'm not imagining things.

Something's going on, but whatever secrets this house is holding, it's not giving them up tonight.

After smearing Neosporin on my hand, I wander into the living room, my heart still racing wildly.

I sit on the sofa and reach for the framed photo of my mom

on the coffee table to the left. Thinking about her always helps center me, and I feel as off-kilter now as I ever have. "What the heck is going on in this house, Mom?" I ask the photo, which was taken on her wedding day. She's standing in the garden, wearing a beautiful gown of layered lace, her red hair done up in an elaborate twist. She's laughing and looking at someone off to the side of the photo, but I can't see who it is. Curious, I turn the frame over and gently begin to slide the photo out. As I do, another picture, which was hiding behind the wedding one, flutters to the floor.

I bend to pick it up, and I'm so surprised that I almost drop it. It's a photo of me when I was two or three months old, my red curls so vibrant that I look like a Raggedy Ann doll. My mother is holding me, her expression serene and happy, but what shocks me is the sandy-haired man beside her, his arm slung around her shoulders, staring down at me lovingly.

It's my father—the father Aunt Bea always told me left before I was born and never returned.

"That's impossible," I say aloud. But the image is unmistakable. I turn the photo over after a moment and am even more surprised to see a note scribbled on the back.

> *I'll watch over Every always.*
> *—Love eternal, Matthias*

Not only had my father come back to see my mother and me, but he'd made her a promise that he'd always watch over me.

The image from the cemetery, the one that hit me so vividly as we entered Carrefour last week, flashes through my mind again as clear as day. *They're coming for you*, my father said. *You have to be ready.*

So was the cemetery recollection a dream, or had he really been watching over me like he promised? And does Aunt Bea know he'd come back at least once? I'm still staring at the back of the photo in confusion when something outside catches my eye.

I blink into the darkness beyond the back window. For a moment, I think I'm imagining things, but then I see it: three faint beams of light bobbing through the gloom of the cemetery beyond the garden wall.

I jump to my feet and press my nose against the glass as I peer out into the blackness. There's no mistaking it: three shadowy figures are making their way through the maze of tombs beyond our back wall. Suddenly, I have the crazy sense that whatever's going on out there is connected to the dreams I'm having and the weird mystery of my own house.

Before I can question my own sanity—and let's face it, I'm pretty sure I'm losing it anyhow—I grab my flashlight and stuff my bare feet into an old pair of Aunt Bea's ballet flats I find laying in the laundry room. I'm careful to open and close the back door as quietly as possible, and I keep the flashlight off. The moon overhead provides just enough light to see.

It's only once I've landed in the mud on the cemetery side

of the wall that I realize exactly what I've done. I've dashed out of my house without leaving a note, climbed into a creepy cemetery in the middle of the night, and am pursuing a group of people sneaking around in the darkness—all because of a completely baseless theory.

"Brilliant, Eveny," I mutter. I'm just about to turn back when I hear it: a faint, female voice in the distance, singing words I'm beginning to know well.

> *For each ray of light, there's a stroke of dark.*
> *For each possibility, one has gone.*
> *For each action, a reaction.*
> *Ever in balance, the world spins on.*

Just like in my dream and on the hallway wall.

Now I'm desperate to know what's happening. My heart hammers faster as I make my way deeper into the cemetery, the light of the half-moon growing fainter above the thick canopy of trees. I can clearly see the three beams of light now, bouncing toward a small clearing up ahead. I flatten myself against a tomb and pray that no one is looking in my direction. Carefully, I peer around the edge.

I notice three things at once in the pale light of the moon.

First, there are at least two dozen candles flickering on the ground, laid out in a circle.

Second, the three people standing in the middle of the circle, eyes closed, hands raised to the sky, are Peregrine,

Chloe, and Pascal.

And finally, Audowido is winding his way slowly down one of Peregrine's outstretched arms, his scaly body reflecting the moonlight as he hisses into the silence of the night.

10

I watch in shock as Audowido slithers to the ground and Peregrine begins calling out loudly to someone or something called Eloi Oke—*El-ooh-ah Oh-key.* "Come to us now, Eloi Oke, and open the gate. Come to us now, Eloi Oke, and open the gate. Come to us now, Eloi Oke, and open the gate."

She pounds on the ground with a big, gnarled stick, while Chloe holds up a huge silver triangle dangling from a string and strikes it once before dropping it. I half expect the earth to open up beneath them, but all that happens is an unnatural calm settles over the cemetery as the air goes completely still.

Peregrine releases the stick and joins hands with Chloe and Pascal, whose eyes are closed. All three of them look like they're in some sort of trance, and I wonder for a moment if they're drunk, or maybe even high. Peregrine says something else, in a language I don't understand, and then she repeats the phrase twice more.

Chloe and Pascal begin to dance slowly, their feet thudding against the ground in an unhurried, deliberate rhythm, their hips swaying in time. After a moment, Peregrine joins in too, and I realize I can hear a distant, musical tinkling sound. Then I see the moonlight glinting off tiny bells attached to all of their wrists and ankles. The breeze that has picked up out of nowhere carries the sound skyward.

The dancing gets faster and wilder as Peregrine chants more urgently in a sultry, velvety voice. Soon Chloe is singing along with her, her voice sweeter and higher. Pascal is the last to join in, his voice gravelly and low. Audowido is coiled in the middle of the circle now, and as the song gets louder, he begins to rise up toward the half-moon, his body weaving in time. Suddenly, he turns his head toward me and freezes as his eyes lock with mine.

It takes all my self-control to keep from screaming. If I didn't know better, I'd think the damned snake had just cracked a small, satisfied smile. After a long moment, he turns his gaze skyward and begins swaying to the music again.

I fall back against the tomb as Peregrine, Chloe, and Pascal abruptly let go of each other's hands and open their eyes. Audowido retreats back into the studded leather bag, and Peregrine waits for him to vanish before she kneels in the dirt and begins digging with her bare hands. After a moment she stands and brushes her hands off.

"It shall be done," Chloe says solemnly. She pulls a cloth bag out of her pocket and sprinkles some sort of black powder in the shallow hole.

"It shall be done," Pascal echoes, pulling a cloth bag from his own pocket and doing the same thing.

"It shall be done," Peregrine says solemnly, sprinkling powder of her own into the hole.

They join hands again, and this time, while their chanting is louder, I can't understand most of the words.

"*Fantom nan sot pase a, tande sa pledwaye nou an,*" they say together. "*Move lespri a sot pase a, tande sa pledwaye nou an.*"

There's a sudden chill in the air, like the temperature has dropped twenty degrees. I shiver and begin to back away slowly, but I stop in my tracks when I hear them say a familiar name—Justin Cooper. I also hear them chant the name of a guy I don't know, someone named Beau Fontenot. I squint into the darkness to see what they're doing, and my eyes widen when I see each of the girls holding up a small rag doll.

They throw the dolls into the shallow hole, then kneel on the ground and smooth dirt back over the open space. When the ground is flat and the dolls have been buried, each of them spits on the earth. Once they're standing again, Peregrine begins to chant: "Dandelion and mojo beans, sandalwood and lemon balm, we draw your power. Spirits, open the gates of Carrefour on Saturday night." She holds up a handful of herbs to the sky, then she drops them on the ground, reaches for the stone that dangles around her neck, and joins hands with the others.

I hear them say twice in unison something that sounds like *"Mesi, zanset."* But before they can say the words a third time, Chloe pulls away.

"We can't do this," she says. "It's wrong."

Peregrine rolls her eyes and tries to grab Chloe's hand. "Oh come on, goody-two-shoes," she says. "You don't have a problem when we're making boys fall in love with *you*, but now you don't want to complete *my* charm?"

Goose bumps prickle up and down my arms as I try to process what they're saying.

"This is different," Chloe says in a small voice. "Especially after Glory . . ."

Peregrine laughs, and the sound cuts through the still night air like a knife. "Glory's death had nothing to do with this."

"But don't you think we should be trying to figure out what happened to her instead of playing?" Chloe asks.

"You don't think I'm doing that?" Peregrine demands. "I'm exhausted. There's no harm in creating a teeny, tiny exception to the protection charm so that we can have a little fun as a reward for all our hard work."

"I just really, really don't think it's a good idea," Chloe replies.

Peregrine's eyes narrow, and she says, "Well, I didn't think it was a good idea to cast a charm on Hazel Arceneaux when she tried to hit on Justin, did I? But I did it because it was important to you."

"That's different," Chloe mumbles. "Justin's my soul mate."

"You're being a hypocrite," Peregrine says calmly. "Now are you in, or am I going to have to throw this party all by myself?"

I wait for Chloe to fight back, but instead she says something under her breath, grabs the hands of Peregrine and Pascal, and says along with them in a low voice, *"Mesi, zanset."*

"There," Peregrine says, dropping Chloe's hand. "Was that so bad?"

"I hate you sometimes," Chloe says, but I can see a small smile on her face, and Peregrine begins to laugh.

Pascal is watching them with his arms crossed over his chest. "Are you sure it worked?"

Peregrine glares at him. "Of course it did."

"I was really looking forward to the idea of hot sorority girls arriving on our doorstep like pizza delivery," he continues. "But usually we can feel it if a charm works, and I didn't feel a damned thing this time."

"Me neither," Chloe agrees. She hesitates and adds in a small voice. "Maybe we're running out of power."

"You two are so tiresome." Peregrine sighs.

"Don't you think it's maybe time we get Eveny involved?" Chloe asks.

What the . . .

"It's not like we have a choice," Peregrine mutters.

"So we'll talk to her tomorrow?" Chloe asks.

"You better hope you're right about her," Pascal says, "or everything goes to hell around here."

Without waiting for a reply, he strides off into the darkness, away from where I'm standing.

"I don't think she knows anything yet," Chloe says stiffly after the sound of his footsteps has faded. "At all."

Peregrine makes a noise. "Well, her hippie aunt is completely useless. What do you expect?"

Chloe kicks at the dirt. "I don't know. In a way, it must have been kind of nice to have a normal life all these years, don't you think?"

"A normal life?" Peregrine repeats. "I can't think of anything more pointless. Not when you have powers like ours."

She grabs her bag from the ground, stomping off before Chloe can respond. After a moment, Chloe scrambles after her.

I stand still for a good five minutes to make absolutely sure Peregrine, Chloe, and Pascal are gone. Then I give in to the weakness in my knees and slowly slide down the tomb until I'm sitting in the dirt. I can't understand why they'd mention Aunt Bea and me.

I knew the Dolls were odd, but is it possible they actually believe they have some sort of magical powers? Though as much as I want to dismiss what I just saw as some sort of sorority ritual, I can't deny the way the air got deathly still the instant they began their ceremony, or how a breeze picked up as soon as they began to dance.

I struggle to my feet and creep into the clearing, which is bathed in lemon meringue moonlight. It appears to be a well-defined crossroads. Three of the four corners are grave plots, filled with shadowy, aboveground tombs and mausoleums of all shapes and sizes. The fourth corner, where I saw them bury the dolls, sits entirely empty, except for the handful of herbs Peregrine threw to the ground. I bend to look at them and am startled to realize they're an ashy, burned black. I could have sworn they were alive when she let them go.

I take a deep breath and begin digging with my left hand; my right is still throbbing from grabbing the parlor door. Side by side in the hole lie two dolls, each with a name written across it, a lock of hair glued to it, and a feather pinned to it. The one that says *Justin Cooper* has a pale pink feather, and the one that says *Beau Fontenot* sports a bright red feather. The dolls have crudely sewn *x*'s where their mouths and eyes should be. Like the real-life Justin, the miniature version has brown hair and is wearing pants and a shirt that vaguely resemble the Pointe Laveau uniform. Beau is sporting a purple letter jacket.

I can't possibly piece together everything I just saw while squatting in the middle of a cemetery, so I shove the Justin doll in my pocket and push the dirt back over the other doll. I stand up, my legs shaking, and make a run for it toward my house, no longer caring if I make noise.

11

A few minutes before seven the next morning, I sit down across from Aunt Bea, who looks wide-awake and cheerful after her successful opening. "Morning, hon," she says through a mouthful of Cheerios. She's reading the *New York Times* on her iPad, just like she does every day at the breakfast table. She looks up at me and the smile falls from her face. "What's wrong?"

I take a deep breath. "Aunt Bea, there's some seriously strange shit going on in this town, and I want to know what it is." I do my best to look threatening.

She sets her iPad down. I can tell she's trying to appear casual as she says, "What would make you say that, Eveny?"

"Drew said something about satanic rituals in town, and I thought he was just being dramatic until I saw Peregrine, Chloe, and Pascal perform a ceremony in the cemetery last night."

She blinks a few times. "What were you doing in the cemetery?"

"You're missing the point."

"Okay." She looks at the table. "Well, first of all, I can assure you that nothing like satanism is going on here. That's just idle gossip."

"Oh come on. This town is cut off from the outside world by a big, creepy gate! Everything's in bloom, even though it's January! But you drive a half mile away across the bayou, and it's winter again." I'm ticking things off on my fingers as I go. "I've been having bad dreams about the parlor, and last night I burned my hand trying to open the door. And now, the daughters of Mom's best friends, who look and dress like supermodel gabillionaires, are sneaking around in cemeteries at night, casting spells on people! You're going to tell me nothing's going on?"

"Charms," my aunt murmurs. "Not spells." As she takes a bite of her Cheerios, her hand is shaking so hard I can hear her spoon clattering against her teeth. "Why are you so sure I'll know the answers, anyhow?"

"Because I heard them mention you—and me. Not to mention the fact that you've been walking around since we got here saying cryptic things about how I have so much more in common with these girls than I realize. What, am I supposed to be out there with them, dancing around with snakes and burying voodoo dolls?"

"They're not voodoo dolls," she says right away. When I

continue to look at her, she sighs and says, "Look, before we get into an explanation, I need you to tell me that you won't get sucked into all of this before you've had a chance to understand what it's all about."

"I'm not making you any promises until you start being honest with me," I shoot back.

"Well, I guess that's fair." She studies her cereal for a moment. "Okay. To start with, I'm guessing that what you saw in the cemetery was a zandara ceremony."

"A what ceremony?"

"Zandara. It's a kind of magic only practiced here in Carrefour."

She stands up from the table and takes her bowl to the sink. I stare at her in disbelief as she washes her leftover cereal down the drain then turns on the disposal. When the rumbling is over, the silence feels dead and all-encompassing.

"Aunt Bea?" I prompt.

"I don't even know where to begin."

"How about at the beginning?"

She nods slowly, and when she speaks again, her voice is firm and steady. "At one time our ancestors were very powerful practitioners of voodoo. But in 1863, they, along with Peregrine's and Chloe's ancestors, struck their own deal with the fates because they felt voodoo was getting too commercialized. The final straw was when your great-great-great-great-grandmother learned that a Confederate general was purchasing potions and using them to defeat Union soldiers in battle.

"Our ancestors didn't want any part of that," she continues, "so they sought out a powerful spirit named Eloi Oke, who agreed to serve as a gatekeeper between this world and the world of the spirits, and—"

"That's the name I heard them say in the cemetery," I interrupt.

She nods. "He agreed to help in exchange for letting him and some of his friends possess them once a year on Mardi Gras so that they could experience life in human form again. A small price to pay for the power he opens them to."

"Oh yes, being possessed by a ghost," I mutter. "Such a small price to pay."

Aunt Bea ignores me. "So zandara developed as a way to trade for what the queens wanted through communication with different spirits. All the magic centers around living things that grow from the soil, because they're a direct link between life and death. Zandara queens just need to find a spirit who's willing to help them channel the power of those plants once Eloi Oike opens the gate to the nether."

It feels like my head is spinning as I try to keep up. "What's the nether?"

"The world between life and death, where some spirits are stranded for a while. It's people who did something wrong in their lives and can't move on to a peaceful death. They long for human comforts because they're closer to the human world than most spirits. That's how queens barter with them, by providing those things through occasional possession ceremonies."

"And you're saying zandara only exists here in Carrefour?"

"It's where the queens decided to make their home, for their own protection." Aunt Bea's expression grows serious. "Just before the turn of the last century in New Orleans, seven French immigrants who believed the magical arts were evil founded a group called Main de Lumière. They zeroed in on zandara and began a 'Crusade of Light.'"

Aunt Bea draws a deep breath before going on. "They started murdering practitioners who were part of your great-great-great-grandmother Eléonore's group, claiming they were cleansing the world of evil.

"In early 1903, a Main de Lumière soldier killed Eléonore's younger daughter, who was three years old at the time." I gasp as Aunt Bea continues. "If he'd killed her firstborn, as he believed he was doing, he would have destroyed zandara forever. You see, only the firstborn daughter of each of the three queens inherits power, generation after generation, so that the balance of power will never change. Killing a future queen would have ended that family's magical bloodline.

"Eléonore and the other zandara practitioners had to leave New Orleans immediately if they were to escape Main de Lumière's bloodlust," Aunt Bea continues. "They chose the land we're on now because it was out in the middle of nowhere. Crossroads are very powerful in zandara— symbolic of the intersection between this world and the nether—so the queens built a crossroads in the cemetery and performed the founding ceremony of Carrefour there, imbuing the town with power and protection.

"Over the years, the queens and their descendants have let in a few thousand carefully screened outsiders to ward off suspicion," she says. "If they had kept Carrefour to only themselves and their *sosyete*—the small group of trusted insiders they practiced their magic with—a town so tiny would have looked suspicious. But allowing the town to grow slowly in a very controlled manner has let Carrefour look from the outside like a typical small bayou town. Most of the families here have no idea that magic is keeping Carrefour afloat, so for a long time, the town existed without raising Main de Lumière's suspicions."

"Wait, Main de Lumière still exists?"

"Unfortunately." Aunt Bea's expression is grave. "In fact, I think it's possible they found you in New York. The way you described the man you thought was following you—pale face, blond hair, slinking around in the shadows—it fits what we know of Main de Lumière soldiers."

"And they're after me because . . . ?"

"As this generation's direct descendant to Eléonore, you're the next in line to the throne."

My mouth goes dry. "I'm a . . . zandara queen?" I manage.

She looks down for a long time before answering. "I wanted to protect you as long as I could, because I think your mother might still be alive if it wasn't for zandara. And because I wanted you to have better values than this town would have given you. You're different from Peregrine and Chloe, Eveny. They may be your sister queens, but that doesn't mean you have to become one of them."

"This isn't possible." I shake my head. "I've never felt powerful or magical or capable of anything close to what you're talking about."

Aunt Bea frowns. "A queen comes into her abilities on her seventeenth birthday, which means that you wouldn't have begun feeling anything magical until last week."

I stare at her in disbelief. I'm not sure what to ask first, so I settle for the simplest question. "Okay, I can see why we had to leave New York if you thought some Main de Lumière guy had found me, but we could have hid somewhere cool and far away like London or Paris or the Siberian tundra. Why come back to Carrefour?"

"You're safest here. The whole town is under a protective charm. Unless someone is in possession of a key, which is passed down through generations and bestowed on new families only by the queens, they can't enter. It's like there's an invisible barbed wire fence all around us.

"In fact," she adds, "we believe Main de Lumière has finally found Carrefour after all these years because, without your mom to complete the triumvirate, the protective charms have weakened. Peregrine's and Chloe's mothers have been able to continue performing the annual Mardi Gras Possession ceremony, so they've accrued *some* favors from the spirits, but their power has greatly diminished and so has the protection around the town because there aren't three queens."

"But now that I'm back . . . ," I say in a hollow voice.

"You, Peregrine, and Chloe are all seventeen. That means you're queens now and can begin casting together, restoring the full power of a triumvirate to Carrefour. But," she continues, her face darkening, "I don't trust them, Eveny, and I don't trust their mothers. They've used their magic selfishly and carelessly, drawing power in ways that are strictly forbidden. The town is dying because of it."

"So what am I supposed to do?" I ask desperately.

"I don't know, I really don't." She leans in to kiss me on the forehead and adds, "Remember, there are only a handful of people in town who know about this. You must keep all of it a secret, or you'll put us in terrible danger." She checks her watch and grimaces. "I'm sorry, but I have to go. We can talk more later."

She walks out of the room before I can get another word out.

A moment later, I hear the front door open and slam closed, then the sound of her car's engine being revved in the driveway. By the time I make it to the front window to look outside, she's already gone, leaving me alone with a thousand questions I don't have the answers to.

I stay home from school that day because I can't go off to Pointe Laveau and pretend that things are normal after everything I've just learned. Besides, my brain feels as muddled as if I'd just downed a half dozen lunchtime gin and tonics in the Hickories. I go out to the garden to try to talk to Boniface, but he's not in his cottage, and I can't find him anywhere on the grounds. I search the house for books or notes that might be related to zandara, but I come up empty on that front too.

I consider calling Peregrine or Chloe, but I realize I have no idea what I'd say. There isn't exactly an approved script for the hey-I-saw-you-performing-a-creepy-ceremony-and-now-I-know-you're-a-queen conversation I'd need to have with them. I pull the Justin doll out and stare at it for a while as if it might be able to provide some answers, but its *x*'s for eyes begin to creep me out, so I shove it back in my desk drawer.

By mid-afternoon, I'm still going crazy over Aunt Bea's crazy revelations when the doorbell rings. I squeeze my eyes shut and hope that whoever it is goes away, but the bell rings again and again. Finally, I hurl myself out of bed and slouch down the stairs. By the time I get to the front hallway, the doorbell has sounded a sixth time, and I'm ready to punch whoever I find standing there.

But when I yank open the front door and see Peregrine and Chloe, my jaw falls. I'm not ready for this yet.

"Why hello, Eveny!" Peregrine trills. She's still wearing her Pointe Laveau uniform, which she has paired with black, thigh-high perforated leather boots and blood-red lipstick. Her smooth black stone with the jagged edge hangs just above the ornate hook and eye of a black fur capelet. She's carrying a huge quilted leather Chanel bag. "We certainly hope we didn't wake you. We were concerned when we didn't see you in school!"

"You were?" I ask skeptically.

"Of course, sweetie!" Chloe chimes in. She's dressed nearly as outrageously in platform ankle boots and a long sable coat that I swear I saw in *Vogue* this month. Her black stone necklace shines against her smooth, tan skin. "Are you all right? Do you need anything?"

I'm not surprised to see that their smiles don't reach their eyes.

"So?" Peregrine prompts after a moment. "Why did you miss school?"

I debate what to say but settle on the truth. "I saw you last night, in the cemetery."

The color drains from Chloe's face, and Peregrine's expression hardens.

"What is it you think you saw, exactly?" Peregrine asks carefully.

"I saw you practicing zandara," I tell her.

Their mouths open into identical *o*'s of surprise.

"You know what zandara is?" Chloe asks. "We figured your aunt hadn't told you yet."

"She hadn't," I say. "Until this morning."

They look at each other and then back at me. "Remarkable," Peregrine breathes. Then she shoots me a dazzling smile. "What I mean to say is, *perfect*. Chloe and I have been studying for years, so there's no one better to learn from than us.

"But first things first," she adds, leaning forward. "Now that you know the truth, let's go have some fun."

12

ive minutes later, I'm folded uncomfortably into the back of Peregrine's cherry-red Aston Martin DB Mark III hatchback, after she has sworn up and down that she's left her creepy snake at home. She guns the engine and roars down the hill toward the center of town while Chloe turns around in the passenger seat and stares at me.

"What?" I finally ask.

"It's just amazing, that's all," she says. "To grow up with no idea about any of this. I can't even imagine what you must be thinking!"

"I don't know what to think."

"Well, I'm sure you have questions," she says excitedly. "Ask us anything!"

"Okay." I hesitate. "How do we cast spells, for example?"

Peregrine rolls her eyes at me in the rearview mirror.

"They're not *spells*, Eveny. You are not a character in *Bewitched*. They're called *charms*."

"Ignore her," Chloe says. "There are a few things to know: First, all charms have to start with asking Eloi Oke to open the gate so that we can talk to the spirits. Second, they all have to involve herbs or flowers, because we channel our power from them. Third, they always have to be specific. Like you can't say, 'Make all the boys fall in love with me.' Instead you'd have to ask for your own beauty enhancements, or ask for the love of a specific guy. Or both."

"Assuming you're completely lame and believe the best use of your immense power is to make boys love you," Peregrine says with a snort.

Chloe turns red. "Peregrine thinks that only losers fall in love," she tells me.

"No, I believe that only losers use their powers for something so entirely pointless." Peregrine glances at me in the rearview mirror again. "But while we're on the topic of losers and powers, Eveny, why don't we have you do a little charm with us today? Our strength is much greater when there are three of us, so really, this should be no big deal. It's just to open the gates of Carrefour for one teeny, tiny night so that we can have a fraternity party."

It's the charm I overheard them trying to cast in the cemetery, the one Pascal thought didn't work. "Look, I'm all for the idea of bringing a bunch of hot college guys to town, but are you sure we should be opening the gates if a bunch of magic-haters are out to kill us?" I ask.

"I told you she'd be a nerd about this," Peregrine sing-songs. "Maybe a better question is why Main de Lumière is after us in the first place. Or didn't your aunt tell you that?"

"Peregrine—" Chloe says in a warning tone.

"It was your great-great-great-grandmother Eléonore's fault," Peregrine says, cutting her off. "*Our* great-great-great-grandmothers were wise enough to realize that if they had this kind of power, they shouldn't waste their time on something as pointless as falling in love. But Eléonore decided she was above all that. She fell for a man and let him get to know her daughters, and look what happened: he killed one of them."

"The murderer was Eléonore's boyfriend?" I ask.

"She was engaged to marry him," Peregrine says smugly. "When she and our ancestors fled to Carrefour before he could finish the job, he vowed that he'd find us, no matter how long it took. It's revenge, pure and simple, passed down through the generations, all because of Eléonore's stupidity."

Chloe takes over. "What she's trying to say, Eveny, is that after Eléonore made that mistake, the queens vowed they'd never let their hearts get in the way again. They need to give birth to continue their bloodlines, but they decided it was easier to have one-night stands and then use zandara to make the men forget. It just uncomplicates things."

It takes me a second to grasp what she's saying. "Wait, your fathers don't have any idea you're their kids?"

"We don't even know who our fathers are," Peregrine says.

"And when you don't know someone in the first place, they can never deliberately let you down, like your father did. I mean, our dads don't know we're theirs, but yours *chose* to abandon you."

Peregrine obviously thinks she's pushing my buttons, but I'm not about to waste my time and push back. Instead, I return to the more pressing topic. "So everyone thinks Main de Lumière has found us? Why?"

The question is greeted with silence. Finally, Chloe says, "Because we're fairly certain they killed Glory."

My blood runs cold. "I thought she killed herself. Didn't she?"

"The police chief is part of our mothers' sosyete," Chloe says. "He helped cover up her murder and make it look like a suicide."

"Otherwise it would have panicked everyone, made them leave town. We can't afford for people to be leaving right now, especially in the Périphérie. Our power has to come from somewhere," Peregrine adds.

"What?"

"What Peregrine's trying to say," Chloe interjects, "is that in every great society, there are people of privilege and people who make sacrifices for the people of privilege. You need that separation to keep things balanced. Though we totally make life as comfortable as possible for the people who don't live in central Carrefour!"

"But you don't treat them as equals," I say. When neither

of them says anything, I push down my annoyance at their snobby attitude and ask why they suspect Main de Lumière of killing Glory.

"Their pattern is always the same," Chloe explains. "They stab practitioners of magic through the heart, because that's the source of our greatest power. And that's how Glory died."

My mind flicks to my mother. If Glory's suicide was staged, is it possible my mom's was too? But her wounds were to her neck, not her heart. . . . I fight off a sense of disappointment and say, "I thought the charm around the gates was supposed to protect us from intruders getting in."

"Main de Lumière could only have gotten to Glory if they recruited someone who already lives here in Carrefour," Peregrine says. For the first time, she looks worried instead of just smug. "In other words, someone who grew up in town, maybe even someone we're friends with, has turned their back on us and joined Main de Lumière."

I gape at her. "No offense, but with all of this going on, doing some sort of charm to let strangers into town doesn't exactly seem like a genius move."

"First of all, opening the gates isn't going to have any impact on the person who's already here," she snaps. "Second of all, we only invited the very hottest fraternity guys from LSU, and they've all passed their background checks with flying colors. Plus, we'll have Oscar and Patrick, two older guys who work for us, checking IDs at the gate. No one will get in if they're not on the list.

"Besides," she adds, "if Carrefour gets any more boring, there'll be no point in protecting it anyway. Don't you see, Eveny? We can have anything we want. Good grades. Fabulous clothes. Immunity from teachers' punishments. Control over everything. Lust and love from whatever boys we choose. It's all ours. Doesn't that interest you?"

I feel a surge of excitement, despite my trepidation. "Of course it does."

"So you'll join us?" Chloe asks.

"Well . . . yeah." I suspect I don't have much of a choice, and I have to admit, the possibilities of what this means are tempting.

Peregrine pulls into a space on Main Street, parallel parking in one impressive attempt. I unfold from the backseat and launch myself onto the sidewalk.

"Welcome aboard," Chloe says, linking arms with me and pulling me toward a pair of pink double doors on the corner. "Now let's get you looking like the queen you are."

Cristof's Salon is opulent and gold-trimmed on the inside, with mirrors lining all the walls, like the parlor of an eighteenth-century French palace. A small, slender man with a goatee and several tiny stud earrings emerges from behind a velvety purple curtain in the back and exclaims, "Dah-lings!" as he rushes over and kisses Peregrine and Chloe on the cheeks. He turns to me. "And *you* must be Eveny." He leans in to kiss me on both cheeks too. "I am Cristof!" he says grandly.

"I see you're not a moment too soon. But don't worry, doll, that's what we're here for. We'll fix you up real nice and pretty.

"Sharona!" he yells at the top of his lungs, startling me. A moment later, a round middle-aged woman with rosy cheeks and spiky purple hair emerges from the back wearing a smock. "Sharona," Cristof says, "this here is Eveny, Sandrine Cheval's daughter." The color drains from Sharona's face as Cristof goes on. "Obviously we have great raw material here, but we have a lot of work to do."

My cheeks continue to flame as Sharona's eyes rake over me. "Dat's a fact," she says in a thick accent.

She takes me over to a chair, leans me back, and begins to wash my hair while Peregrine and Chloe talk in hushed tones with Cristof. By the time Sharona has blotted my hair and led me over to a chair facing a huge oval mirror, the girls have settled into seats behind me.

"So, my dear, what can I do for you today?" Cristof asks as he approaches.

Peregrine answers for me. "She'd like a gloss treatment, of course, and those shaggy split ends will have to go. Also, if her bangs could sweep to the side rather than cut across her forehead like she's a second grader, that would be ideal."

I turn. "I like my bangs," I say. "They're ironic."

Peregrine just looks at me. "They're hideous."

Cristof chuckles. "The gloss, I can do. The bangs, well, that's your department. I cut. I don't make hair grow."

"Right," Peregrine says. She exchanges looks with Chloe, and together, they get up and walk toward me. Peregrine grabs my right hand and Chloe grabs my left. With her free hand, Peregrine reaches up and plucks a single strand from my bangs.

"Ow!" I exclaim.

"Oh give me a break," Peregrine says, rolling her eyes. She grabs my hand again and gestures for Chloe to do the same. In her right hand, she holds up the strand of hair. "Cristof? A flame, please?" she asks.

But he's already approaching with a lit red candle. He hands it to Chloe, who thanks him and thrusts it toward Peregrine. They squeeze my hands tighter as Peregrine holds my strand of hair over the flame.

Chloe fishes in her pocket for something. Finally, she withdraws a handful of squished herbs, which she hands to Peregrine as she looks toward the ceiling and begins to speak in a low voice. "Come to us now, Eloi Oke, and open the gate. Come to us now, Eloi Oke, and open the gate. Come to us now, Eloi Oke, and open the gate."

There's a subtle shift in the air after she speaks the last word. The room is silent and heavy. Chloe takes a deep breath and continues in a singsongy voice:

> Rosemary roux, marigold dust,
> Violet leaf, we draw your power.
> Spirits, let there be bangs where there weren't before,
> Beauty for Eveny, let it be done.

They release my hands, and as soon as they do, I feel a gust of wind blow through. The herbs in her hand turn to black dust, and the flame on the candle goes out. "*Mesi, zanset*," she murmurs.

"Not bad," Peregrine says.

"See for yourself." Chloe turns my chair so that I'm facing the mirror.

My jaw drops. My hair is still damp from the shampoo, but I can plainly see that my choppy Bettie Page bangs are no longer there. In their place, there's an elegant swoop that skims across my forehead, grazing my right eyebrow and falling ever so slightly over my left eye. "How did you do that?" I whisper.

Peregrine rolls her eyes. "Seriously?" she asks. "You're impressed with *that*?"

"But you made my bangs grow," I say in astonishment.

"Oh for goodness' sake," Peregrine says. "Get your big girl pants on. This is nothing."

"*I* think you look pretty," Chloe whispers, meeting my gaze in the mirror.

"All right, Cristof," Peregrine says, waving a hand at him. "Do your thing."

"Of course!" Cristof says, sweeping over to us dramatically with a pair of scissors. He reaches for my long bangs and holds them up. He lightly snips the ends and lets them fall gently back on my forehead. "Now, let's get a conditioning treatment on you."

He smears a gel that smells like lavender all over my head and then rolls a big hair dryer over. It looks like a giant helmet, and he instructs me to sit under it for five minutes while the conditioning treatment warms up. "Then we'll rinse and work some magic," he says, winking. "Well, stylistic magic."

He heads toward the velvet curtains in back, leaving me alone with Chloe and Peregrine.

"I thought we weren't supposed to practice zandara in front of people," I say as soon as he's gone.

"Cristof is one of us," Peregrine says.

"Sharona too," Chloe adds.

"They have powers?"

The girls laugh. "No, silly," Chloe says. "But they're both members of our mothers' sosyete. It's fine to work magic in front of those who are part of the sosyete because they're sworn to secrecy, punishable by death."

Peregrine adds, "Not that it's ever come to that. The sosyete members don't have powers of their own, but they're in on the Secret of Carrefour, and they help increase the queens' power as they channel the power of the spirits."

"So if the sosyete members don't have their own powers, what are they there for?" I ask.

"The spirits like to know they have humans who will do favors for them," Peregrine explains. "So only the queens can call upon the dead or use the power they give us, but the sosyete members can enhance our strength during ceremonies just by chanting or dancing along with us. Plus, when they allow themselves to be possessed, the spirits are more likely to help us."

"So in our sosyete it's us three plus Arelia, Margaux, Pascal, and Justin," Chloe adds. "Oscar and Patrick, who you'll almost never see, work with us sometimes. Oh yeah, and Caleb Shaw."

I can feel myself flush at the mention of Caleb. I look away as Peregrine raises her eyebrows at me.

"Everyone in our sosyete is a descendant of people who have been involved with the Secret of Carrefour for generations," Chloe goes on. "Once we're a little older, we get to add a few new members too, people we pick and choose. But that doesn't happen until after we've all turned eighteen."

Cristof reemerges from the back room then, brandishing a pair of scissors. "Ready to be transformed, Eveny?"

I take a deep breath. "Ready as I'll ever be."

Forty minutes, one zandara-charmed facial mask, and one cut and blow-dry later, I look like a different person.

My frizzy hair is gone, replaced with shiny waves that cascade over my shoulders, down to the middle of my back. My bangs sweep perfectly to the side and frame my glowing face. My pimples have all vanished, and my skin looks like it's lit from within. Even my eyelashes, which usually need multiple coats of mascara, have turned dark and lush, and my lips have become pinker and fuller.

"Not bad," Peregrine marvels.

I just stare at myself in the mirror as Chloe squeals, "Eveny, you're gorgeous!"

"I don't even look like me," I say.

"Exactly the point," Peregrine says smugly. "Now, we've taken the liberty of picking out some shoes and accessories for you. The way you've been styling your school uniform"—she pauses and shudders—"just won't do. They should be at your house by the time you arrive home."

"Oh," I say awkwardly. "You shouldn't have done that. What do I owe you?"

"It's our treat," Peregrine says. "Now, let's work on that charm and see what you can do."

They lead me behind Cristof's purple curtain, where several candles flicker in the corner of a small room. Sheer gold scarves are draped over lamps, and incense burns from a small pot on a coffee table. I see three tiny bells, each hanging on a long piece of string, sitting on a chair. Beside them is a cluster of various flowers and herbs.

"Aren't you excited?" Chloe asks. "Think about it, Eveny. You have the power to give yourself anything you want."

"How do you even know I'll be any good at this?" I ask.

Peregrine shrugs. "We don't." She slips a bell on a long piece of twine around my neck. "But there's only one way to find out."

13

My heart hammers as Peregrine and Chloe grab each other's hands and then mine, so that we're standing in a circle of three.

"I can feel it already," Peregrine says, a dangerous gleam in her eye. "Power."

Chloe turns to me. "Just relax, Eveny, we'll do all the work. Clear your mind and think of this as a two-way street back and forth from the spirit world. It'll just be an easy little ceremony."

Like I saw them do in the cemetery, Peregrine and Chloe call out three times to Eloi Oke to open the gate. Chloe stomps her right foot and the room suddenly goes still. The air feels thick and heavy, as if we're underwater. It's hard to breathe for a moment, but when Chloe and Peregrine release my hands and begin to dance slowly, the air thins out again. Their feet move in a steady right-left-right, left-right-left sashay, with their hips swaying gracefully. I try to follow, and although I feel clunky, I'm sort of getting the hang of it.

As the three of us move in time to Peregrine's voice, I feel a breeze picking up. The candles are snuffed out, and we're plunged into near darkness, the only light coming from a lone scarf-draped lamp in the corner.

"Dill, fern, and five-finger grass, we draw your power," Peregrine chants. "Spirits, please open Carrefour's gates to the outside world Saturday night until the hour just before dawn."

Chloe takes over the chanting. "Dandelion and mojo beans, sandalwood and lemon balm, we draw your power. Spirits, please make all of our LSU visitors forget they were here after the gates have closed again." She pauses and adds, almost as an afterthought, "And coriander and cumin, I draw your power. Spirits, please keep Justin faithful."

Peregrine snorts in the darkness but joins Chloe in reciting, "Spirits, open our gates. Spirits, open our gates. Spirits, open our gates. *Mesi, zanset, Mesi, zanset. Mesi, zanset.*"

They stop abruptly, and I'm about to tell them it isn't working when I feel a rush of icy coldness wrap around me. Something solid pushes on my skull from the inside out, and my head throbs. When I try to pull away, I find that my hands are frozen, as if my brain is no longer firing impulses to my limbs. I begin to tell the girls to let me go, to reverse whatever they've done, but my mouth isn't working either. I'm getting colder and colder until my entire body is prickling with icy pain. The room begins to look blurry, and I wonder fleetingly if I'm dying.

Suddenly, something moves inside me, and my fear turns to flat-out terror. It's like there's another person fighting for room in my body. Before I can do anything about it, I hear myself whisper in a thick southern accent, "My killer is among you."

I'm a puppet, a shell; someone else is moving my jaw, speaking through my mouth. I scream, but no sound comes out. Through my blurred vision, I see Peregrine and Chloe staring at me. *Get out!* I cry in my head to whatever's inside me.

"Glory, who did it?" I hear Peregrine ask, but she sounds muffled and far away. "Who killed you? Was it Main de Lumière?"

I feel the spirit inside me gathering its strength to reply. "Yesssss," the voice hisses.

"Did you see your killer?" I hear Peregrine demand, a desperate edge to her voice. "Is it someone we already trust?"

The only thing that comes out of my mouth is, "In your midst."

The coldness begins to fade, and I can once again feel the tips of my fingers and toes. *Eveny*, says an urgent voice in my head just before the icy chill is gone. I recognize Glory's drawl immediately. *I didn't see my killer, but it was someone who knew exactly where I'd be. It must have been a friend.*

And then she's gone, and I can move again. I jerk away from Chloe and Peregrine. "What the hell just happened?" I demand. My tongue still feels thick and heavy, but at least I have control of it.

"You were possessed," Chloe whispers. Her face has gone pale, and she's looking at me with wide eyes. "Glory must still be in the nether."

"How remarkable," Peregrine says.

Chloe clears her throat. "It's not the possession itself that's so unusual. . . ."

"It's that we've never seen it happen so easily before," Peregrine says. "And we've never seen it happen uninvited like that."

"I can't believe you didn't tell me that would happen!" I'm out of breath, dehydrated, and weak. I don't know whether to be excited or terrified.

Peregrine's eyes narrow. "Power to communicate with the spirit world like that is a great gift. It figures you wouldn't appreciate it."

I want to ask them what Glory meant when she said her killer was in our midst, but my eyelids are growing heavy, and it's getting harder to stay on my feet. "Guys?" I say. "I think something's wrong with me."

"That's what it feels like after you've been possessed," Peregrine says. "The spirits take your energy with them."

"We should get her home," Chloe suggests.

Peregrine nods. "Well, the good news is that we know she's definitely one of us. She's a natural."

I see Chloe's forehead crease in concern, so I ask the

obvious question. "And the bad news?"

Peregrine's tone is somber as she turns her attention back to me. "The bad news is that now you're definitely a target for Main de Lumière too."

My house is dark and silent when Peregrine and Chloe drop me off, and I head straight upstairs. I'm swaying on my feet by the time I finally make it to my room and collapse into bed.

That night I dream again of the parlor and blood pouring out from beneath the doors. But this time, the images are blurry and vague, as if my brain can't muster the energy to form them whole.

Still, I wake up with my heart racing, the alarm clock blaring on my bedside table next to me.

I haul myself out of bed and head toward the bathroom. As soon as I catch a glimpse of myself in the mirror, I stop in my tracks and stare.

It would be no exaggeration to say that I look like a model. The so-called magic mask seems to have continued working overnight, making my lips even fuller, my skin even more luminous, and my eyelashes even thicker. My hair, which is normally creased and wild when I wake up, looks like it's been professionally blown out.

I dress quickly in my school uniform, then dig into the box of accessories Peregrine sent to my house and pull out a pair of huge diamond studs. I've only ever had the fake kind you can buy at stalls in Chinatown, though I have the feeling these are the real thing. I put them on and study myself in the mirror, admiring the way they catch the light. I'm about to venture back into the box to see what else is there when Aunt Bea's words from yesterday flash through my head. *They may be your sister queens, but that doesn't mean you have to become one of them.*

I'm hit with a surge of guilt. Am I doing something wrong by embracing the advantages zandara can give me? Then again, my ancestors risked their lives so that we could have this kind of power. After a minute, I close the box up, but I keep the earrings on.

Downstairs, there's hot coffee in the pot on the counter, and Aunt Bea has left a note saying she had to get to the bakery and will see me this afternoon. I guess that means I'll be walking to school. I shoot Meredith a text saying, *You'll never believe the makeover I got*, toast a Pop-Tart, pour myself a paper cup of coffee, and head out the door. Maybe the walk will clear my head.

But Peregrine's Aston Martin is already idling in my driveway. "Get in," she says through her open window, looking me up and down. "No, on second thought, go back inside, change your shoes, and get in."

I glance down at my loafers then back at her. "What are you doing here?"

"Giving you a ride," she says calmly. "Unless you insist on wearing *those* hideous things. The least you can do after we went out of our way to help you yesterday is to wear some heels."

"But I don't *want* to wear heels."

"There are at least six pairs in the box I sent," she says. "Seriously, go. The purple stilettos will look perfect with your skin tone."

I retreat back inside and throw the shoes on, grateful that Aunt Bea isn't here to see this. When I totter back out, Peregrine calls from the car, "Now roll up your skirt. What are you, a nun?"

I suppose she has a point, so I roll it once at the waistband, raising the hem an inch from my knees.

"Roll it again!" she commands.

I shake my head vehemently. "I'm not a nun," I grumble as I climb into the passenger seat, "but I'm not a prostitute either."

She makes a face. "This would be so much easier if you'd just accept my fashion advice." She revs the engine, puts the car in drive, and roars down the hill toward town. It's only when I glance absentmindedly toward the backseat that I realize her creepy snake is sitting there, his eyes fixed on me. I shriek, and Peregrine swerves.

"Crap, Eveny, what's the problem?" she snaps. "You're going to get us into an accident!"

I flatten myself against the door. "Your snake is staring at me."

"So?"

"So it's creepy," I say.

"Oh for goodness' sake, grow up. Snakes are an important part of zandara. Did you know that in some parts of the world, people who practice magic even worship them?"

"You're never going to get me to worship your snake."

Peregrine laughs. "Of course not. If anything, *he* worships *us*." I look back at Audowido, who's still staring at me with his beady little eyes. I shiver as his tiny tongue darts out of his mouth.

"Aw, he likes you," Peregrine says. "That's his way of blowing kisses."

Peregrine laughs, and I could swear that I can see Audowido crack a small, snakey smile.

As I walk down the hall toward first period flanked by Peregrine and Chloe, people turn and stare. And it's not the who's-the-new-girl? stares I got on Monday or the what's-she-doing-with-the-Dolls? stares I got Tuesday. No, these stares are disbelieving and appreciative. A few guys whistle at me, and I feel myself turning red.

As we take our seats in English class, everyone turns to look at me. A cheerleader is openly glaring at me from the front of the room, and a guy wearing a Pointe Laveau baseball uniform and glasses is actually drooling.

"You're welcome," Chloe says, beaming at me.

"This is all because of my makeover yesterday?" I whisper.

"Maybe you're underestimating how unfortunate you looked before," Peregrine says.

I grit my teeth. "So this is your secret? You cast charms on yourselves, and boys just fall all over themselves with lust?"

Peregrine pouts dramatically. "You say that like it's a crime! You're forgetting that *we're* both beautiful to start with, so it's not like we need as much work as you do."

"Leave her alone, Peregrine," Chloe says wearily. "You know she's pretty." She turns to me and adds, "Just between us"—she gestures to her ample cleavage—"this is magic too!"

"Your chest?" I ask incredulously.

"Our whole *bodies*," she replies. "Our moms created a charmed floral mud; the effects last about six weeks. It works amazingly."

"Maybe if you play your cards right, we'll let you have one too," Peregrine says. She looks meaningfully at my chest and adds, "Your A cups will thank you."

As much as I'd love to magically have the perfect body, Aunt Bea's warning echoes in my head again. But can I really turn down something like this? I settle for saying, "Let me think about it."

Peregrine snorts. "Suit yourself. But don't blame me when the frat boys at our party mistake you for an eight-year-old girl."

When I slink into my seat in third-period French class with Mrs. Toliver, trying to avoid the catcalls in the hall, I'm surprised to see that Drew's back.

"Hey! I didn't know you had this class with me!" I say. "Are you feeling better?"

But Drew just stares. "What happened to you?" he asks.

I'm not sure whether the question is appreciative or critical.

"A little makeover. No big deal."

"Whoa," is all he says. But the smile doesn't quite reach his eyes.

I clear my throat. "So you were out sick?"

"Yeah, must have been a stomach bug or something. I woke up Monday morning feeling totally gross. So how was your first week?"

"It was okay. I made some friends."

"At this school? You must have magical powers or something."

He's just joking, but knowing how close he's come to the truth makes me flinch. "Liv Jiménez is nice," I say. "She says she knows you."

"Liv? Yeah, we went to grade school together."

"You don't hang out with her now?"

"Not at school too much, just because we have different classes. But she comes to see my band play sometimes. She knows a lot about the music industry, actually. She's a real cool girl."

The bell rings, and Mrs. Toliver tells us to quiet down. Drew takes the seat beside me and scoots his desk a bit closer. "So what other classes do you have?" he whispers.

I dig my class schedule out of my backpack and hand it to him. "Bummer," he says. "This is the only one we have together. Figures you'd be in all those smarty-pants AP classes."

"Eveny? Drew?" Mrs. Toliver asks. "Think your conversation could wait until after class is over?"

"Sorry," we say in unison.

After class, Drew walks me to my locker. "So," he begins as I pull out my economics book and stuff it in my bag, "my band's playing at this bar tonight. I was wondering if you might want to come." He looks nervous and hopeful.

The truth is, I want to stay home and think about all the bizarre developments that have come with moving back to Carrefour. But I have to admit, it would be nice to have a few hours off from my weird new reality.

"Sounds cool," I say. "Where is it?"

He jots down the name and address of the place. "It's in the Périphérie, though. Is that going to be a problem?"

I look at him blankly. "Of course not. Why would it be?"

"I don't know." He looks me up and down. "You just seem to be adjusting real quickly to this side of town."

14

I'm standing in line in the caf when Liv and Max walk by without so much as a glance.

"Liv!" I call out.

She turns and does a double take. "*Eveny?*" she asks. "What happened to you?"

"Holy face-lift," Max says.

I look down. "I just got a haircut and a facial. No big deal."

Liv looks me up and down and waits for me to meet her gaze. "You look like a different person," she says flatly. It's not a compliment.

I open my mouth to explain, but I'm interrupted by Peregrine's voice behind me.

"Eveny?" she trills. "Why in the world are you standing in line?"

"Yeah, come on," Chloe, who of course is standing beside

her, cuts in. "Up in the Hickories, Margaux and Arelia are serving smoked salmon blinis and caviar, and they brought Veuve Clicquot today."

"Veuve what?" I ask.

Peregrine makes a face. "It's a brand of champagne, Eveny. Obviously."

How was I supposed to know that? "Well, can Liv and Max come eat with us too?" Liv is glaring at Peregrine, and Max just looks nervous. His eyes dart back and forth between Liv and me.

"I'm sure Liv and Max would prefer to eat with their own people," Peregrine says. "Isn't that right, Liv?" Somehow, Peregrine manages to make her name sound like a dirty word.

"Whatever," Liv mutters, calling Peregrine a few dirty words of her own under her breath. "See you in class, Eveny. Have fun with your new friends." She storms off, dragging Max behind her.

I start to follow after her, but Chloe grabs my arm. "Let her go," she says gently. "She's a nice enough girl, but this is bigger than her. She's not one of us." She and Peregrine begin walking away without waiting for me. I glance after Liv and Max, but they're already gone.

After a moment's hesitation, I follow Chloe and Peregrine toward the Hickories. I know it's where I'm supposed to belong, but I can't help feeling like I've just made a mistake.

Arelia and Margaux openly glare at me when I sit down, but when Peregrine tells them to pour me a glass of champagne,

Arelia grudgingly does so, and Margaux shovels a spoonful of caviar onto a plate and thrusts it in my general direction. My nose wrinkles when I taste it; it's salty, and the texture is peculiar.

"Take a sip of your drink," Peregrine advises. "It brings out the flavor."

I take a small sip of champagne and am surprised to realize she's right.

"You forgot the verbena in Eveny's champagne!" Peregrine says, shooting daggers at Arelia.

"Sorry." But Arelia doesn't look sorry at all as she grabs a sprig of purple flowers, leans across the picnic blanket, and shoves it into my drink.

I'm about to ask her if she needs help refilling people's glasses, but I'm interrupted by the arrival of a cute guy with huge, broad shoulders, dark hair that curls at his ears, and empty-looking brown eyes. His sleeves are rolled up to reveal bulging muscles, and he has a letter jacket slung over his left shoulder. "Hey, baby," he says dully, plunking down next to Peregrine. He doesn't look at anyone else; he immediately busies himself with giving her a shoulder massage while sniffing her hair adoringly.

"Oh sorry, Eveny, perhaps you haven't met Beau yet," she says. "Beau, this is Eveny. Eveny, Beau."

Beau grunts what I assume is a greeting, but he doesn't tear his eyes away from Peregrine for even a millisecond. "Beau Fontenot?" I ask. It's the name I heard them utter in the cemetery on Wednesday night. I realize in an instant that this is what his part of the charm was about: making him fall blindly in lust with Peregrine.

"Yes." Peregrine narrows her eyes at me. "Anyhow, as I was saying, people who aren't in on the Secret of Carrefour are not welcome to eat in the Hickories. This is *our* place."

"Well, what about Beau?" I ask.

Beau goes on massaging her shoulders lovingly. Peregrine laughs. "Oh, Eveny, he's so enthralled with me that he's not listening. Isn't that right, Beau?"

"Baby, you're hot," Beau mumbles robotically.

"See?" Peregrine says.

I glance at Chloe and realize she's not paying attention to us at all. She's staring at Justin, who's sitting down in the courtyard outside the cafeteria, laughing with a few other guys. I turn my focus back to Peregrine. "I thought you didn't believe in using zandara to make people fall in love with you."

"Love? Don't be ridiculous. This is just lust, which is much easier to control. Besides, you've been in Carrefour for, like, thirty seconds. I don't think you're exactly in a position to judge me."

"Whatever." I scoot away from them and toward Chloe. "What's the matter?" I ask her as I reach her edge of the blanket.

The expression on her face is mournful as she watches Justin. He's grinning, and from the way the three guys around him are laughing as he talks, I'm guessing he's telling a joke, which surprises me because this is the first time I've ever seen him exhibit anything resembling a personality.

"Did something happen with you two?" I venture.

"I don't know what's wrong," she says. "He's totally ignoring me."

"At least he's not hitting on other girls," I point out. I'm trying to think of something else comforting to say when I realize that his behavior is probably my fault. If Peregrine cast a charm to make Beau fall in love with her that night, Chloe was surely doing the same with Justin. When I dug his doll up, I must have reversed it. "Um, sorry if this is a personal question," I say, "but did you cast some sort of charm to make him like you?"

Chloe looks at me sharply, but then her face softens and there are tears in her eyes. "Maybe," she says. "But he liked me before that. I just helped things along. He's really shy."

I look up at Justin, who's carrying on an animated conversation.

"Shy with girls," Chloe amends, following my gaze. She sighs heavily. "Anyway, things were really good between us. And now . . . I don't know what I did to screw things up."

I swallow hard. "Sorry."

She gives me a watery smile. "Oh, Eveny, it's not your fault," she says, which makes me feel even worse. She turns back to watching Justin with a dreamy, troubled expression on her face.

I open my mouth to reply, but Pascal interrupts our conversation with a long, low whistle as he makes his way up the hill to the Hickories. "Damn, girl!" He's staring at me with a predatory grin. "You look *fine*."

I notice Peregrine's attention snap in our direction. Her eyes narrow at Pascal as he sits down next to me. "You're the hottest chick in this whole school now, Eveny," he continues. "What do you say we spend a little alone time in the teachers' lounge?" He makes air quotes over *alone time*.

"No thanks," I say.

"Ignore him," Peregrine says coldly. "He's just trying to get in your pants. He's exaggerating. *Obviously*."

"About me being the hottest girl in school?" I ask with mock innocence. I know that's exactly what she's talking about; her eyes burn with jealousy.

"She's not as beautiful as you, Peregrine," Arelia says, shooting me a smirk.

"Not nearly," Margaux adds helpfully as she gazes in adoration at Peregrine.

To my surprise, Peregrine seems unmoved. "Give it a rest, girls," she says. "She's one of us. She has been long before you two joined the sosyete."

Arelia's and Margaux's heads swivel toward me in surprise. "But she's new!" Margaux whines.

Peregrine narrows her eyes at them. "For goodness' sake, you *know* she's a queen. Now quit being ridiculous and pour me another glass of champagne."

I turn away from them in annoyance just in time to see Caleb walking up the hill toward us. My heart does a little flip-flop, and I feel color rising to my cheeks. I glance away as our eyes meet, but a second later, I look back and realize he's still gazing evenly at me.

"Hey," I croak.

"Hey," he replies. He settles on the far side of the cashmere picnic blanket, facing away from me.

My heart hammers, and I'm not sure whether to be grateful that he doesn't appear to be impressed by my magically enhanced looks, or disappointed that he's obviously still avoiding me.

Peregrine purses her lips at our exchange. "So, Caleb, catch any good waves lately?" she asks, turning to him. "I heard conditions are supposed to be ideal in the Gulf right now."

"Since when do you follow the surf forecast?" Caleb asks suspiciously.

"I've always been interested in your hobbies," she says sweetly.

"You know I haven't left town, Peregrine," he says. "Give it a rest."

She laughs as he turns away, and I have the feeling she's not as over him as she wants everyone to think.

Twenty minutes later, I sit down next to Caleb in American history, expecting his usual inexplicable silent treatment. So I'm surprised when he says, "I see Peregrine and Chloe have gotten their hands on you." His voice is deep and warm, and it makes my stomach feel like Jell-O.

My cheeks heat up. "You could say that. It feels . . . different."

I take a deep breath and ask, "So what do you think?"

"You look pretty," he says, and for a moment, my heart both soars and sinks at the same time. "But I thought you looked pretty before too."

He doesn't say another word for the rest of class, and he strides out of the room at the end before I have a chance to talk to him. But his words stay with me and echo in my head for the rest of the afternoon.

I call Meredith on my walk home, but she doesn't pick up. I swallow back a lump in my throat and leave her a message saying that I miss her. I call Liv next, because she avoided me in physics and was gone by the time I reached the hallway.

"Look, I'm sorry about lunch today," I say to her voice mail when she doesn't answer. "I don't know why Peregrine and Chloe are so picky about who eats in the Hickories."

I spend the rest of my walk hoping that Caleb will pull up alongside me like he did my first day of school, but only a few cars whiz past, and none are his. I try not to feel disappointed.

When I arrive home, I wander around the rose garden looking for Boniface, but he's nowhere to be found, nor is Aunt Bea.

Liv calls back at four, and before I can even say hello, she says, "There's no law saying you have to eat with the Dolls just because they invite you."

"I know," I reply. "I'm sorry." I wish I could explain to her that like it or not, I'm linked to Chloe and Peregrine forever.

But of course Liv's not in on the Secret of Carrefour, so all she sees is that I'm choosing popularity and power over real friendship.

She's silent for a moment, then she says, "No big deal," but her tone tells me she's still pissed off.

"Hey, so Drew invited me to go see his band play tonight," I say.

"At Domion? Yeah, I was planning to go."

"Cool. So would you want to go together, maybe?"

"What, are Peregrine and Chloe busy?" The bitterness is creeping back in.

"I didn't ask them," I tell her. "I'm asking you."

"Oh." She pauses. "Yeah, all right. And I'll come get you. But dude, you need to get your driver's license."

"I know."

"And Eveny? Don't invite the Dolls, okay?"

"Don't worry," I tell her. "I definitely won't."

15

Aunt Bea gets home fifteen minutes before Liv is due to arrive, her navy T-shirt and skirt smudged with flour. She looks surprised to see me in skinny jeans, boots, and a flowy top, all dressed for a night out.

"Don't tell me you're meeting up with Peregrine and Chloe," she says, looking at me suspiciously.

"No, my friend Liv is picking me up. We're going to see Drew's band play in the Périphérie."

She chews her lip. "Who's Liv? One of the girls in Peregrine and Chloe's sosyete?"

"Actually, she pretty much hates Peregrine and Chloe."

Aunt Bea's expression relaxes a little. "Well, I was hoping we could talk."

"Me too. But Liv'll be here in a few minutes."

"The morning's fine, I guess," Aunt Bea says. She kisses

me on the cheek and walks away without another word.

Five minutes later, I hear a horn honking outside. I look through the peephole and see Liv sitting in a pale blue VW Bug with rusted bumpers.

"I'm heading out!" I call up to Aunt Bea, who doesn't respond. "Back by eleven!"

I lock the front door behind me and climb into the passenger seat of Liv's car. "Hey," I say, but she doesn't reply. My heart sinks; she's obviously still annoyed about today. "Look," I say after she's pulled out of my driveway and is sputtering down the hill. "I know you don't like Peregrine and Chloe."

She snorts. "Understatement of the year."

I glance down. "It's complicated with them, Liv. I knew them when we were kids. They're kind of part of my life whether I like it or not."

Liv's shoulders relax a little. "I don't want you to get sucked into their little circle of clones, that's all."

"Just because I'm hanging out with them doesn't mean I have to *become* one of them." But the words taste like a lie, because of course I *am* one of them.

Fifteen minutes later we're walking into Domion, a run-down looking restaurant heaving with people. At least half the crowd inside is our age, and I tag along after Liv as people come up to her to say hi. A few of them I recognize from the crawfish boil, but most are unfamiliar and don't pay any attention to me.

Liv seems completely in her element. Dressed in a denim

miniskirt, faded leather cowboy boots, and a sheer blouse with a cami underneath, she also appears more relaxed than she does at Pointe Laveau.

"You see why I don't exactly fit in with your new friends?" she asks as we settle into seats at a high-top table to the right of the stage. "Unlike them, I realize there's more to life than looking hot and messing with guys' heads."

Liv's smile is bright, but her eyes are hard. I wish I could explain that their snubbing her has nothing to do with money and everything to do with birthright. But of course I can't, so I settle for changing the subject. I ask Liv about her family, and she tells me she has a little brother named Davy, a freshman at Carrefour Secondary, and that they live with their dad; their mom left when Liv was three.

"My dad disappeared before I was born," I tell her. "So I get it."

She looks up at me with an expression of surprise. "I didn't know that," she says. "Where did he go?"

"No idea. I only know that he's from somewhere back east and that my aunt hates him." I hesitate and add, "I've been thinking about him a lot since we got here, actually. My aunt says I've never met him, but I found a photo of us together, and I have a weird, hazy memory of talking to him at my mom's funeral."

"So you've never heard from him other than that?" she asks.

I shake my head.

Liv studies me for a moment. "Maybe Peregrine and Chloe know something about what happened to him, since their moms knew your mom."

"Maybe," I agree. Truthfully, I hadn't thought to ask.

Liv is looking at me differently now. "I guess I can see why you'd want to hang with them sometimes," she says grudgingly. "Even though I still think they're pretty worthless human beings."

I open my mouth to answer, but I'm interrupted by a mash-up of guitar strings behind the small stage. A moment later, Teddy, the guy who threw the crawfish boil, bounds out and hurls himself into the seat behind an impressive drum set. He begins banging the cymbal with a drumstick, and a moment later Drew runs out with an electric guitar, and two other guys I don't recognize come out playing a banjo and a bass guitar. Teddy whales on the drums while the guy with the banjo leans toward one of the microphones and begins to sing in a low voice that reminds me of John Mayer.

Drew looks up and grins at us after the first verse is over.

"They're good, aren't they?" Liv says once he looks away. "Good chord structure. Good hooks. They've got a good look too." She pauses and adds, "Especially Drew."

I realize she's staring at Drew raptly as he launches into a solo to begin the second song. I see a blush creep up Liv's neck, and I wonder for the first time if she likes him as more than a friend.

We both clap along as the band rocks out to the next song,

which reminds me a bit of an Irish drinking anthem with a hard rock rhythm and a smattering of banjo strings.

"I'm Tallon Duchovny!" announces the banjo-playing singer after Drew has strummed his last chord. "And we're Little Brother, from right out here in the Périphérie!"

The room explodes into applause, and Drew grins at us again as he strums a few chords to lead off the third song. Tallon is singing lead again; the lyrics are about a girl who goes around breaking hearts. After the chorus, Drew and Tallon lean toward each other and engage in a few minutes of dueling licks; Tallon plucks out complicated melodies on the banjo, which Drew mimics while Teddy and the bass player keep time.

"I've never heard anything like this before," I shout to Liv over the music as Little Brother launches into a fourth tune.

"They're something special!" she shouts back.

After their first set, Teddy bounds over to our table, still clutching his drumsticks, while the other guys head into a back room to put their guitars down.

"Hey, Eveny!" he says. "Hey, Liv!" His forehead is glistening with sweat, and he's grinning. "Anyone want to go do a shot with me at the bar?"

I say, "No thanks," at the same time Liv says, "Sure, why not? There's something I want to run by you anyway." I give her a look, because after all, she's the one driving home after the show.

"They're not real strict with IDs in this town, are they?" I ask.

Liv and Teddy both laugh. "The Dolls aren't the only ones who can get away with breaking the rules," Liv says. I watch as she follows Teddy, giggling about something he's said.

I turn my attention back toward the stage just in time to see Drew emerge without his guitar. He heads straight for me.

"You came to my show," he says, giving me an awkward half hug.

"Yeah, me and Liv both." I gesture toward the bar.

He glances her way then grins at me. "You look beautiful tonight, Eveny. Really."

"You looked pretty good up there yourself." I change the subject before it gets uncomfortable. "I'm really glad we came. The band's amazing."

"Thanks!" He launches into a long explanation of how they're trying to get a record deal with some New Orleans–based music label, and I'm listening until a familiar deep voice somewhere off to my left catches my attention. I do a double take when I see who's sitting there.

It's Caleb, all by himself at a table near the back of the room, giving a pretty waitress his order.

I feel my heart leap into my throat. *What's* he *doing here?*

Caleb catches me staring and half raises his glass in greeting, then turns away as if he has no interest in interacting with me at all.

As I force myself to refocus on Drew, I feel a river of heat flowing through me, and I hope it's not showing on my face. Drew's still talking, and when he leans in and touches my arm to make a point, I pull away and feel instantly guilty when a hurt expression flickers across his face. But what if Caleb thinks I'm *with* Drew?

Drew makes it worse a second later by giving me a peck on the cheek. "Seriously, Eveny, thanks so much for coming out tonight. It's really cool of you."

Then Tallon beckons from the stage, and Drew says sadly, "Looks like I have to go. But see you in a few, okay?"

Liv sits down next to me a moment later holding two drinks. She pushes one toward me. "They're both Sprite," she says.

I thank her, and I'm about to open my mouth to ask what she thinks Caleb is doing here when she asks eagerly, "So did Drew say anything about me?"

I look over at Caleb's table. He's deep in conversation with the waitress, who's in short shorts, a tight white T-shirt, and cowboy boots. I shake off a surge of jealousy. "He's really glad you came," I tell Liv.

"Awesome," she says.

The band begins playing, and we turn back to the stage. Drew keeps grinning at us, and Liv is squirming in her seat. Meanwhile, Caleb doesn't appear to be paying the slightest bit of attention to me. I'm puzzled that he's here, considering that the Périphérie isn't exactly the Dolls' domain.

"So would you think I was totally crazy if I told you I'd offered to help Drew's band?" Liv asks after a few minutes.

"Help them how?"

"I was thinking I'd offer to manage them," she says.

When I shoot her a confused look, she hurries to add, "I know it sounds kind of nuts. But I'm always listening to indie bands and reading *Spin* and *Rolling Stone* and all that. I've been saving up for this program that'll basically turn my Mac into a home recording studio—what if I offer to cut a song for them?"

"You know how to do that?"

"I'll learn," she says confidently. "Then maybe I can get out of this town and take Drew and his buddies with me. I mean, look at those guys." She points at the stage. "Girls will go crazy for them. They're all really cute, right?" Her eyes linger on Drew several beats too long.

"You sure this isn't just a way to hit on Drew . . . ?"

"No!" she exclaims. Then she shoots me a guilty look. "Maybe. But only a little. If you tell anyone that, though, I'll have to kill you."

I laugh and settle back to watch Little Brother's set. Just before the band finishes, Liv grabs my arm and says, "Wait, is that *Caleb Shaw*? What's he doing out here?"

I sneak a glance at his table again. He's reading the menu like it's a fascinating book. "I don't know," I say, trying to pretend I don't care.

Liv stares at me. "Wait, do you *like* him?"

"No," I protest unconvincingly. "He's just, uh, a nice guy, you know?"

"You don't have to lie. Every girl in Carrefour has had a crush on Caleb Shaw at some point. *I* even liked him for thirty seconds. But sooner or later, everyone realizes he just doesn't date."

"But I thought he used to date Peregrine."

Liv frowns. "That was really short-lived. I wasn't at Pointe Laveau yet, so I don't know all the details, but I hear he just wasn't that into her, and everyone sort of knew it except her."

I'm embarrassed by how happy this makes me. But then something occurs to me. "Maybe he's gay," I say, my heart sinking a little.

"No. Believe me, Max has asked. Several times."

I laugh, but before I can say anything in reply, Liv's already standing up.

"I have an idea," she says before waving her hands dramatically in the air. "Caleb!" she yells across the bar. "Over here!"

He hesitates before getting up and walking slowly in our direction. I can feel the hairs on my arms standing on end as he comes closer.

"Hey," he says in a low voice. His sky-blue eyes flick to me for an instant and land back on Liv. "What's up?"

"Well first of all, Caleb, I didn't know you hung out in the Périphérie."

"I do sometimes."

"But you live in central Carrefour, right?"

"Right."

"So Caleb, I was wondering if you could do me a favor," she continues. "I picked Eveny up, and I don't *mind* driving her home. But seeing as you live right by her, maybe you'd be willing to do it?"

Caleb looks startled, so I jump in to say, "Liv, that's really not necessary."

"Oh, but Eveny, I have to talk business with Drew and the band." Liv turns to Caleb with a faux-serious expression. "Plus, I've been drinking," she says. "Like, a *lot*."

"Liv, I'm sure Caleb is busy. And you said yourself you only did one shot."

"Caleb, are you really that busy?" Liv asks immediately. "I mean, you're going home anyway, right?"

"Uh, yeah, sure, that's fine," he says. "But I was about to leave, actually. I don't want to cut your night short." I feel like curling up and vanishing; it's so obvious he doesn't want to give me a ride.

I open my mouth to tell him to forget we even asked, but Liv elbows me in the ribs.

"Would you excuse us for a minute, Caleb?" I ask. He looks uncertain as I grab Liv's arm and drag her a few feet away. "What are you doing?" I demand.

"Just getting you a little alone time with the hottest guy in Carrefour."

"I didn't ask you for that!" I exclaim.

"You didn't have to," she says with a shrug. "Besides, I was kind of hoping this would give me some time to talk with Drew."

"Talk? Or make out?" I tease.

Her cheeks turn a little pink. "To talk about the *band*, Eveny."

I'm about to argue further when Caleb comes up behind

us. "You ready to go?" he asks.

"If you're sure you don't mind taking me."

Liv's already slinking away from us. "Later, you guys," she says, winking at me.

"My Jeep's this way." Caleb begins walking toward the exit without waiting for me, and even when I hurry to catch up, he keeps a few feet of distance between us.

"I'm sorry about that," I say. "I didn't ask Liv to do that."

"I know."

"What are you doing here, anyhow?" I ask when he opens his passenger door for me.

"Driving you home," he says in an even tone. "We're neighbors, and Liv asked me to, in case you don't remember."

He waits for me to get in and buckle my seat belt, then he shuts my door and goes around to the driver's side. Once he's buckled in and has started the engine, I say, "What I mean is, what are you doing *here*? At Domion?"

"Listening to music, same as you," he says. "Why, are you implying I'm following you?"

"No, of course not!" I feel like an idiot.

For a moment, I'm sure he's about to say something else. But he puts the car in gear, mumbles something to himself, and backs out of his parking space.

It's not until we're almost out of the parking lot that I realize I've walked out without saying good-bye to Drew.

16

The first few minutes of the drive are silent. I feel nervous and tongue-tied in Caleb's presence.

"So, Liv and Drew? I didn't know she liked him until tonight," I say in an attempt to cut through the awkwardness.

"Yeah," Caleb says, his eyes glued to the road.

"I mean, Liv seems so tough sometimes, like she doesn't need anyone," I add when it's clear he's not going to say anything.

"Yeah."

I take a deep breath. "But when you think about it, they're kind of perfect for each other."

"Yeah."

This is getting ridiculous. "Okay, so the way that conversation works is that I say something, and then you say something back—preferably something other than 'yeah.'"

This finally elicits a reaction from Caleb. He chuckles. "Yes, I know what a conversation is." He hesitates and adds, "I'm sorry. I'm not making this very easy, am I?"

"I just don't understand why you're avoiding me."

"I'm not," he says instantly.

I continue to stare at him until he clears his throat and says, "All right. Maybe I've been avoiding you a little."

The words hit me harder than I expect. "Why? Does it have something to do with zandara?" I ask after a moment of silence.

He hesitates. "It's hard to explain. I think it's better if we just don't talk about this."

"Look," I say, "I didn't even know anything *about* the Dolls or the sosyete or anything until two days ago. I wasn't raised with any of this, so you can't hate me because of it."

"I don't hate you," Caleb says immediately. His voice is husky as he turns and repeats, "I don't hate you."

"Well, it sure feels like it," I reply.

"It's not that. It's just . . ." His voice trails off. "It's just that certain people in town have certain responsibilities. And feelings make those responsibilities that much harder."

"Feelings?"

"Oh, that's not what I meant."

"Right," I say, feeling foolish. "Me neither."

"It's just . . ." He hesitates and starts again. "There are some things in this town that you don't understand."

I grit my teeth. "You know, I'm getting pretty tired of

everyone talking in mysteries and riddles over my head."

"Eveny . . ." For a moment, I think he's going to tell me what he means. But instead, what he says is, "It's complicated."

"Seriously, no explanation? Are you *trying* to drive me crazy?"

"No," he says quickly. "I'm trying to warn you. This town, it sucks you in. It's like all your choices start to disappear, and you realize your life's been planned out for you long before you got here."

"Well, that makes everything a lot clearer," I say sarcastically. I realize that he actually looks upset, so I soften my tone and add, "That's why you disappear to go surfing, isn't it? You're just trying to get out of here."

He looks surprised. "You remembered." When I nod, he continues, "I love that feeling of anonymity when I'm out there alone in the water." He pauses. "But now that I'm not going as much anymore, it sometimes feels like this town is closing in on me."

"Because of the Dolls?"

"I just have this feeling that there's a storm coming, and they're the ones bringing it here." He hesitates. "They told me about the possession at Cristof's. You should be worried too."

"Gee, thanks for making me feel better."

"This is life-and-death stuff, Eveny. I know Peregrine and Chloe think this is all fun and games, but I need to know that you know better. Tell me you know better."

"Of course I do."

He's silent for a moment before changing the subject. "So Drew. Has he said anything to you about Glory?"

"Drew?" I repeat, surprised. "No. Why?"

"I think he was seeing her," Caleb says. "I was just wondering if Liv knows."

"Caleb, that's crazy," I say. "The Dolls act like Drew's not even alive. Besides, Drew would have told me if there was something going on."

He shrugs. "I saw them together. A week before she died."

"Saw them doing what?"

He clears his throat. "It just seemed like they were together, okay? I thought it was great that something was going on between them, being that she was a Doll and he's from the Périphérie. About time someone shook things up around here. But then she died, and he kept right on acting like he didn't know her."

I shake my head. "Are you sure they were together? Like *together* together?"

"No. Not one hundred percent."

"So don't you think you're being a little unfair?"

"Then ask him, Eveny," Caleb says. "I just want to make sure Liv is aware. She's your friend, and if she's interested in him, she deserves to know that something might have been going on."

We're pulling into my driveway now, and I feel a sense of disappointment. Even if we're disagreeing, I want to keep talking to Caleb. Forever, if possible.

"I'm only being cautious, Eveny," he says as he puts his car in park. His eyes are wide and concerned as he turns to me. "You should be too."

I open my mouth to respond just as he leans forward to jiggle my door handle. "It sticks sometimes," he explains. Our eyes meet, and for a moment, as he goes still, I have the weirdest feeling he's going to kiss me. But then he retreats to his own seat and looks out the windshield with his hands gripping the wheel, like he can't wait to get out of here.

"Bye," I say softly as I climb out of the car.

He doesn't reply. Instead, the moment I shut his car door, he guns the engine and pulls away.

But he lingers at the bottom of my driveway until I've unlocked my front door and slipped inside my house. I watch from the window as his taillights disappear.

Aunt Bea is already in bed when I get home, but I'm not even slightly tired. I sit down at the kitchen table and dial Meredith's number.

When she answers on the third ring, all I can hear at first is club music pumping through the earpiece.

"Mer?" I ask loudly. I repeat myself a few times, until I hear her voice faintly over the music.

"Eveny?" she yells. "Hang on, I'll go outside!"

A moment later, the music fades and is replaced by New York street sounds: people talking, car horns honking, brakes screeching. I realize with a pang just how much I miss being there.

"Hey, girl!" she says excitedly.

"What are you up to tonight?" I ask.

"Nick and Holly heard about a party in Chinatown," she says. "So Colton and James and I grabbed a cab and came out here. This place is amaze, Ev! No cover, and the door guy didn't even look twice at my ID."

"Sounds cool."

"Totally wish you were here! What're you doing tonight?"

"Just got home from seeing a friend's band play," I tell her.

"Ooh, you have a friend in a band?" she asks. "Is it a *boy*?"

"Just the guy I told you about the other night. The one I knew when I was a kid. But the other guy drove me home."

"Who?"

"Caleb. The one who's insanely gorgeous."

She makes a noise. "Girl, the hot ones are the ones you've got to look out for." She pauses. "So are you coming back to visit soon, or what?"

I think about it for a minute. A few days ago, I was dying to return to New York. Now, I feel like there are a thousand answers I need to figure out here in Carrefour first. "Probably not," I tell her. "Not for a while, at least."

"Seriously?" she asks. "Why, your aunt won't give you money for a plane ticket?"

"It's not that. It's just that so much of my family's history is tied in to Carrefour." I try to stay as vague as possible. "I know it sounds crazy, but I think I belong here for now."

"In the boonies?" she asks with a laugh.

"It's not so bad," I say, actually meaning it.

"Well, in that case," Meredith says after a moment, "I've been meaning to ask you a question."

There's something in her voice that makes me pause. "What is it?"

"Do you still like Trevor Montague?" she asks quickly.

"I guess." I've had a crush on Trevor for as long as I can remember, though nothing ever happened between us. "Why?"

"Well, he kinda asked me out," Meredith says.

"Trevor, who I used to ask you for advice about on a daily basis? Trevor, who I used to draw pictures of in my notebook in middle school? Trevor, whose name we carved into that tree in the park in ninth grade?"

"Yes," Meredith replies, her voice flat.

"Well, you said no, right?"

"Not exactly."

The silence is heavy between us. "You didn't?"

"It's not like you're coming back, Eveny. You just said so yourself. And I've liked him for a while too."

"No, you haven't," I protest. "You've never said anything about liking him."

"Well, maybe I do!" Her tone is defiant, and it wounds me. I close my eyes and try not to think of them together. After all, she's right; I might never be coming back. But that doesn't mean my best friend has to go out with the guy I've liked forever.

"Meredith—" I begin, trying to sound calm.

But she cuts me off. "You don't get to call dibs on someone if you're not here."

She hangs up without another word. I try calling her back, but it goes right to voice mail. Finally, I settle for texting Drew. *Your band was awesome*, I tell him. *Did you and Liv have fun?* But there's no reply.

When my phone stays silent, I head up to bed, feeling more alone than ever.

I wake up the next morning to a return text from Drew.

Thanks again for coming, he writes. *And yeah, Liv is cool.*

I grab my phone and text back, *Anything happen with you guys?*

Nah. We just talked about music and stuff. There's a pause, then he writes, *So I hear you went home with Caleb Shaw??*

My cheeks heat up as I text back, *He only gave me a ride cuz I was on his way.* But even over text, I can sense Drew's jealousy. I feel like adding, *Caleb acts like the very thought of me is offensive, so you don't have to worry*, but instead, I settle for, *Call me later*, before I head down to the kitchen.

Aunt Bea is sitting at the table, sipping a cup of coffee, when I round the corner.

"Morning," she says. Her eyes flick up to meet mine, and I realize they're bloodshot and underlined in deep blue half-moons.

"You okay?" I ask.

"I didn't sleep well last night," she says. "A lot on my mind."

That's when I notice a small purple jewelry box and a yellowed envelope on the table in front of her. She follows my gaze. "I picked this up yesterday while you were at school," she says.

"What is it?"

Aunt Bea just shakes her head. "Sit down," she says, sliding the envelope and box over to me. "They were left in a safe-deposit box for you many years ago. Your mom wrote the letter the year you were born, in case anything ever happened and she wasn't here when you turned seventeen."

She pauses and looks down at the table. "I should have given them to you on your birthday, but I was hoping to prolong the sense that our lives are normal. Now that zandara has found *you*, though . . ." Her voice trails off, and there are tears in her eyes when she looks up again.

"You knew it would when you brought me back here, didn't you?" I ask, turning the box over in my hands.

"I was doing what I had to do." She nods at the envelope, and with shaky hands I open it carefully. A dried rose flutters out first, and I recognize it as one of my mother's gold-tipped Rose of Life blooms. There's also a single piece of thick paper, yellowed at the edges. I unfold it shakily and begin to read.

My dearest Eveny, my mother writes.

Happy seventeenth birthday. If you're reading this, it means I am no longer with you, and for that, I am sorrier than I can ever say.

As I'm sure you've realized by now, Carrefour is full of secrets, and only you can make the decision about what's right for your future— although I suspect others around you will have opinions of their own. Remember that zandara can be used for good or evil, selfishly or selflessly. But one thing remains true: it exists always in balance with the universe.

Dark times are coming, and in order to survive, you'll have to tap into everything inside of you. You have the chance to become the greatest queen the world has ever known.

I have always loved you, Eveny, and I always will. I hope that one day, you'll understand everything.

Then, in verse form, she has printed the poem from the front hallway:

For each ray of light, there's a stroke of dark.
For each possibility, one has gone.
For each action, a reaction.
Ever in balance, the world spins on.

But there's a second verse too.

> *Blood of my blood, in dreams I will come*
> *To show you the way, soul to soul.*
> *The pieces are shattered, a puzzle undone.*
> *You must piece them together to make it whole.*

Beneath the second verse, the letter is signed simply, *Love forever, Mom.*

When I finish reading, tears cloud my vision. I slide the letter over to Aunt Bea. "I don't understand. Why would she write all this if she was going to kill herself?"

Aunt Bea doesn't reply. Instead, she looks up from the letter a moment later with tear-filled eyes and pushes the box toward me. "Open it," she says.

I take the top off gently. Inside, a smooth black stone with one jagged edge hangs from a long, thin gold chain. I pick it up, and as my fingers touch the stone, a jolt of electricity shoots through me. "It's just like the necklaces Chloe and Peregrine have," I say.

Aunt Bea is watching me closely. "It's a third of the Stone of Carrefour. When the town was founded, Eléonore and the other two queens channeled a huge amount of magical energy into a piece of obsidian. And when they cast the protective charm, the stone itself was so laden with power that it split into three. The reigning zandara queens in Carrefour each have one, passed down to them on their seventeenth birthdays.

"Only a zandara queen can harness its strength," she continues. "Once you put it on, it will hang from your neck until you die, or until you pass it on to your own daughter on her seventeenth birthday. If someone tries to take it from you, the magic within the stone burns them. And as long as you're wearing it, it's all you'll need for minor charms."

"You've lost me," I say, confused.

"As long as you're touching the stone with your left ring finger," Aunt Bea explains solemnly, "you can channel any herb or flower, without actually having it in your grasp. The queens designed it that way so that they didn't always need access to their gardens. Actually holding the plants in your hand always makes a charm stronger, but the stone is sort of like a backup plan."

I touch the stone, and it throbs with possibility and foreboding.

"If you channel a specific herb while you're using it, somewhere in the world, one of those herbs dies," Aunt Bea continues. "Zandara always requires balance, which means power always comes from somewhere.

"Now," she adds, looking up at me, "about your mother's letter—"

"It sounded like she knew what might happen with Main

de Lumière," I cut in, "and like she thought I should do all I could to learn about zandara."

"But that's an easy thing to say in the abstract, Eveny. You were just a baby when she wrote this. She never had the chance to know you as a young woman, and she didn't have a chance to see you blossom outside of this town. She assumed that your choices were already made for you, like hers were for her."

"But my choices *are* made, aren't they?" I ask. "If I walk away, the town will get weaker, until Main de Lumière figures out a way to destroy us."

"On the other hand, perhaps if zandara wilts here, we'll fall off Main de Lumière's radar," Aunt Bea says. "Maybe losing its magic is the one thing that will allow Carrefour and zandara to survive."

17

That evening, I wander out to the garden, the place I feel closest to my mom.

I have no doubt that Aunt Bea has my best interests at heart, but in the last fourteen years she has watched her sister take her own life, assumed custody of a child she never expected to raise, and left behind everything she ever knew. All because of zandara. It's no wonder that her feelings about magic would be less than glowing.

But if my mom wrote me a letter telling me that the only way through the storm is to stay strong and tap into everything inside of me, there must be a reason. Suddenly, it occurs to me that there might be a way to ask her directly.

My heart thudding, I stand up and put my left ring finger on my Stone of Carrefour like Aunt Bea told me to do. "Come to us now, Eloi Oke, and open the gate," I say uncertainly.

"Come to us now, Eloi Oke, and open the gate. Come to us now, Eloi Oke, and open the gate."

There's an almost imperceptible shift in the air, and a small gust of wind picks up around me, swirling like a miniature cyclone. I take a deep breath and realize I don't know what to do next.

"Eveny?" A concerned voice from behind me startles me, and I release the Stone of Carrefour and whirl around. In an instant, the air pressure regulates and the air stops spinning.

It's Boniface, and he's holding pruning shears and staring at me worriedly.

"Oh, hey," I say casually, trying to act normal.

"Sweetheart, what were you doing?"

"I was trying to talk to my mom." I feel suddenly silly and childish.

His expression is sad as he shakes his head. "I'm afraid you can't. Her spirit has moved on. Zandara queens can only communicate with spirits in the nether."

"Oh," I say.

Boniface puts his shears down and pulls me into a hug. "What brought all of this on?"

"Aunt Bea gave me a letter from my mom, and I was just trying to find some answers."

I sit down on the edge of one of the big rose planters, and Boniface settles beside me. After a moment he says, "This is all very new to you, isn't it?" When I nod, he adds, "And very unsettling."

"I don't know what I'm supposed to do," I tell him, "or how I'm supposed to become this great queen my mother thinks I'll be."

Boniface seems to consider this for a moment. "I've been around these parts—and your family—for quite some time now. I reckon I've picked up a few things. How about you learn to work a bit of magic on your own?"

I feel a flutter of excitement. "Really?"

"For something minor like charming roses, you don't need the herbs themselves as long as you're touching your stone with your left ring finger and as long as you're thinking about the herbs you've chosen." He strokes his chin for a moment and appears to be thinking. "You always want to look for herbs and flowers associated with what you're hoping to achieve. For this one, let's invoke squaw vine and master root. They're both used to foster growth. Are you familiar with both plants?"

"Yep," I say, and Boniface looks impressed.

"Great. Start with something simple, like, 'I draw the power of the squaw vine and the master root.' Then command the roses to grow."

I take a deep breath and touch my Stone of Carrefour as Boniface and I say in unison, "Come to us now, Eloi Oke, and open the gate. Come to us now, Eloi Oke, and open the gate. Come to us now, Eloi Oke, and open the gate."

Boniface nods to me, and I take a deep breath. "I draw the power of the squaw vine and the master root," I chant, touching one of the rosebushes with my right hand. My stone hums against my breastbone. "Spirits, please grow this rose, raise its height."

Nothing happens. I try again but still nothing. "What am I doing wrong?"

"The words you say don't matter as much as the things you're channeling as you say them. You touch the stone with your left ring finger because people believed in the *vena amoris,* a vein that runs from the ring finger to the heart. That's one of the reasons that finger is used for wedding rings, you know."

I look down at my ring finger and touch it to the stone again.

"Touching the stone with your ring finger links your magic to your heart," Boniface explains. "It has to do with harnessing specific memories, times when you've been filled with love. Harnessing feelings that pure can enhance a queen's magic tenfold. Love is power."

"Then how can Peregrine be so powerful?" I mutter. "She doesn't exactly seem like the warm and fuzzy type."

Boniface chuckles. "Love of oneself is also a very powerful emotion, not to mention love of material things." He leans in and adds, "What she's missing, though, is the power of someone loving you in return. That can magnify your magic too.

"So think of a memory in which you loved and were loved," Boniface says, "and try again."

I close my eyes. When I recite the invocation, I think about my mother smiling proudly at me in our front yard when I was a little girl as I showed her the cartwheels I'd just learned to do. I feel a sizzle shoot from my left ring finger through my heart to my right hand, which is touching the rose. I open my eyes and see that the bush has grown a foot taller and has sprouted three new rosebuds.

"So somewhere out there, a squaw vine shrub and a master root plant just died?" I ask.

He nods. "*For each action, a reaction, ever in balance, the world spins on.* Now try again."

I touch another rosebush. This time, I reach even further back, to my oldest memory of my mom. I'd fallen in the driveway and skinned my knee, and when I looked up, there she was, with a look of concern on her face so deep that I felt instantly soothed. I recite the words and crack my eyes open.

"Even better." Boniface looks approvingly at the second bush, which is blossoming in a rainbow of colors now. "You were thinking of your mother again?" When I nod, he says, "Try again, thinking of someone else."

This time, I'm intending to think of Aunt Bea and everything she's given up for me, but when I close my eyes what I see is Caleb leaning across me to open the passenger door of his Jeep last night, during the split second in which I thought he was going to kiss me.

When I open my eyes, not only has the bush I was touching grown and sprouted dozens of new blood-red roses, but every bush *it* was touching is flourishing too. I pull my hand away.

"Who were you thinking of?" Boniface asks.

"Um, Aunt Bea," I lie.

"Hmm. Well, she clearly loves you very much." He checks his watch. "In any case, I must get inside. I have a few things to do tonight. Besides, I'm guessing you're tired; working zandara can be exhausting."

I yawn and thank him. As much as I want to keep going, to keep learning, I have the feeling he's right. And even though it's only a few minutes after eight, I feel like I could crawl under my covers and sleep for the next sixteen hours. As I head off to bed, all I'm thinking about is Caleb and the power that surged within me as he flashed through my mind.

It feels like I've barely drifted off when my phone begins ringing. I swat at it to silence it and snuggle deeper into my covers, but it rings again. I reach for it on the third cycle and, still half asleep, mumble into the receiver, "Hello?"

"Eveny? It's Peregrine. Where on earth are you?"

I yawn. "Sleeping," I mumble. "Good night."

I start to hang up, but I can hear her yelling something, so I reluctantly hold the phone back up to my ear. "Are you there?" she's asking angrily.

"Hmm mmm."

"Are you seriously in bed? It's eleven p.m. on a Saturday, you lame-o!"

"I'm tired," I tell her. I don't really care if she's judging me or not.

"Boy, you must have been the life of the party back in

Brooklyn," she says, her voice dripping with sarcasm. "Nevertheless, I need you here, pronto. Frankly, I'm rather disappointed in you for not making this a priority."

Now I'm confused. "You need me *where* pronto?" I ask.

She lets out a frustrated huff. "Our *party*, Eveny! You know? Frat guys in togas? Hunch punch? All sorts of secluded corners to make out in?"

I sit up in bed. "What does that have to do with me?"

"Seriously, Eveny? This is your first party as a Queen of Carrefour. Your sosyete needs you."

"But—" I start to protest.

"I'm not taking no for an answer," she says. "Be here in twenty. Your toga is hanging by my front door."

"I don't even know where you live."

"Geez, Eveny, do you need me to spell everything out for you?" When I don't reply, she sighs heavily and says, "Walk out your front door and turn right. We're the mansion next door, just down the hill and up the next one. Obviously."

She clicks off and I'm left holding a dead phone. A moment later, against my better judgment, I haul myself out of bed, slouch into the bathroom to brush my teeth, and head back to my vanity mirror to add a bit of mascara and lipstick. Thanks to the facial mask from Cristof's, my face and hair are otherwise perfect, so I'm ready to go in under five minutes.

Aunt Bea is snoring in her room at the end of the hall, so I don't bother disturbing her. Instead, I leave a note on the table in case she wakes up before I'm back.

As soon as I'm outside, I can hear the party. Loud music and muffled laughter float through the trees, and as I begin to walk down the driveway on the back side of the hill, I can see Peregrine's house glowing. As I get closer, I realize there are blazing torches all over her property, casting shadows and light everywhere.

There's music blasting from the speakers on the grand, columned front porch when I arrive, and since the door is open, I don't bother ringing the bell. I squeeze inside past a big group of hot, toga-clad guys.

"Eveny!" Peregrine exclaims, emerging from a hallway off to the right. "It's about time!" She's wearing sky-high chocolate leather stilettos and a white toga so short that I'm pretty sure it's supposed to be a top, not a dress. "Come in, come in! Here's your toga!" She grabs a slip of white, drapey fabric from the coat hook beside the door and thrusts it at me. "I'll show you where to change. Follow me!"

As she leads me down the front hall, through a throng of muscular, square-jawed guys whose eyes follow her, I look around in awe. The Marceaus' mansion is a little smaller than ours, but it's a thousand times fancier. The front hallway is all ivory marble with gold leafing and gold trim. An enormous crystal chandelier hangs over the entryway, sending little rays of light cascading everywhere.

As we emerge into a larger room, which Peregrine calls the ballroom, I suck in a deep breath. The chandelier here is even larger than the one in the entryway, the floor is all done in black and white marble, sleek white furniture hugs the walls, and the ceiling soars several stories high. There are torches blazing everywhere, and the place is teeming with guys and a handful of girls, all of whom are wearing togas too. I recognize Arelia and Margaux gyrating on the dance floor, but the rest of them are strangers.

"Pascal appreciates the sorority girls we added to our guest list," Peregrine says as we whisk past. "It's nice to be able to appease your friends."

Indeed, I spot him grinding on a leggy blonde whose toga has ridden up almost to her crotch. A tall black girl with perfect features and close-cropped hair is pressed up against his back. "Well, he definitely looks appeased," I say, and Peregrine laughs.

She leads me into a huge, sprawling bathroom. "Change in there," she orders.

I slip inside and quickly shrug into the tiny swath of fabric Peregrine has shoved into my hands. I'm unsurprised to see that it hits above mid-thigh, but at least I'm not flashing anyone. I tug it down uncomfortably and, clutching my own clothes in my hands, open the door.

"You look hot," Peregrine says. She snatches my clothes and adds, "I'll put these away. On second thought, perhaps I should burn them, since bootcut jeans are totally passé."

"They're comfortable," I protest, but she just snorts. "Why are we wearing togas, anyhow?"

"Parties are so much more fun when they're themed," she

says. "And since Chloe and I went through the whole Greek system at LSU and chose only the hottest people, we figured Hot Greek would be a great theme for our little soiree. Try to keep up."

Back in the ballroom, Peregrine drifts away and I stand against the wall awkwardly until Chloe walks up wearing a toga even shorter than mine.

"Have you seen Justin?" she asks over the music. The dance floor is full of hot guys ogling Arelia and Margaux and casting looks at Chloe and me in the corner. I feel conspicuous, and I tug on the too-short hem of my toga again.

"No," I say. "Isn't he with you?"

She shakes her head. "He keeps disappearing with this group of frat guys," she says miserably. "Do you think he's doing drugs?"

"Doesn't seem like the type," I tell her.

"At least he's not trying to get with the sorority girls," she says.

"Yeah, I think Pascal seems to have the monopoly on that." We look back to the dance floor, where Pascal's gyrating sandwich seems to have grown. There's a girl with long brown hair giving him a come-hither look and a girl with the biggest fake breasts I've ever seen jiggling pointedly in his direction. He looks delighted. "Is Caleb here?" I ask uneasily.

"Maybe he's with Peregrine," she suggests. My stomach swims.

Chloe snaps to attention as soon as Justin strolls in from

the direction of the front hallway. "I have to go," she says quickly. "Have fun."

She's already making a beeline across the dance floor before I can reply. I'm about to turn and go look for Caleb when I feel a hand brush against my arm. "What are you doing standing over here all alone?" says a male voice in my ear.

I turn to see a blond guy with brown eyes and glasses smiling at me.

"Just hanging out," I tell him.

"Well, you want to just hang out with me?" he asks. He doesn't wait for an answer before introducing himself. "Blake Montoire, Lambda Delta Epsilon."

"I'm Eveny," I reply.

"Which sorority are you in?"

"I'm not. I live here in Carrefour."

"Wow, cool," he says. "Pretty amazing town you've got. I've never seen houses this gorgeous. Built around the turn of the last century, right? Maybe 1904 or so?"

"How'd you know that?"

"I'm majoring in architecture. Although I have no desire to talk about school tonight. I'd rather talk about you."

He looks down at me flirtatiously, and I can feel my cheeks heating up. I'm flattered by the attention, but there are fifty guys here and only a dozen girls; maybe he's just run out of other options.

"I'm going to go get a drink," I tell him.

His expression falters. "I'll come with you. Protect you

from all those other guys who'll want to hit on you."

"Thanks, but I'm good," I tell him, already inching away. "I'll be back in a little while."

Instead of returning, I circulate around the party for the next hour, feeling a bit like a character from *The Great Gatsby*. Champagne's flowing from a big fountain out back, people are getting drunker and wilder, and the dance floor heaves with more frat boys every few minutes. I would have thought that a bunch of partygoers in togas would look sort of dorky, but because Peregrine and Chloe only invited the hottest people, the backyard is filled with Adonis look-alikes. I'm scanning the party for a glimpse of Caleb when I spot Arelia and Blake disappearing upstairs together. So much for his interest in me.

By one in the morning, I'm ready to go. I find Peregrine to thank her for the party and ask where my clothes are, but she's too busy making out with a tall, muscular guy with a tattoo of a tiger on his arm to say anything other than, "Just wear the toga home, for goodness' sake, Eveny."

Arelia, Margaux, and Chloe are in the corner of the ballroom whispering to one another, so I say a quick good-bye to them before heading out the front door.

Blake is sitting on the step and jumps up as I walk by. "Hey, Eveny, where are you off to?"

"Heading home," I say without stopping.

He hurries to catch up with me. "I'll walk you. You never know what might be lurking out there this time of night."

"I'll be fine," I tell him. I can't resist adding, "Maybe Arelia could use an escort back to her place, though."

He looks surprised. "She was just showing me around the house. Nothing happened." He grasps my forearm as he adds earnestly, "You're the girl I've been thinking about all night."

"Eveny?" comes a voice from the darkness behind me. I turn to see Caleb striding out of the house. Somehow, the toga looks better on him than it does on anyone else at the party. "What are you doing?"

I open my mouth to answer, but Blake beats me to it. "Hey, man, I was just about to walk her home."

"I'll do it," Caleb says instantly. He walks right past Blake and offers his arm to me. "C'mon."

"Look, man, I was talking to her—" Blake begins, but Caleb cuts him off.

"She's my girlfriend," he says, which makes my cheeks immediately heat up. "And I'm taking her home."

He turns and begins striding down the driveway, pulling me with him, before Blake can respond.

"Hey," I say, my heart fluttering madly as soon as the sounds of the party have faded behind us and we're alone. "Where'd you come from? I haven't seen you all night."

"I was around."

"You called me your girlfriend," I say after a minute. I'm thankful for the darkness, because he can't see me blushing.

"Oh," he says. "I didn't mean it, obviously."

I shake my head. "Yes, because that would be horrible."

"Sorry," he says. "That came out wrong."

I blink a few times. "Well, if I'm so repulsive to you, why did you drag me away from the perfectly nice, cute guy who was hitting on me?"

He stops walking and looks at me in surprise. "You were interested in that guy? I thought I was saving you from him."

"I didn't ask you to save me," I snap.

"And you're not repulsive," he says after a pause. "At all."

"Gee thanks," I say. "I can't think of the last time someone said something so flattering to me."

"Eveny—" he begins, but he stops as I pull my arm away from his.

"I can take it from here," I say, already quickening my pace toward my own front porch, which is visible on the hill up ahead. "Good night."

"But—" he begins to protest.

"I said good night," I say stiffly. I double my pace and continue ahead without looking back.

That night, the dream about the parlor returns, and it's even more vivid than last week. I hear screaming and crying as the blood pours out, and I see someone creeping from the room, hugging the shadows. I can't make out his face or any of his features in the darkness, so I follow him as he walks through the front door.

But the moment I leave the house, it begins to crumble. I run into the yard, but I lose the man in the darkness as I turn in horror. My beautiful mansion, the one my ancestors built, disintegrates, its bricks and stones crashing to the ground with a mighty roar. "No!" I cry.

But the tide of blood from the parlor is rising around me now, hot and sticky. I try to run from it, but as I get to the edge of the cemetery, it drags me down and pulls me under.

18

On Monday morning, I wake up to a missed call from Meredith. When I play back her message, I grit my teeth as I listen to her chirp, "I hope you're not still mad at me. What Trevor and I have is special, and I know you'll be a good enough friend to understand." What irks me about her behavior has little to do with the feelings I once had for Trevor. With the distance of a few weeks and a thousand miles, and with destiny and power swirling around me in ways I never could have imagined, Trevor feels irrelevant.

What bothers me more is how easily Meredith has rejected the idea that my feelings could be hurt. The reality is, she simply doesn't care.

I'm still grumbling to myself as I head out the front door, and I almost trip over Caleb, who's inexplicably sitting on my doorstep. He hastily stands and brushes his hands off. "Sorry,

I didn't know if your aunt was up yet, and I didn't want to wake anyone."

"What are you doing here?" I ask. Even though I have bigger things to worry about, his instant dismissal of me on the walk home from Peregrine's still stings.

"I wanted to explain what I meant on Saturday night."

"Oh, I think it was pretty clear," I tell him. I lock the door behind me and start walking down the driveway. "Let me recap: You could never imagine dating me, even though you don't find me *entirely* repulsive. That about the gist of it?"

He falls into step beside me, even though his Jeep is still parked in my driveway. "You don't understand."

"Don't I?"

"Eveny—" He attempts to interject, but I'm on a roll.

"I know I'm an outcast here. I know I don't really belong with the Dolls. But if you're not interested in me, why do you keep lurking around being all sexy and intriguing?"

He stops walking. "You think I'm sexy and intriguing?"

I groan. He's missing the point.

After a moment, he hurries to catch up with me. "Eveny, I'm not trying to jerk you around."

I snort. "Yeah, well, your social skills could use a little work."

"I know." He hesitates. "The thing is, I do like you. A lot."

This time, I'm the one who stops walking. "What?"

"I like you, Eveny."

A whole fleet of butterflies invades my stomach. I try to

keep my face neutral. "Well, you have a funny way of showing it."

"The thing is, I'm trying my best to stop having these feelings for you."

The words hit me hard, and I start walking again so that he can't see my face. "Gee, sorry to be such an inconvenience."

He grabs my arm and spins me around. "Would you stop being sarcastic and listen to me?" He takes a deep breath and blurts out, "I'm not *allowed* to be in love with you. I'm not allowed to date you. I'm not allowed to be feeling this way at all."

"What are you talking about?"

"I'm your protector, Eveny," he says. "For as long as Carrefour has existed, my family has protected your family."

"My protector?"

"It was all established in the town's founding ceremony," he explains. He looks miserable. "There's one protector for each queen. We're specially charmed and trained to guard you, and there are rules that go along with it, just like there are rules dictating everything else in this damned town."

I realize what he means. "And one of the rules is that you can't have feelings for the person you're protecting."

He nods. "As long as you're inside Carrefour's walls, I'm supposed to be able to sense when you're in danger. But the more I feel for you, the fuzzier the protectorate link gets. Like, I don't know, the way Wi-Fi slows down when there are too many people using it."

I choke out a laugh, despite everything. "You're comparing your feelings for me to a slow internet connection?"

"Maybe not the best analogy ever." He half smiles, but the expression quickly disappears as he adds, "Look, I'm sorry. But if I keep letting myself feel this way, I'm putting you in danger. And I can't do that."

I take a deep breath, trying to absorb what he's saying. "But what if I'm willing to risk not being protected?"

"Why would you do that?" he asks, his voice catching.

"Because I like you too," I say, "and I'm getting sick of some ancestral pact controlling my life."

There's sadness etched across his face as he says, "I can't run from who I am any more than you can. I'll just have to figure out a way to stop having these feelings." He pauses and says, "I just thought I owed you an explanation."

Without another word, he walks back up the hill and gets into his Jeep. I stay glued to the spot as he guns the engine and comes down my driveway to where I'm standing. "Get in," he says as he pulls up alongside me.

"I'm okay walking," I say, trying not to think of the first time I climbed into his car, when electricity crackled between us and anything felt possible. It feels like an eternity has passed since then.

"Eveny, you know I have to keep an eye on you. It'll be a lot easier if you're in my passenger seat."

"Fine," I say after a minute, climbing into his car and slamming the door behind me.

We ride the rest of the way to school in silence, and when he drops me off in the parking lot, he says that he has to go.

"Go where?" I ask, surprised.

"Training," he says, his jaw stiff, "with Patrick and Oscar, Peregrine's and Chloe's protectors."

"Oh," I manage. "What does this training involve, exactly?"

"It's part intensive workout, part martial arts, part reflex training and speed. But the biggest thing is reviewing years' worth of intel our fathers, their fathers, and their fathers' fathers have gathered on Main de Lumière. It's about knowing exactly how they might hurt you and staying one step ahead."

"So you're training to be a killing machine?"

I expect him to laugh, but instead, his mouth straightens into a thin line. "We're trained to kill, but that's always the last resort."

"I was joking."

He looks sad. "I know. So I'll see you later, okay?"

"Wait," I add. "All this protector stuff. Why tell me now?"

He hesitates for a moment before saying, "All these years, I figured I'd hate you, which would make protecting you easy because there wouldn't be any feelings involved. But then I saw you for the first time, and I felt exactly the opposite. I still do." He drives off without another word and my Stone of Carrefour, which is hidden under my standard-issue oxford shirt, heats up against my chest.

I'm floating down the hall in a fog of my own making a few minutes later when I hear Mona Silvestre from my French class saying to a guy near her locker, "Holy crap, did you hear what happened to that guy from LSU?"

"I heard he was murdered right outside the gate to Carrefour!" the guy replies.

I hurry to my own locker, where more people are gossiping around me as I grab my books. "Dude, some frat guy was stabbed to death," a soccer player named Phil Demetroux is saying. "I heard it was so gruesome that the police chief hurled all over the crime scene."

By the time I make it to first period English, I've managed to piece together the full story through snippets of hallway gossip, and I'm chilled to the bone.

Apparently, sometime on Saturday night, one of the LSU guys on Peregrine's guest list was stabbed to death just outside the city walls. But since his car wasn't found, police speculate that someone stopped him on the road, perhaps pretending to be injured, and killed him to steal his car.

"What the hell?" I hiss at Peregrine as soon as she takes her seat beside me in class. "You said nothing bad would happen if we opened the gates for a few hours!"

She looks at me defiantly. "I don't know what you're talking about."

"Someone is *dead*!"

"Quiet down, okay?" I'm surprised to see Peregrine looking tearful. "I didn't mean for it to turn out this way. I swear, Eveny, I don't know what could have happened!"

Chloe slides into her seat then, looking equally disturbed.

"Eveny's pissed at us," Peregrine mumbles.

"We didn't know," Chloe says miserably.

"Well, this should really help us keep Carrefour off Main de Lumière's radar," I mutter. "Nice work."

Chloe and Peregrine spend the remainder of class staring straight ahead. When the bell rings, they pick up their things and dash out without another word. My Stone of Carrefour continues to hum against my chest.

In third-period French, before the bell rings, Drew pulls his desk over to mine and whispers, "You heard about that dead frat guy?"

I nod without looking at him. I don't want to give anything away with my eyes. "Pretty awful."

"Doesn't it seem kind of strange to you that someone would be stabbed to death right outside our gates for no apparent reason?"

I shrug and look away. "Totally strange."

"What was he even doing here?" Drew asks.

I'm saved from answering as Mrs. Toliver calls the class to order and begins talking about irregular verbs. Drew reluctantly scoots his desk back, but I can feel his gaze on me all through class.

At lunch, I deliberately avoid locking eyes with Peregrine or Chloe; instead, I grab a lunch tray and get in the caf line with Liv and Max, who look surprised to see me.

"You're not eating with the Dolls today?" Max asks.

"I'd just rather eat with you guys."

"See?" Liv says to Max. "I told you she wasn't one of them."

Max shrugs. "Yeah, but who wouldn't want to be? *I* even want to be a Doll."

Liv rolls her eyes at him, and I force a laugh. I order some gross-looking lasagna from the cafeteria lady, grab a carton of chocolate milk, and follow Liv and Max to a table in the center of the caf once we've all paid. I've just taken my first bite of the lasagna, which isn't as bad as it looks, when a shadow falls over me. I know without looking who's there.

"Eveny?" It's Peregrine, her voice hushed. "Can I talk to you for a minute?"

Beside me, I hear Max drop his fork. He and Liv stare, and I'm not sure if it's because she's gracing us with her presence in the cafeteria, or because even with her Louboutin boots, a fitted fur vest, and perfect makeup, she looks terrible.

"About what?" I ask. I take another bite of lasagna and do my best to ignore her.

"You know," she says. She's being uncharacteristically meek, and it's freaking me out a little. "Please?"

"I'm eating now," I say stiffly.

She leans down and whispers in my ear, "*Please?* There's a serious problem."

"No kidding," I reply.

"What's the problem?" Max pipes up eagerly from across the table. His eyes dart over to Peregrine. "If you need help with something, I'll help you."

Liv smacks him on the back of his head, but Peregrine acts like she hasn't heard him. "Just come talk to me for a minute, Eveny. I'm asking nicely."

I slam my fork down. "I'll be right back," I say. I stand up and follow Peregrine outside. She begins to head for the Hickories, but I say, "No. I'm eating with Max and Liv today. If you have something to say, say it to me here."

She looks wounded. "How come you don't want to eat with us?"

"For real?" When she doesn't reply, I say, "Look what you've done! You wanted to have a party so you could have more hot guys than usual drooling all over you. And someone ended up dead because of it!"

"But I didn't mean for that to happen!" she protests.

I look back toward the cafeteria and see through the window that Drew has arrived at the table and is deep in conversation with Liv. Max is staring at us with wide eyes. "Well, Liv, Max, and Drew don't create situations where innocent people die," I say.

"This isn't totally my fault," she says. "Look, I know I screwed up. But there's a bigger issue here. The guy they found dead was killed *before* my party."

"So?"

"*So*, everyone at the party was accounted for," she says urgently. "We had a guest list at the door. Every single person signed in. So how did that happen if one of them was already lying dead outside the gates?"

My blood runs cold. "What are you saying?"

"That someone stole the dead guy's identity and used it to get into town. Into *our party*. For all we know, he's still here."

"But the gates are closed again, right, so we're protected?"

"Not exactly," she says miserably. "If someone got into town when the gates were open, he'd still be able to do what he pleased here. Including kill us."

"So fix it!" I cry.

"I *can't*," she says. "Not alone, anyway. Just like I couldn't open the gates on my own, I can't restore the protection by myself either."

I shake my head. "I should never have taken part in this," I say, more to myself than to her.

"You didn't know," Peregrine says. "Please, Eveny. If you, Chloe, and I work together—"

"Why should I trust you?" I interrupt her.

Peregrine looks at me blankly. "What are you talking about?"

"I know there are more important things to worry about, but you're obviously keeping things from me. Like, couldn't you have clued me in about the fact that Caleb's my protector? Or were you having too much fun watching me make a fool of myself?"

"So he told you." The corner of her mouth twitches. "Well, it was kind of amusing watching you stare at him like he was God's gift to earth." When I just glare at her, she adds, "Fine, so Chloe and I thought it might be too much for you to handle along with everything else, okay? In case you haven't noticed, we've been trying to ease you into this whole zandara thing. It's obvious that you like him, so why hurt your feelings right away by telling you that you two can never be together?"

"Yes, you're a benevolent angel," I say drily. "So while we're on the subject, is there anything else you're keeping from me? Any other secrets about my own life I should know about?"

"Now you're just being a drama queen." She sticks out her lower lip in a dramatic pout. "So are you going to keep yelling at me, or are you going to help us fix this?"

"Obviously I'm going to help you. Tonight?"

Her shoulders sag. "It'll take us a day or two to put together the necessary herbs to render the intruder powerless. We'll need the help of the whole sosyete too. This is a big deal."

"I don't understand," I say. "Can't we just reverse the charm we cast to let him in on Saturday?"

"We have to find out who the guy is first. As long as one of us in the sosyete actually saw him at some point that night, as long as we know what he looks like, we can harness that memory in a ceremony and cast against him."

"And we can't just cast a charm to learn his identity?" I ask.

Peregrine purses her lips. "You don't think we would have done that already if we could? No, the spirits rely on our eyes. If we didn't see something, the spirits won't know it either. It's exactly why we have no way to learn who killed Glory. No one saw what happened, except for Glory herself and the killer."

The words send a shiver down my spine. "Well, what's the name of the guy who was killed outside the gates?" I persist. "Obviously the killer used his identity to get in."

"The police haven't released his name yet. But I'll keep trying to find out."

"You do that," I say tightly. I can't resist adding, "I don't believe this is happening. All because you wanted to have a party."

Peregrine's eyes narrow. "You can quit blaming me, Eveny. You know *nothing* about how this town works. Nothing."

With that, she spins on her stiletto heel and walks away toward the Hickories.

Back in the cafeteria, Max, Drew, and Liv stare at me as I slide into my seat and pick up my fork. I take a bite, but the lasagna's cold. I've lost my appetite anyhow. "What?" I ask after a moment.

"Did you just stand up to her?" Liv asks.

"She had a question she needed to ask. It was no big deal."

"It's like she thinks she runs this town, like she thinks she's *so* much better than the rest of us," Liv mutters. "It's about time someone lets her know she's not the queen of the world."

Liv returns to chatting with the guys, and I watch them for a moment, feeling like I'm miles away. Although Peregrine may not be the queen of the world, she *is* one of the Queens of Carrefour. And like it or not, I am too.

19

That afternoon after school, I'm changing into jeans and a T-shirt in my room when I spot my mother's letter lying on my desk. I pause and sit on the corner of my bed to read it again. It feels like the answers about what I'm supposed to do should be there in her words. Then again, maybe that's the wishful thinking of someone who's just stepped into the weirdest situation of her life.

I head outside to look for Boniface, who I'm hoping will be able to help me understand. He's not in the rose garden, but I eventually find him in the toolshed, organizing a rack of hammers and screwdrivers. He turns when I enter. "Hi, honey," he says. "How was school?"

"I need to talk to you," I say instead of replying.

He stops what he's doing and looks at me with concern. "What is it?"

"We think there's a Main de Lumière soldier in town," I tell him. "Not just the one who killed Glory. But someone from the outside."

"That's not possible." He looks suddenly unsteady on his feet. "How would they have gotten in?"

I reluctantly explain the fraternity party and the guy whose body was found outside the gates. "I know it was the wrong thing to do," I conclude miserably, "but at the time I thought it was a harmless sort of wrong."

"Of course you did," he says. "But Peregrine and Chloe, they know better. They've gotten out of control."

I pull my mother's letter out of my pocket and hand it to him. "I feel like there's something in here I'm supposed to understand, something connected to what's going on now. Can you take a look?"

"Of course." He unfolds the letter, and a shadow crosses his face as he begins to read. "This sounds just like her," he says when he's done. "God rest her soul."

"What do you think the two verses are supposed to mean?" I ask. "Or her line that dark times are coming?"

"She knew her sister queens well enough to realize that if she was gone, they might resort to practicing zandara in a way that defies your ancestors' rules. And she knew enough to be afraid of what that might lead to."

"I don't understand."

"The universe is like a seesaw—when one side is lifted up, the other has nowhere to go but down—and zandara exists in the middle. Action and reaction. But when your mother died and Carrefour lost its triumvirate, her sister queens' power was greatly reduced, and they could no longer cast with the strength they were accustomed to. In other words, they can use herbs, but there's nothing to magnify their power anymore."

"Right, it's why the protective charms around the town are crumbling. I know all that."

"But did you ever stop to wonder why the wealth of central Carrefour hasn't crumbled too?" Boniface asks.

My stomach swims uneasily as he continues.

"A few years after your mother died they realized there was another source from which they could draw power," he says. "They're still able to execute small charms with herbs and flowers, and they do so when they can. But the bigger things—new cars, great wealth, unnaturally good looks— those have to come from somewhere else. So they tapped into the Périphérie."

"What do you mean?" I have a bad feeling about this.

"The Périphérie was always less privileged than central Carrefour, but it wasn't like it is today," he says. "That's a result of Annabelle Marceau and Scarlett St. Pierre realizing they could achieve great things by taking from the other side of town. Casting a charm to get a new sports car, for example. Because they can't draw a large amount of power from flowers and herbs without having three queens working together, they cast using the Périphérie's good fortune instead. So they get their car, but something of value crumbles in the Périphérie, the same way an herb dies in the world when it's drawn for a simple charm. That's an overly simplistic explanation, but you get the idea. There's always a balance, and when it doesn't come from plants, it has to come from somewhere."

"So they've been taking from the Périphérie all these years, making themselves richer while people out there get poorer and poorer?" I whisper.

"Yes. I don't approve, and neither do most of the people in the sosyete. But they're the queens. They don't need our permission. And until you came back, Chloe and Peregrine were doing the same thing. Now they won't have to; they have you."

My mind is spinning. "But look at all the destruction they've caused."

Boniface nods, and that's when I realize he hasn't addressed the second verse my mother wrote. "What do you think the rest of her letter means?" I ask.

He looks away. "I'm not sure."

I take the letter back from him and read it. *Blood of my blood, in dreams I will come to show you the way.* And suddenly, I know.

"I need to get into the parlor, Boniface," I say. "There's something in there I'm supposed to see; I think that's what the verse means." I quickly explain the dreams I've been having and the way the door burned my hand when I tried to open it. "My mom's letter specifically mentions blood and dreams," I conclude. "That can't be a coincidence."

He looks into my eyes for a long moment, like he's trying to figure something out. Then he sighs and says, "There's no missing key, Eveny. The room is charmed. It hasn't been opened in fourteen years."

Well that explains the burning-hot handle. "Who charmed it?"

"Ms. Marceau and Ms. St. Pierre closed the parlor off years ago. It holds memories that they wanted to forget—but that they couldn't afford to lose altogether."

"Memories connected to my mother?"

"I think I'd better call Annabelle and Scarlett," he says.

"No." I shake my head. "I'm going to uncharm the room myself." I don't trust the mothers, especially now that I know they've been destroying the Périphérie. If they're hiding something connected to my family, I have to find out.

I stride toward the house, and Boniface follows me. "Please, Eveny, I think you should wait until someone can be here to explain things to you."

"Explain *what*?"

He looks uneasy, but he doesn't answer the question. Instead, he says, "How about I call Peregrine and Chloe? Perhaps they should be here for this."

"*They* know about the parlor too? Unbelievable." Once again, everyone has been keeping me in the dark. I feel a surge of anger as I storm away, my mind spinning through the herbs and flowers I've studied over the years.

What comes to mind as I reach the closed parlor doors is

something I once planted in our community garden. Its technical name is *Euonymus americanus*, but it's more commonly known as bursting-heart or burning-bush. Superstitious people put it over their doorways to repel unwanted magic.

It may not be the perfect plant for what I'm trying to do, but it should work. I stand in front of the doors and ask Eloi Oke to open the gate. Then I take a deep breath, think of my mother, hold my left ring finger against my Stone of Carrefour, and say, "Bursting-heart, *Euonymus americanus*, I draw your power. Please, spirits, open this door to me and reveal the secrets that lie inside."

For a moment, nothing happens. Then I hear a click, and one of the doors opens a crack. Musty air escapes in a whoosh, and I drop my stone and reach for the handle, my heart racing in anticipation as I push it open.

As my eyes adjust to the dim light, I realize the room is exactly as it appears in my dreams—except now enormous spans of cobwebs hang from the chandeliers, and the mirrored walls are covered with a film of dust and smoke so thick that the images blinking back at me are dark and hazy. Candles still stand, half melted and covered in dust, on big candelabras.

I walk across the room to the spot where I've seen my toddler self standing in my dreams. I bend to touch the floor, and as I do, I can see a huge, dark stain on the hardwood. It vanishes as soon as I pull my hand away. A chill sweeps through me, and I turn around slowly to find Boniface looking at me.

"This is blood, isn't it?" I ask.

"Yes," he says sadly.

"Whose?" I ask. But the look on his face tells me all I need to know. "My mom's?" I ask in disbelief. "But she died miles from here. Didn't she?"

Boniface frowns. "Eveny, I really think you should wait until your aunt comes home. She'll explain everything."

"If she'd wanted to explain," I say, "she would have already." I clench and unclench my fists. "Are there herbs that will let me see what happened in this room?"

"Eveny, your aunt will be furious with me," he says.

"Please!" I exclaim. "I promise, I'll tell Aunt Bea you tried to stop me. I deserve to know what happened."

"Yes, I suppose you do." He crosses the room and stands in front of the bookcase for a moment before pulling a narrow, leather-bound volume from the shelf. He flips through it, seems to find what he's looking for, and returns to me. "I believe peppermint leaves and flax seed will call the past into focus."

"What's that book?"

"Your mother's herb journal. It's incomplete, but she took notes on herbs and charms that worked particularly well for her. It's yours now." He hands it to me. "I hope this is the right thing. Good luck. But I can't be here for this," he says as he walks out of the room.

I put the journal down on the coffee table and take a deep breath. I again call on Eloi Oke to open the gate, then, with my left ring finger on my Stone of Carrefour, I invoke peppermint and flax seed and ask the spirits to show me what happened here. As the wind picks up, the candles around me flicker suddenly on, their flames growing and shrinking like the room itself is breathing. Suddenly, all of the flames go out, and I'm plunged into darkness. I hear the faintest of whispers, a woman's voice saying, "It shall be."

When the candles flicker on again, the cobwebs are gone and the parlor looks entirely different. It's just like it was fourteen years ago, just like it has looked in my nightmares the last few weeks. Suddenly, three figures appear in the middle of the floor. They're hazy at first, but they quickly materialize, and I gasp as I recognize my mother and younger versions of Peregrine's and Chloe's mothers. All three are dressed in long, gauzy gowns that catch the candlelight and make them look like ethereal fairies.

"Mom!" I cry and take a step forward. The women don't hear me, though, and when I reach out to touch my mother, my hand goes right through her. It's like I'm watching a projected image on a movie screen.

The three mothers begin to chant and dance, and then the candles flicker out again. I hear a panicky voice ask, "What just happened?" I'm pretty sure it's Chloe's mother.

Another voice—Peregrine's mom—replies shakily, "I don't know. It must have been the wind."

Then there are heavy footsteps and the sound of something sliding. "Who's there?" says a voice I recognize as my mother's. Hearing her after all this time pierces my heart.

There's silence for a few seconds, then a pealing scream and a soft thudding sound before footsteps retreat and a door slams. A moment later, the overhead light flickers on, and I see Peregrine's mother near the light switch, blinking into the sudden illumination. "Sandrine!" she cries.

I follow her eyes to see my mother lying with her neck sliced open in a rapidly spreading pool of her own blood.

I sob uncontrollably as the rest of the scene unfolds. Peregrine's and Chloe's moms are screaming. Chloe's mom tries to revive my mother, but she's drifting in and out of consciousness. "We have to go get Bea," Peregrine's mother says.

Chloe's mother stands up, and when she does, I see that she's covered in my mother's blood. Her mascara is running down her face in teary rivers. "And Boniface," she adds weakly. She turns back to my mom. "Sandrine, we'll be right back. We're going for help. Hang on, sugar."

They run out of the room and, in the sudden quiet, I can hear my mother gasping for air. It breaks my heart. I move toward her, and that's when I see my younger self amble into the room, blinking in confusion. She's wearing the same nightgown from my dreams, and I know this is the moment I've been seeing. I watch as she rushes over and wraps herself around my mother, trying to fix her, trying to stop the blood.

My mother whispers something, and I can just barely make out her words: "You're the only one who can save us all. I live on in you," she says, and then her whole body goes limp.

"Mommy?" I hear three-year-old me ask in a small voice. "Mommy, wake up!"

I'm full-out sobbing as the images slowly fade away and the room returns to the present. Dazed, I stumble out of the parlor and into Boniface's waiting arms.

"You saw everything, didn't you?" he asks gently as he rubs my back.

"I saw my mother die," I sob. "She didn't kill herself. She was murdered. Why has everyone been lying about it all these years? Lying to *me*? Why has everyone let me believe my mother took her own life?"

"Honey, no one knows exactly what happened that day. But we couldn't have the police asking questions, not if her death was linked to zandara. So a decision was made to stage a car crash. It was for the good of the sosyete, and it made sense at the time. Your aunt asked that everyone play along for your sake too. She didn't want you to remember your mom dying this way."

"It was better that I think she'd killed herself?" I whisper incredulously. "That I'd think she deliberately abandoned me?"

"Bea was just trying to protect you. While Peregrine's and Chloe's mothers took care of staging the accident, your aunt and I calmed you down, got you back into bed, and convinced you it was just a bad dream. Chloe's and Peregrine's mothers gave you a charmed potion to make you forget what you'd seen."

"They should never have done that."

"But no child should ever, ever grow up with that kind of sad memory, and we were all afraid that if the police were called, you'd let the cat out of the bag about the ceremonies that were going on here. The police chief was a member of the sosyete, but none of the officers were. We couldn't take the chance of anyone finding out."

"So who killed her?" When he doesn't answer, I add, "Was it Main de Lumière?"

"You didn't see her killer in your vision?" he asks. When I shake my head, he sighs. "At first we assumed it was Main de Lumière, but tradition and ritual are very important to them, and none of us really believed they'd kill your mother by slitting her throat instead of stabbing her through the heart."

"So if it wasn't them . . . ," I say.

"No one knows what could have happened," he says simply, looking away.

"Okay, I get why no one wanted a little kid to have a horrible memory like that," I concede. "But I'm seventeen now. Why hasn't anyone said anything?"

Boniface looks sad. "It wasn't my place to tell you, honey. I can't speak for the others."

I clench my fists, a wave of frustration rising within me. All the lies, all the half truths—I'm suddenly furious. "Peregrine and Chloe knew, didn't they? They've known all along." I don't wait for an answer; my blood is boiling. "I'm going over there."

"Eveny—" Boniface begins, but I'm already on a mission, already moving toward the front door. I have to confront them, to find out what else they've been hiding from me. "Wait, Eveny!" Boniface calls after me. "Come back!"

"I can't," I say as I shut the door behind me. I take off running toward Peregrine's opulent mansion on the next hill over.

20

I pound on Peregrine's front door with both fists and am surprised when she and Chloe answer together.

"You lied to me!" I cry, still breathless from my run.

They look at each other and then back at me. "Lied about what?" Chloe asks.

"About the night my mother died!" I say. "Your mothers were there. I just charmed the parlor and watched the whole thing play out. Your mothers saw *everything*. You knew all along, and you let me keep believing my mother had left me on purpose!"

"Calm down, Eveny," Peregrine says crisply. "Anger isn't getting you anywhere."

But her words only make me madder. "Could you cut the whole icy superiority thing for a minute and be honest with me? Or is that too much for you?"

Chloe takes a step forward and reaches for me without saying a word. At first I pull away, but she just steps closer and stays there until I crumple. She folds me into a hug as I start to cry. "We're sorry, Eveny," she says. "We're sorry we didn't tell you. And we're sorry about what happened to your mom." She pulls away after a moment and tilts my chin up so that I'm staring right at her. "If you come inside, we'll tell you what we know."

I reluctantly follow her in, glancing at Peregrine as I go. She's being strangely silent, and her lips are set in a thin line.

"Are your mothers here?" I ask once we're seated in the living room.

Peregrine shakes her head and looks almost apologetic. "They're at Chloe's house. We can wait until they're back if you want. . . ."

"No," I say immediately. "I want to know the truth. Now."

"What did you see?" Chloe asks gently.

"Wait, go back," Peregrine interrupts. "You said you charmed the room? How?"

"I used my Stone of Carrefour."

The eyes of both girls widen. "You have your stone?" Chloe asks in a whisper. "We thought it was lost with your mother."

"This is a huge deal," Peregrine says flatly. "I can't believe you didn't tell us."

"Kind of like you didn't tell me that my mother was murdered?" I say through gritted teeth.

Chloe puts a hand on Peregrine's arm and says to her, "We can talk about the stone later. Right now, Eveny's trying to tell us about her vision."

I recap what played out in the parlor. The ceremony. The plunge into darkness. The screams. My mother gasping for breath as Peregrine's and Chloe's mothers ran for help. My mother dying.

"Our mothers aren't sure whether your mom was a target because of something personal, or whether it was someone trying to weaken the power of Carrefour by eliminating the triumvirate," Chloe explains when I'm done.

"Without your mother," Peregrine adds, "our mothers were greatly weakened, and it's been harder for them to . . ." Her voice trails off and she adds, "Harder for them to cast their magic."

"So I've heard," I say stiffly. "Somehow you've all managed to convince yourselves that it's fine to use the Périphérie to keep your own lives floating along perfectly."

"You don't understand; they owed it to us," Peregrine says right away. "Our ancestors have been providing for the people in the Périphérie for over a century."

"That doesn't justify taking from them now!" I exclaim. "All the crumbling houses, the people who have lost their money, the dead lawns, the decaying trees . . . That seems right to you?"

"We had to keep central Carrefour up somehow," Chloe says in a small voice.

"Even the weather?" I ask.

"The sunshine on this side of town doesn't create itself," Peregrine says. "We don't use it every day, though. You can see there's a storm coming now." Peregrine's eyebrows knit together in annoyance. "You can't expect us just to stop *living*."

"I don't," I say. "But you have no right to live in luxury that's built on other people's lives falling apart. That's disgusting!"

Chloe quickly picks up the thread of Peregrine's argument. "It doesn't have to be that way anymore, Eveny. That's the great thing about you being back. We have a triumvirate again. We can start drawing our power purely from plants. We can even restore the Périphérie."

"If you join us," Peregrine says, "our lives can be just as we want them to be. You seem to keep forgetting what a gift this is." She reaches out to take my hand, but I pull away.

"But you and your moms have already destroyed so much. You can't possibly justify that."

Peregrine rolls her eyes. "Whatever," she says. "Don't goody-goody us. You've adjusted quite well to the perks of zandara since you've been back, haven't you? Your beautiful house, your huge property, your instant popularity, the money to attend Pointe Laveau. It's all zandara, Eveny. All of it."

"We don't deserve those things," I reply. "None of us do."

I stand up and look at the two of them. They're perfect on the outside, exactly what any girl would want to look like. Perfect hair, perfect skin, perfect bodies, perfect *everything*.

But none of it's real. It never was. "I can't do this," I say. "Not until I've figured out what's right and wrong here."

"Do you have any idea how much you'd be walking away from if you turn your back on us?" Peregrine demands.

"None of those things matter to me," I say. "Besides, if we stopped—no magic, no charms—Main de Lumière wouldn't have a reason to punish us anymore."

"Sure, it's possible they'd stop coming after us," Peregrine says, "but in the meantime, we'd have nothing! We'd be like everyone else."

"That's better than being dead," I tell her. I take a deep breath. "You've gone too far, Peregrine. You know that. I'll do the ceremony with you whenever we figure out the identity of the Main de Lumière soldier who snuck in during the party, but after that, I quit."

"You can't quit!" she cries.

"Watch me," I say.

With that, I stride out of Peregrine's perfect mansion, slamming her perfect front door behind me as I go. I don't look back.

Boniface is sitting in the parlor with his head in his hands when I storm through the front doorway of my house a few minutes later.

"Eveny?" he asks, standing up right away. "Are you okay?"

"Just peachy." I move past him without making eye contact.

"I never should have let you into the parlor," he says, wringing his hands together and following me into the room.

I stop and look at him. "I wish someone had told me before."

"Eveny—" he begins.

"Any other secrets you're keeping from me?" I interrupt. "How about my dad? Is everyone lying to me about him too? I know he's been back since I was born."

"Yes, he's been here, Eveny," Boniface says slowly. "But he's gone now."

"Where?" I demand. "Where did he go?"

But Boniface just shakes his head. I throw my hands up in frustration, grab my mother's herb journal from the coffee table where I left it earlier, and head upstairs to my room without saying another word. I can feel his concerned gaze on my back as I go.

I flip through the little book until I find a page in my mother's hand entitled *The Removal of Charms from Inanimate Objects*. She's written that you must focus intently on the specific things you want uncharmed. I fold the page and dash downstairs. I don't know if her charm will successfully remove magic from this house, but I intend to try. It's the first step to making things right again.

I close myself in the parlor, and with the herb book open in front of me, I ask Eloi Oke to open the gate to the spirit world. The air in the room shifts, and I touch the Stone of Carrefour with my left ring finger. I focus on our house and property as I read the words from my mother's charm.

"Mint, nettle, and rue, I draw your power," I say. I pause and try to feel the request with my heart, like Boniface advised. "Spirits, magic killed my mother, and it's destroying this town. I want it gone from this house."

For a moment, nothing happens, but then I notice my Stone of Carrefour getting colder and colder, and something begins leaching from the parlor. I can feel it, like the air is being sucked out. The lights flicker, and a huge, crimson stain appears on the hardwood floor, just where my mother died. I stifle a scream, and it takes me a moment to realize that her blood had never really been gone at all; someone had simply cast a charm to make it disappear.

I run toward the door and pull it open, but the moment I stagger into the hallway, I almost fall over. I stare around me in horror.

It's not the same hallway I entered through just a few minutes earlier. Or rather it is, but it appears that the hall hasn't been touched in decades. It's caked with dust and cobwebs, the marble floors are cracked and chipped, and the walls sag under the weight of the house. Above me, the chandelier hangs at a precarious angle, like it's going to crash to the ground at any moment. The front door is splintered, and light slices through in jagged beams. Several of the windows are broken, and wind whistles in.

"What have I done?" I whisper, but I know the answer to my own question before the words are out of my mouth. I hadn't thought it through enough to realize that the mansion itself is mostly a product of magic. Without zandara, it's just a dilapidated old shack, and the room where my mother died still looks like a crime scene.

I have to fix this. And I'm certainly not going to turn to Peregrine or Chloe for help. Boniface will know what to do. In a panic, I run across the rotting floorboards of the living room and out the back door, which is hanging from its hinges and swaying in the breeze.

As soon as I'm through the doors, I stop dead in my tracks. My mother's beautiful rose garden, her pride and joy, is dead and decaying. The few roses that still cling to vines are wilted and gray; the rest of the garden looks like it hasn't been tended in decades. It's overgrown with weeds and smeared with mud.

"Boniface?" I cry out. But then I see him, and for a moment, I'm so stunned I can't move. He's lying motionless beside one of the rosebushes, a pair of garden shears still in his hand. "Boniface?" I whisper. I run to his side, but when I bend to help him, my breath catches in my throat, and I scramble backward in terror.

Not only has he collapsed, but he looks like a skeleton with graying skin stretched haphazardly over the sharp juts of his bones. He's gasping for breath, but his skin is so thin and decayed I can see his lungs rising and falling inside his chest. He looks like a rotting corpse. "Eveny . . . ," he rasps. "Help me." It sounds like a death rattle.

Boniface's eyes close and as he goes still, I back away,

horrified, sure that I've somehow killed him. I'm sobbing with my hands over my mouth when Peregrine and Chloe stroll into the rose garden, looking as glamorous and unperturbed as usual.

"The front door was unlocked—well, more like unhinged—so we let ourselves in," Peregrine says casually, her stilettos clicking across the stone path as they approach me. "Come to think of it, you're looking rather unhinged yourself."

"What did you do to Boniface?" Chloe asks, staring at his collapsed, sunken frame. "We came over because we figured you might do something rash after our talk, but we didn't think you'd hurt someone."

"I didn't mean—I mean, I didn't want—I didn't know . . ." I'm still stammering nonsensically, my teeth chattering, when Peregrine holds up a hand to stop me.

"Just tell us what you've done," she says calmly. "Quickly, before Boniface expires."

I take a deep breath and quickly recap what happened. "I was only trying to get rid of zandara's influence in my life," I say. "H-how did I hurt Boniface?"

"Well," Peregrine says coolly, "it's probably because in actuality, he's one hundred seventy-six years old, and zandara is the only thing keeping him alive. Or it *was*, anyhow, before you cleverly removed it. Nice work."

My whole body goes cold. "What?"

Chloe interrupts in a gentler tone. "Eveny, Boniface is one of several people in town who rely on the zandara queens to extend their lives. He's been in his seventies for more than a century now."

"Same with our groundskeeper, Milo, and Peregrine's groundskeeper, Samuel," Chloe explains. "When the town was founded, they made a bargain: They'd help watch over the Queens of Carrefour and continue to keep up our homes without pay, in exchange for lodging and continued life."

"Like indentured servants?"

"Not really," Chloe says. "They could leave at any time."

"But if Boniface leaves, he'd die?"

"Yes, unfortunately he would, when the magic wears out," Peregrine says nonchalantly. "That's one thing *zandara can't* reverse—death. Once someone has expired, it can't be undone."

I gape at them. I have a hundred questions I want to ask. But first: "Please, help me save him," I whisper.

"Of course we'd be happy to help you," Peregrine says sweetly.

"But you have to agree to join us," Chloe adds. "We need you, Eveny. It's the only way."

"We know it's a lot to absorb," Peregrine says diplomatically. "But we promise you'll like it. And you'll have a one-third vote in how we handle things from now on."

"Like, I can tell you I think you're a real snob, and you treat people outside your *sosyete* like crap?" I ask coldly.

Peregrine looks surprised, but she laughs. "Eveny, I can't be wonderful to *everyone*. I simply don't have the time."

I just glare at her until she sighs heavily.

"Fine," she says. "I'll try to be more decent to your little friends. Are you happy now?"

I look down at Boniface, whose breathing is growing shallower by the moment. "Fine," I say. "I'll do it. Just help me fix this."

"Wise choice, Eveny," Peregrine says. "Come on."

She and Chloe lead me reluctantly away from the gasping Boniface and back into the parlor. While Chloe lights some candles, Peregrine asks me to remember exactly which herbs I invoked. When I tell her, she walks out the door.

"You'll have to focus your energy on this house and the grounds like you did when you cast the original charm," Chloe says while we wait for Peregrine to come back. "Feel the energy as deep in your heart as you can."

Peregrine returns a moment later with a handful of mint, nettle, and rue. "Fortunately, you didn't destroy the herb garden entirely."

"Casting with the herbs themselves instead of only relying on your Stone of Carrefour to channel the herbs will help make us stronger," Chloe explains. "Now put your left ring finger on your stone, and your right hand here."

I do as she says, reaching for my stone and then folding my right hand over Peregrine's, which is upturned and clutching the herbs. Chloe's hand comes down over ours, and as soon as she touches us, I feel a surge of power. "When Peregrine's done, you'll recite the words *Mesi, zanset* with us,"

Chloe instructs. "It's what finishes an important charm."

"What does it mean?" I ask.

"*Thank you, ancestors*," Chloe replies. "It's Creole. When our great-great-great-grandmothers founded Carrefour, they dealt with a lot of Haitian immigrants who had lived and died in this swamp. Some of their words became a part of zandara."

"Are we going to have a history lesson here," Peregrine asks, glancing from Chloe to me, "or are we going to fix what you messed up?"

I take a deep breath while Peregrine calls on Eloi Oke. I feel the air in the room shift, and then Peregrine chants:

> *Mint, nettle, and rue were invoked to cast a charm.*
> *Reverse it now, oh spirits, before it's too late.*
> *A mistake was made here, and it must be righted.*
> *We humbly beg you for your sympathy and assistance.*

Together, the three of us say, "*Mesi, zanset. Mesi, zanset. Mesi, zanset.*"

I feel a whoosh of air, and suddenly the whole house is shifting beneath our feet. The walls straighten, the crimson pool of blood vanishes, and the peeling wallpaper turns vibrant and new again.

When Chloe pulls away a moment later, her eyes are wide. "Did you feel that?" she whispers to Peregrine.

Peregrine nods, looking just as shocked. "Power," she whispers.

I felt it too, but I don't have time to dwell on that. "I have to make sure Boniface is okay." I run out of the parlor toward the backyard.

I find Boniface sitting on the ground, rubbing the back of his head. I exhale in relief when I see that he looks like he's seventy-something again instead of a hundred and seventy-something. He appears to be breathing normally.

"I don't know what happened there!" he says, looking up as I approach. "I must have fallen and hit my head. I feel a little woozy."

I hurl myself at him and wrap my arms around his solid body. "I'm so glad you're okay," I tell him.

"Well, that sure is the best greeting I've gotten in a long time," he replies, hugging me back.

Peregrine and Chloe step out on the deck and call to me. "Come on, Eveny!" Peregrine says impatiently. "We have things to discuss!"

My stomach twists itself into a knot as she turns and disappears inside, followed by Chloe.

"When did they get here?" Boniface asks.

"Just in time," I tell him in a shaky voice. With a heavy heart, I stand up and head toward my fellow zandara queens.

21

*P*eregrine is standing in my living room filing her nails when I reenter the house. Chloe is applying lipstick in the mirror on the wall.

"You're welcome," Peregrine says as I linger in the doorway, watching them.

I give her a look. "I don't remember thanking you."

Peregrine shrugs. "I assumed that was just an accidental lapse in manners on your part. After all, I *did* just save your house and Boniface's life."

"So I made a mistake. But can we agree that we won't do any more big charms without consulting each other? Like I won't destroy my house, and you won't endanger everyone just because you've run out of guys to make out with?"

Peregrine glowers at me. "You're being awfully bossy for someone who's new at this."

Chloe elbows Peregrine. "Eveny's right," she says. She turns to me and says, "We'll scale it back until we know for sure what happened to Glory and that frat guy. Deal?"

I nod.

Peregrine doesn't look happy. "I still get to work zandara on guys, though."

I open my mouth to protest, but Chloe cuts in. "Don't bother arguing," she says to me. "Peregrine would wilt without male attention."

Peregrine walks out of the room without another word to me. "I'll be in the car, Chloe!" she calls over her shoulder.

I hear the front door open and close a moment later. I turn back to Chloe, expecting that she'll leave too, but she's just standing there. She shifts from stiletto to stiletto for a moment and twirls her honey-blond hair nervously as she stares at me.

"What?" I finally ask.

"Look, I'm not accusing you of anything, but did you dig up the Justin doll? In the cemetery that night that you spied on us?"

"Oh, crap," I say. "I'm sorry. I was just trying to figure out what was going on."

"You need to put him back." She looks like she's about to cry. "You don't mess with another queen's magic! I mean, I know you didn't know, so I'm not mad this time. But Justin's been acting weird, and I had no idea why. Just rebury him before I have to break up with him, okay?"

"Chloe," I say slowly, "is *everything* between you and Justin magic?"

She gives me a look. "Not everything. It's just easier when there's a little charm involved. I don't have to worry about stupid stuff like him checking out other girls."

"It's called real life," I say.

Chloe makes a face. "But why would I want to go through that if I don't have to?"

"Maybe because it would be great to know that Justin likes you for you, and not just because you've forced him to?"

She studies the ground. "But he wouldn't like me," she says so softly that her words are almost inaudible. "He'd like Peregrine."

"You don't know that."

"Every guy in town is into her, Eveny. And I've been in love with Justin for a really long time. I can't lose him."

She looks miserable, and I feel sorry for her. It's not worth arguing about. "Fine. I'll rebury the doll tonight."

"Thank you so much. I'll write down a super easy reinstatement charm."

She grabs a pen and notepad out of her Louis Vuitton bag, jots something down quickly, then rips out the page and hands it to me. I stuff it in my pocket. "You have to mix damiana with balm of Gilead buds," she says. "When you use them together, they strengthen a charm's ability to bring back a drifting lover."

"You sure you want to do this?" I ask.

"Of course, Eveny." She pauses, then brightens suddenly.

"Hey, want me to write a love charm for you too?"

My mind immediately goes to Caleb and how drawn I feel to him, how many things stand in our way. "Nah," I say. "Thanks, but I think I'll do it the old-fashioned way."

Chloe looks perplexed. "Suit yourself," she says and disappears out the door to find Peregrine.

Exhausted from working the charms in the parlor, I go to bed early and set my alarm so I can make a quick trip to the cemetery on Chloe's behalf under cover of darkness.

At nearly two a.m., clutching the Justin doll, I slip out the back door and over the garden wall by the light of the moon.

"Don't freak out. Don't freak out," I say to myself as I move past fog-draped tombs. I don't think there will ever be a time when I'm not nervous to be in a graveyard in the middle of the night. But I promised Chloe, and I'm eager to see if a charm like this works when I do it alone.

Standing at the crossroads, I touch my Stone of Carrefour and call on Eloi Oke. I feel the now-familiar change in air pressure, and I know the door to the spirit world has once again opened. I take a deep breath and quickly skim the words Chloe has jotted down. I shake my head in amusement when I realize she's written them in rhyme, then I chant them quickly aloud.

> The magic lifted, and some were hurt.
> I restore it now, back in the dirt.

The charms of Chloe will work through this doll
On Justin's heart, through it all.

I rebury the Justin doll and a flannel sachet of damiana and balm of Gilead buds along with it. As I kick the dirt over the doll, concealing him completely, I feel a quick whoosh of wind, and the dust settles.

I stand there for a moment, then bend and touch the dirt again. I reach for my Stone of Carrefour with my left ring finger and say, "Also, spirits, if you're still listening, if Justin isn't a good guy, or if he doesn't care about Chloe at all, please make her realize that before he breaks her heart."

I hastily straighten up, brush my hands off, and turn to walk back toward my house, and that's when I suddenly hear pounding footsteps getting rapidly closer. I gasp and flatten myself across a tomb. Someone's running toward me, and I'm out here in the darkness all alone. I curse my stupidity. What if it's the faux frat boy who's unaccounted for, or the person who murdered Glory?

A moment later, a figure shrouded in darkness bursts into the clearing less than a foot away from me, breathing hard. I scream before realizing that it's Caleb Shaw—a shirtless Caleb Shaw, with ripped biceps, taut abs, and caramel skin sparkling with moonlit perspiration.

He whirls to face me and pulls out his earbuds. "What are you doing out here?" he demands. "You scared me to death!"

"*I* scared *you*?" I manage. Just as quickly, my heart is

racing for a different reason entirely.

He wipes his arm across his forehead and then puts his hands on his thighs as he catches his breath. He's wearing olive-green running shorts, dark gray running shoes, and nothing else. "You shouldn't be out here, Eveny," he says. "It's not safe."

"Well, what are *you* doing out here?" I counter.

He looks a little embarrassed. "I like running in the cemetery at night when I can't sleep," he says. "My dad's buried here, so I kind of see it as my time to visit him."

"Oh, I'm sorry. About your dad, I mean. I didn't know."

"I don't talk about it much."

I study him for a minute. "How old were you when . . . ?"

"Four," he says. He wipes the sweat from his brow again, and the moonlight highlights the tendons and muscles in his arm. "Not much older than you were when you lost your mom." He scratches his head and says, "What are you doing in the cemetery anyways?"

"A favor for Chloe."

He grimaces. "Zandara?"

"Yeah."

He gazes at me for a moment but seems to accept this. He leans beside me against the tomb, and suddenly I'm acutely aware of his near-naked body just inches away.

"You shouldn't be here all by yourself," he says, and I have the strange feeling that he's as nervous as I am.

"Nothing happened," I mumble.

"But it could have." He shakes his head and changes the

subject. "So Peregrine and Chloe have swayed you to the dark side?"

"I don't know that I'd call it dark, exactly."

"I'm not sure this qualifies as light either. You're standing in a cemetery in the middle of the night, all alone."

"But now you're here," I say before I can second-guess myself.

For a moment, we just stare at each other. In the silence, I can hear both of us breathing rapidly.

"So this protector thing," I say after a minute. "I don't get it. Before I got back to Carrefour, you weren't responsible for me?"

"We're only officially responsible for our queens when they're inside the gates. But before you got here, it was kind of like sitting around, waiting to be called into active duty in the military. There was always a good chance I'd have to step up." He half smiles. "You know, the day I heard you and your aunt were returning, I was out on Sailfish. The waves had been epic that day, so I was feeling great. But then I got home, and my mom was crying. She told me you were on your way back to Carrefour, and she kept telling me I had to figure out how to get out of this."

The words wound me. "I'm sorry. If you know a way out— if there's any way to get you out of the obligation—" I begin, but he cuts me off.

"No, you don't understand," he says. "I didn't want to do this. Not at first. But it's in my blood, same as being a queen is in yours. And then I saw you at Glory's funeral and a day later, I talked to you for the first time." He shakes his head and says, "When you said, 'Reading's cool. . . .' "

He trails off, so I say, "You realized I was the biggest dork you'd ever met?"

He laughs. "No. I realized you were different from the rest of this town. You weren't trying to be anything you weren't. It was the moment I realized I wouldn't be able to forgive myself if I ever let anything happen to you."

"But you can't have feelings for me," I say softly.

"That's the rule," he says.

We're silent for a little while. Finally, I move us into less depressing territory. "So what do you want to do with your life, anyways? I mean, after we graduate next year."

He looks surprised. "No one in this town talks about life after school. Everyone just . . . stays."

"Is that what you want?" I ask.

He turns to look at me, and we're so close that I can feel him breathing. For a moment, all I want him to say is *No. You're what I want.* But of course he doesn't. Instead, he says, "No one's ever asked me that." He hesitates. "The truth? I just want to go somewhere else. I want to have a future that hasn't already been picked out for me. I want to go to college and live in a big city and have a normal life. But I can't just run from the responsibilities I have here."

"But you didn't choose the responsibilities."

"Neither did you. But here we are."

"Here we are," I murmur. And this time when our eyes meet, we look at each other for a long, frozen moment, and then Caleb leans down slowly, very slowly, until his lips brush against mine. He kisses me gently, weaving his hands through my hair as he cradles the back of my head. He tastes like cinnamon. I couldn't have imagined a more perfect moment.

But suddenly, he pulls away, and when I blink up at him in confusion, I see pain in his eyes. "What?" I ask, still breathless.

"Shit. I can't believe I just did that." He shakes his head. "That can't happen again. Do you understand?"

Before I have a chance to reply, he's already running away, back in the direction he came from.

I stand still in the cemetery, touching my lips, my heart hammering, until the sound of his footfalls has faded into the darkness.

22

*I*t takes me until the beginning of fourth period the next day to realize that Caleb isn't at school, which makes the knots in my stomach twist even tighter. Either he's off training somewhere with Oscar and Patrick again, or he just doesn't want to see me. Regardless, I'm reminded just how much my arrival in Carrefour has disrupted his life.

On the way to lunch, Peregrine and Chloe flank me in the hallway. Peregrine's in thigh-high leopard-print stiletto boots, and Chloe's wearing elaborately spiky platform heels that add a good six inches to her height. I see Audowido poke his head out of Peregrine's studded tote bag, and I shiver and inch away from him.

"So?" Peregrine asks in a sour tone. "I suppose you're off to ask those little peons to join us?"

"Who?" I ask.

"Liv, Max, and Drew." She makes a face. "After your big speech yesterday, I figured that I was supposed to be more *decent*, or whatever it was you said. So here I am, acting like a nice person by inviting your grimy friends to eat in the Hickories."

I try not to show my surprise. Instead, I say evenly, "My friends aren't grimy."

"Well," she says haughtily, "let's just say I've already asked Arelia to dry-clean the cashmere picnic blanket after today's lunch."

I just give her a look and she giggles and walks away.

Chloe lingers for a moment longer. "So you did it?" she asks furtively. "The charm? Justin?"

"Yes."

She looks relieved. "I thought so. Thanks, Eveny. See you in a few!"

Liv, Max, and Drew are all in line for food when I enter the cafeteria a moment later. "Unless you're dying for congealed mac and cheese," I say, shooting a glance at the orange globs the caf lady is lobbing onto plates, "you should all come eat with me in the Hickories today."

The three of them just look at me. "Wait, what?" Drew manages.

"The Hickories," I repeat. "You can eat up there today, if you want."

"Us?" Liv asks blankly. "In the Hickories?"

Max lets out an excited whoop and dashes out before I can

say anything else. Drew and Liv follow several paces behind, looking stunned.

"You're sure this isn't just some trick the Dolls are playing on us?" Drew whispers, hurrying to catch up with me.

"I'm sure. Things are going to be different now," I tell him.

"Sure they will," he says under his breath.

Liv hurries to catch up with us too. "Why, exactly, have Peregrine and Chloe deigned to allow us to eat with them?"

"No idea," I lie. "But Peregrine invited you herself. Anyways, it's really not a big deal."

But judging from the horrified expressions on the faces of Margaux and Arelia as we approach, it *is*, in fact, a big deal.

"What are *they* doing here?" Margaux demands, not even bothering to address Liv, Max, or Drew directly. Liv and Drew glower at her, while Max walks around, checking out the picnic basket, the china, and the champagne bottles with a huge grin on his face.

"This is amazing!" he declares.

Margaux glares at me. "Well?"

"Peregrine and Chloe are fine with it," I say.

Margaux opens her mouth to retort, but Peregrine cuts her off. "Seriously, Margaux, give it a rest, and pour me a drink, would you? I'm completely parched."

Margaux opens her mouth then clamps it shut almost comically. "Just don't expect me to serve *them* lunch."

"They are our *guests*, Margaux, and you *will* serve them," Peregrine snaps.

"But—" Margaux begins. She trails off when Peregrine's eyes narrow even further. "Fine," she grumbles. "Champagne?" she asks Liv, Drew, and Max, her voice dripping with bitterness.

The three of them accept and follow me to sit beside Peregrine and Chloe.

"This is, like, the best day of my entire high school career," Max enthuses once we've toasted and taken sips of our bubbly. Arelia and Margaux are both glaring as they prepare a platter of sandwiches for us to share.

"Here," Margaux barks, shoving the platter so hard at us that a few sandwiches topple over the edge.

Max seems oblivious to their coldness, though, and begins chattering away a mile a minute, asking if they're going to the Mardi Gras Ball, what they're wearing, and where they got a cashmere blanket this big. Eventually, Margaux and Arelia seem to warm to him. In fact, they even look vaguely amused.

But though we're all eating together, Liv and Drew sit on one side of the blanket, staring suspiciously at Peregrine and Chloe, who stare suspiciously back until they're distracted by the arrival of their guys. Justin immediately drapes himself over Chloe, and they spend the rest of the lunch hour making out. Peregrine, not to be outdone, has charmed a skater named Tyler into fawning all over her today.

"They are *so* gross," Liv says. "It's like watching porn."

"Uh-huh," Drew agrees vaguely.

"Hey, hotness." Pascal interrupts my train of thought as

he approaches from the other side of the Hickories. He grins at me lasciviously and then turns to Liv. "I see you've brought someone new to lunch. Hey, baby."

She wrinkles her nose, and I see Drew stiffen beside her.

"She's with me," Drew says.

I exchange looks with Liv, who looks thrilled that Drew has come to her defense.

Pascal gazes at him evenly. "And you are . . . ?"

"You know who I am, man," Drew says stiffly. "We've been in school together for years."

Pascal looks amused. "Well, *man*, I can't notice everyone. But this pretty thing, well, with a little makeup and a wardrobe makeover, she'd be damn fine. Just the kind of woman I'd like to get to know in a special way."

Liv opens her mouth to reply, but Drew beats her to it. "I *said*, she's with me."

Pascal crosses his arms. "I'm sorry. Did you not understand that I don't give a damn about that?"

Drew glowers back. "Did *you* not understand that you can't just take whatever you want?"

Pascal's eyes flicker for a moment, and then he chuckles. "Dude, you really have no idea. I'll have her if I want her. And there's nothing you can do about it." He calls over to Peregrine, "Hey, who invited this douche up here anyhow?"

"He's with Eveny!" Peregrine singsongs, breaking away from her make-out session long enough to smirk at me. "I told her it was a bad idea."

Pascal turns back to me. "Way to go, Eveny. We have a firm no douchebag rule in the Hickories."

"Then how do *you* manage to eat lunch here every day?" I ask evenly.

His face darkens for a moment, long enough to make me feel uneasy, but then he laughs. "Touché," he says. "But seriously, babe. You can't just let commoners up here." He turns to Liv and adds, "Although *you're* welcome anytime. Preferably with fewer clothes on."

He shoots Drew a challenging look, but I put a hand on Drew's chest and say, "Don't."

Drew appears to relax after a moment, turning to Liv. "I've been meaning to ask you: would you be my date to the Mardi Gras Ball?"

Liv turns pink. Her eyes dart to me for a second and then back to Drew. "For real?" she squeaks.

Drew grins at her. "I'd love to take you."

"I mean, I guess, yeah, that would be fine." She's trying to play it cool, but when her eyes meet mine, I can see her fighting a grin.

"Oh, puke," Pascal says, rolling his eyes. "Eveny, you want to be my date to the ball?"

"Not a chance," I reply sweetly.

On the walk back to class after lunch, as Drew and Max head toward the north wing of the building, Liv catches up with me, grabs my hand, and asks, "So did you hear Drew ask me to the ball?"

I nod and give her hand a squeeze before letting go. "That's awesome."

"You think?" Her brow creases with worry. "What if he was just asking me to piss off Pascal?"

"He wasn't. He likes you."

"How can you be so sure?"

"I just am," I tell her.

She grins. "So how about you? Do you think you'll go to the dance?"

Caleb flits across my mind, but I dismiss the thought. If I'd had any hope that we could get around the protector rule, it was dashed last night, when Caleb swore me off then literally ran away. "Probably not," I say.

"You shouldn't miss out on it," Liv says. "What if you and Max go together? As friends, I mean."

"Maybe," I say. "I'll probably just skip it."

Liv looks disappointed but lets it go. "So that was weird today, huh? In the Hickories?"

I laugh. "That's a pretty normal day up there."

She wrinkles her nose and shakes her head as the bell rings. "They all creep me out. Those cookie-cutter girls and those guys who don't seem to think for themselves—"

"So what's going on with Drew's band?" I interrupt her brightly.

She stares at me for a minute. "You're changing the subject."

"Yeah, you caught that," I say with a smile.

She laughs. "All right, have it your way." And as she starts
to tell me about a gig they're trying to book in New Orleans,
and a producer who's expressed some interest in them, I relax
into the conversation and appreciate what it's like to talk to
someone whose life isn't already prewritten.

My cell rings at five thirty that evening, startling me. I'd been
poring over my mother's herb journal, trying to memorize the
plants, roots, and potions that seemed most important to her.
Lemon for protection. Blackberry to send evil back to enemies
who try to inflict it upon you. Wormwood to prevent car accidents. Bayberry for good health. Chia seed to quell gossip.

I reach for my phone and see Liv's name on the caller ID.

"What are you doing right now?" she asks after I've said
hello.

I look at my mother's journal, open on my lap to a hand-
drawn sketch of a zandara doll. "Not much," I tell her.

"Good," she says. "Come out with me and Drew, then."

"You and Drew?"

She's silent for a minute. "He just called and asked me to
dinner tonight. I already had plans with Max, and I don't want
to just bail on him."

"Sooo . . . ," I prompt.

"So could you be Max's platonic date for the night? It
would really help me a lot. Plus," she adds, "I kind of want
to get your read on whether Drew's actually into me. Please
come?"

I'm about to say no, but then I think about Meredith and how different Liv is from the girl I'd always thought of as my best friend. Liv may not approve of everything in my life—and I can't exactly blame her for disliking the Dolls—but she's never been unsupportive of me. I've only known her for a few weeks, and I realize that already, the friendship I have with her means more to me than the one Meredith is so casually tossing aside. The least I can do is have her back.

I close my book and push it to the side. "Okay, I'm in."

"Woo-hoo!" she cheers on the other end of the line. "You rock, Eveny. I owe you one. Can you meet us at Cajun Eddie's at seven? It's out in the Périphérie, and it's Drew's favorite."

"Sure," I agree. I check my watch. I know Liv's not thinking about the fact that I don't have a car, and I don't want to bug her while she's getting ready for a date. The weather's supposed to be nice out, and I should have enough daylight left to ride my bike. "Just text me the address."

"You're the best!" she says before hanging up.

I cast one last reluctant glance at the herb book. As I head to the bathroom to put on some makeup for my "date" with Max, I'm repeating some of my mother's favorite herbs in my head in an attempt at memorization.

I've just started applying tinted moisturizer when my cell rings again. Drew's name flashes on the screen, so I pick up. "I hear we're doing dinner in an hour," I say.

"Word travels fast. Liv said you're meeting us, but I know you don't have a car. Want me to come get you?"

I pause. "You don't have to," I tell him. I don't want Liv to get the wrong idea if I show up with Drew.

"I don't mind," he says. "How else would you get here, anyhow?"

"Bike?" I venture.

He laughs. "I'm not making you ride your bike all the way to the Périphérie when it'll barely take me any time to swing by your place."

I'm ready to go ten minutes later in a black tank maxi-dress and a striped cardigan with ballet flats. While I wait for Drew, I boot up my laptop and check my email, which I haven't done in days. Along with a few dozen junk messages and a bunch of ads for Sephora, *Glamour* magazine, and some online bookstores, there are a few forwarded chain emails from Meredith, which I delete instantly, and a note from a guy named Ross I had a few classes with back in New York asking whether I want to go see a movie with him. I laugh out loud at that; a date with a guy who hasn't even noticed I'm gone doesn't sound like the best idea.

I check the time and see that I still have a couple of minutes, so I pull up Google and enter *LSU newspaper* into the search box. It sends me to the site of the *Daily Reveille*, the official school paper. I enter *Carrefour* into the search engine and am relieved when nothing comes up. Then I type in *murdered + fraternity*, and one result, from earlier today, is returned. I click on the article and begin to read.

The body of a Louisiana State University senior was found

early Sunday afternoon in the Fantome Swamp region of Louisiana, about an hour outside Baton Rouge, after Louisiana State Police received a call from the man's fraternity brother Sunday morning. I nearly drop my laptop when I get to the next line: *Blake Montoire, 21, a member of the Lambda Delta Epsilon fraternity, was stabbed several times before his car was stolen, police say.*

Blake Montoire was the name of the guy who was talking to me at Peregrine's party, the guy who tried to walk me home before Caleb stepped in. But the grainy photo featured on the website doesn't match the person I met, except for the glasses, which can only mean one thing: I was talking to Blake's killer. Worse, he'd seemed overly interested in getting to know *me*.

"Eveny?" Aunt Bea's voice from the door startles me. I look up to see her staring at me suspiciously. "What were you reading?"

"School assignment," I lie as I quickly shut the computer.

"You look awfully freaked out for an assignment," she says.

"Math scares me," I say as innocently as possible. I know that if I tell her there's a Main de Lumière soldier inside our gates who's set his sights on me, she'll insist we leave Carrefour. But if I go, the town will have no chance of surviving now that the enemy has gotten in.

Like it or not, this is my fate. And I have no choice but to face it head-on.

23

I shoot Peregrine and Chloe a quick text telling them that I saw the probable killer—the fake Blake Montoire—then I shut off my phone and try to forget about zandara and death for the evening. There's nothing I can do for the next few hours except be on guard.

Drew arrives at 6:45 on the dot, and when I open the door, he grins. "You look real pretty," he says. Once we're in his pickup, he turns to me. "You know I wanted to ask you out, right? When you first got back to town?"

"What? No!"

He gives me a look as we rumble down the hill. "What'd you think that invitation to the crawfish boil was?"

"I thought it might be a date," I admit. "But then you kind of acted like we were just friends."

"Admittedly, I don't have the smoothest mackin'-on-the-ladies moves," he says.

"Mackin'-on-the-ladies moves?" I repeat, stifling a laugh.

"Fine, so maybe I'm not good at talking about my moves either," he concedes. "But then you came to my show, and I figured, hey, girls go for musicians, right? But you disappeared with Caleb Shaw before I could do anything."

"I'm sorry," I say. I want to explain to Drew that our shared history makes him feel more like a brother to me. But I have the feeling that'll only make things worse.

Before I can say anything, he says, "I guess I was stupid to think you could like someone from my side of town."

"That's not it at all!" I say instantly. "Look, if I did anything to hurt your feelings—"

He cuts me off. "I wasn't trying to make you feel bad, Eveny. I was just saying that I'm glad. I mean, it worked out the way it was supposed to. I hadn't really thought of Liv like that, but then I kept running into her because of you, and . . ." He shrugs and says, "Well, anyway, I'm really happy she said yes to going with me to the Mardi Gras Ball."

"She's a great girl," I tell him.

We're halfway out to the Périphérie when I finally ask the question that's been on my mind since Caleb mentioned it. "Before she died, were you dating Glory Jones?"

Drew looks at me in surprise. "Where'd you hear that?"

"It doesn't matter," I say. "And I don't care if you were. I just want to know."

"No," he says after a pause. "But we were friends. Really good friends, actually."

"So why did you act like you barely knew her at her funeral?"

"Because I promised her I'd keep our friendship a secret. I'm still trying to honor that, Eveny, so I'd appreciate if you didn't say anything to the Dolls." There's bitterness in his voice, but there's pain there too. "You know about the line between people from central Carrefour and the Périphérie."

"If she liked you, if you two were friends, she should have been open about it. People would have had to be okay with it."

"I used to tell her that. But it meant a lot to me to have her in my life at all. I don't have a lot of good friends, and I didn't want to hurt her by making Peregrine and Chloe turn their backs on her because of me."

"You really think they would have done that?" But I know the answer to my own question. They treated people from the Périphérie like sources of power, not human beings.

"Peregrine and Chloe aren't the people you think they are, Eveny," Drew says. "They're not nice, they're not good people, and I think they were ruining Glory's life. She died before I had a chance to figure out how to help her."

"You must miss her."

"Sure I do," he says. "All the time. But we were from two different worlds." He clears his throat and adds, "Kind of like you and me."

"I'm not from a different world than you," I say instantly.

"Could have fooled me, with that big mansion of yours."

"I'm sorry," I say, but I'm not even sure what I'm apologizing for. "I'm not like them, you know. The Dolls, I mean."

Drew glances at me as he turns onto a side street in the Périphérie, but he doesn't reply.

The silence between us stretches long and thick until we pull up to the restaurant, close enough to the town wall that you can see the bricks and stones that separate us from the outside world. "Welcome to Cajun Eddie's," Drew says as he puts his truck in park and turns off the engine. "You're going to love this place. Best jambalaya on the planet."

Liv and Max are already waiting by the hostess stand, and although a flicker of worry crosses Liv's face when she sees me and Drew arrive together, she relaxes when I hug her and whisper in her ear, "He talked about you the whole way here."

Twenty minutes later, I'm staring down at the first bowl of jambalaya I've ever ordered.

"You've got shrimp, chicken, andouille sausage, onions, peppers, celery, and all sorts of amazing Cajun spices," Liv explains enthusiastically as she eyes the piping hot mixture on my plate.

"Go ahead," Drew says, smiling at me as he pushes my glass of water toward me. "Try it. But it's gonna make you thirsty."

As I take my first bite, my taste buds tingle with the assault of flavors. But I have to admit, it's smoky and delicious.

The others dig into their own meals: fried oysters for Drew, a blackened fish sandwich for Max, and a Caesar salad for Liv, who nibbles nervously while looking at Drew out of the corner of her eye. *Relax*, I mouth to her when Drew's distracted by a debate with Max over the merits of the Beatles versus the Rolling Stones. *He likes you.*

Thanks, she mouths back, visibly calming.

As we eat, we talk about having lunch with the Dolls in the Hickories, our upcoming tests in French and physics, and the fact that we're all weirded out by the death of the fraternity guy just outside our gates. "I don't get what happened to him," Drew says, glancing at me. "It's so odd."

"Beats me," I say as innocently as possible as I wash down another spicy mouthful of jambalaya.

By the time we're done, Drew and Liv are gazing at each other with googly eyes, and I'm trying not to feel jealous. It's not that I'm interested in Drew at all, and of course I'm glad that he likes Liv. I just wish someone would look at me that way. Specifically Caleb. Instead, I evidently inspire cursing and fleeing.

"Earth to Eveny," Max says. I realize I was so lost in thought that I'd spaced out for a moment.

"Sorry. What were you saying?"

"Just asking if you had a date to the Mardi Gras Ball," he says.

I shake my head. "No. Do you?" I'm hoping he won't ask me to go as friends, because I'm holding out hope that something will change with Caleb.

So I'm relieved when he says in a stage whisper, "I'm thinking of asking Rob Baker." When I look at him blankly, he adds, "He's in my Spanish class. I'm, like, ninety percent sure he's been flirting with me lately."

"Do you like him?" I ask.

"I guess. He's a nice guy. And he'd be fun to pass the time with until Justin Cooper stops pretending to be straight."

I gape at him. "Wait, what? Justin who's dating Chloe?"

He leans in conspiratorially. "I don't know what's up with him. He and I were flirting like crazy for a year. He finally told me he was going to officially come out to his parents over the summer. Next thing I know, he's dating Chloe St. Pierre."

"No way," I whisper. I'm absolutely positive Chloe has no idea about Justin's sexual orientation. "What do you think happened?" I ask carefully.

"Maybe his parents weren't cool with it, and he felt like he had to pretend to be straight? Whatever it was, though, he's not worth it. If he can't be true to who he is, I don't need that." I see sadness in his eyes behind the forced nonchalance.

"Maybe there's an explanation," I begin, but when Max gives me a questioning look, I realize I can't explain further.

"What, that he'd rather be popular than be with me?" Max asks bitterly.

Drew interrupts us then to ask how we want to split the bill. As Max and I dig in our wallets for cash, Max leans over and says, "Don't say anything, okay? Liv's the only one who knows what happened. I figure that whatever's going on with Justin is his business."

I agree to keep Max's story to myself, but I know it's on

me to fix this—not just for Max and Justin, but for Chloe too. As the four of us walk out together, I think how lucky Liv and Drew are to have a chance at a relationship. Whatever's between them is real. Max deserves that too.

Drew and Liv hug awkwardly in the parking lot, then Drew gestures toward his pickup. "You ready?" he asks me.

I nod and say good-bye to Liv and Max before following after him.

"That was fun," I say once I'm strapped in and we're pulling out of the parking lot.

"Liv's a great girl. And Max is kind of growing on me."

"Growing on you?"

"I always thought he was sort of eccentric, with his Buddy Holly glasses and all those vests he likes to wear. But he's okay." He pauses. "You know, now that you have friends like that, I don't know why you'd want to keep hanging out with the Dolls."

I glance at him but don't say anything. Defending Peregrine and Chloe to him is getting old. I get that he's probably still hurting over losing Glory, and blaming the Dolls for making her life complicated is an easy thing to do. But the more I find out about this town, the more I realize that there are no clear-cut lines between right and wrong, good and bad.

"So, anything new with your band?" I ask, changing the subject. "Liv says you have a producer interested."

"Yeah, he wants us to come to New Orleans and meet with

him, maybe play him a few of our originals."

"For real?" I grin at him. "Drew, that's a huge deal! Why didn't you say anything?"

"I'm just trying not to get ahead of myself," he replies, but he looks excited. "Besides, I have to tie up a few loose ends here before I even think about getting out of this town."

We've just turned on to Cemetery Road when Drew's truck pulls sharply to the right, sending us skidding off the shoulder into a muddy embankment. I cry out and reach for the door to steady myself as Drew struggles to regain control.

"What the hell was that?" I demand once we're back on the street. His face is pale, and his knuckles are white on the wheel.

"I have no idea," he says unsteadily. "Something's wrong with the steering."

The words are barely out of his mouth when the truck jerks to the right again, but this time Drew loses the fight with the steering wheel, and the truck goes spinning wildly toward the cemetery. I scream and do my best to brace myself between the dashboard and the door. Drew tries desperately to overcorrect, but we're only spinning faster.

Just as the driver's-side wheels of the truck begin to lift off the ground, and I can feel us starting to flip, I'm hit with a wave of calm and clarity. I can save us.

I touch my Stone of Carrefour and say, "Lemon and wormwood." I don't even have to talk to Eloi Oke or think of what I want to ask the spirits, because every cell in my body knows what it wants: to live through this accident.

And then, as suddenly as the truck started to career out of control, it slams back to the ground and skids to a halt with the passenger door—my door—mere inches away from a huge oak tree. Another few feet and I would have been crushed.

We're silent for a moment as the car's engine hisses and dies. My breath comes in ragged gasps.

"Eveny," Drew says, turning to me with a horrified expression on his face. "I don't know what happened. I—I could have killed you."

"But you didn't," I reassure him in a shaky voice.

We scramble out of the truck. Drew's hands are trembling as he grabs his phone and calls 911. I hear him tell the police officer that he's had an accident. "Are you hurt?" he asks me, covering the mouthpiece with his hand.

I do a quick once-over and am astonished to realize that aside from my rapidly thudding heart, I'm physically fine. "No," I tell him. "Are you?"

He shakes his head and reports to the officer that we're both okay. He hangs up after explaining where we are. I watch as he sinks to the ground and puts his head in his hands.

"How did you survive that?" he asks in a hoarse voice.

"I don't know," I whisper. But against my chest, my Stone of Carrefour is burning. *Lemons for protection and wormwood to prevent car accidents*, I think, sending a silent thank-you up to my mother for having the foresight to include both of those plants in her herb journal. "*Mesi, zanzet*," I add.

"What did you say?" Drew asks, but I just shake my head.

As we wait for the police to arrive, I see a flash of something in the cemetery, and for a second, I'm sure it's Caleb, out for his nightly run. But the figure doesn't stop, and a moment later, I have the strange feeling that we're being watched.

24

The next day, the buzz around school is all about my accident with Drew. Apparently, his truck is still stuck in the cemetery, and lots of people saw the wreckage on their way to school today. Everyone keeps telling me they can't believe I walked away unscathed.

As for the Dolls, they're all quiet and on edge, which I suspect is because tonight's ceremony to disempower the killer inside our gates is a big deal. Even lunch in the Hickories is subdued and mostly silent. It's only the chatter of Max, Drew, and Liv, all of whom have joined us on the cashmere blanket again, that breaks up the monotony. Caleb glares openly at Drew and entirely ignores me all through lunch.

On the way out of American history, Caleb catches up with me and puts a hand on my arm. "I'm really glad you're okay," he says, and the depth of concern in his eyes holds me captive until he turns and hurries away.

After school, I tell Aunt Bea that I'm working on a school project with Liv and spending the night at her place. I'm expecting her to be suspicious, but she's too shaken up by the accident to guess that I'm lying.

"Eveny, what if someone was trying to kill you?" she asks. "What if someone saw you arrive with Drew and cut the steering fluid line or damaged the brakes of his truck or something?"

"Relax," I tell her firmly. "It's just an old pickup truck. Nothing sinister."

I'm not sure I believe my own words, but I don't need Aunt Bea freaking out on top of everything else. She'll never allow me to leave the house tonight if she thinks I'm in danger. "Besides," I add, "I'm fine. Drew's fine."

"Because of a stroke of good luck," she says.

"No, because of zandara," I reply. "I used my Stone of Carrefour."

She blinks at me, her expression darkening. "Well, it sure didn't take you any time to become an expert, did it?" she asks. Without another word, she strides out the front door, slamming it behind her. A moment later, I hear her car's engine rumble to life.

I'm still thinking about Aunt Bea's reaction when I head down our driveway just after eleven. I arrive at Peregrine's mansion twenty minutes later, wearing a flowing, gauzy emerald dress of my mother's that I found buried in the back of my closet. I feel beautiful in it, and I hope it will make Caleb see me that way too.

But when the door to the Marceau mansion opens, my heart sinks. I'm dowdy in comparison to Peregrine and Chloe. As usual, they both look like supermodels in five-inch heels, perfect makeup, and slinky designer dresses. Peregrine's is a black leather sheath with a diamond-encrusted snake-shaped zipper, and Chloe's is a gold lamé minidress that catches the light and makes her skin look even tanner.

"What look, exactly, are you trying to achieve?" Peregrine asks. "Thrift store hippie?"

"It was my mom's," I say defensively.

"I think you look pretty," says a low voice from behind Peregrine and Chloe. I look up to see Caleb gazing at me. In a crisp charcoal suit, he's too good to be real. Locking eyes with him hits me so hard that I can't breathe until he turns and walks away.

Peregrine rolls her eyes and air-kisses me dramatically. "Well, come on in," she says, nearly shoving me inside. "We don't have all night. Are you feeling better after your accident?"

"Still a little freaked out," I say. I follow Chloe and Peregrine into the house. The rest of the Dolls are mingling around, all of them as dressed up as Peregrine and Chloe. Arelia and Margaux are in matching hot pink minidresses with sky-high heels, and Pascal is standing behind them, leering at their legs. He's in a black suit with a silvery shirt and a black tie. A few feet away, Justin lounges on an armchair, looking uncomfortable in a navy suit and a yellow tie, which he keeps tugging at.

I clear my throat as Peregrine announces, "Eveny's here! Someone get her a drink!"

Margaux purses her lips but makes a move toward the bar.

"Gin and tonic?" she asks in a bored voice. "Or champagne?"

"Neither, actually," I say quickly. I want to stay as sober as possible.

Peregrine makes a face and rolls her eyes. "Fine," she says. "Someone go get Eveny some sweet tea instead."

Margaux hustles off toward the kitchen as quickly as her stilettoed feet can take her. Not to be outdone, Arelia scrambles after her.

A moment later, Margaux reappears at Peregrine's elbow and thrusts a tall glass of iced tea at me. "Happy?" she grunts.

"Thanks," I say, put off by her weirdness as usual. I take a few long sips, then set my glass down on a coaster. The grandfather clock chimes midnight, and the energy in the room shifts.

"It's time," Peregrine says solemnly.

I'm the only person who seems not to know what this means, but I follow the others toward a pair of closed double doors, which remind me a lot of the parlor in my own house. Peregrine and Chloe pull open the doors, and I follow the others into a large, dark room lit with candles that send flickering shadows dancing across the walls and ceiling.

The group moves silently into a circle in the center of the room. I'm surprised when it's Caleb who winds up on my left side and even more startled when his large, warm hand folds around mine. I'm elated for a second until I look up and realize that everyone in the circle is joining hands. In the center of the circle sit a bottle of bourbon and the coiled form of Audowido. I swallow back my discomfort, and I keep a close eye on him as his tongue darts lazily in and out of his mouth.

"What's happening?" I whisper to Caleb.

Caleb looks at me with concern. "The girls didn't explain this ceremony to you?"

I shake my head.

"It's a possession ceremony called a *Renmen Koulèv*." Caleb's voice is flat and grim. "They probably thought it would freak you out."

"Why? I've already been possessed."

"It's—" He hesitates, as if searching for the right words. When he looks back at me, his expression is pained. "This ceremony is weird to watch. We use a snake—Audowido in this case—to call the spirits in from the nether. Then Peregrine and Pascal will allow themselves to be possessed by two spirits who already do a lot of favors for us."

"And it's weird to watch because . . . ?" I ask.

Caleb clears his throat. "Because it's kind of . . . sexual. The spirits don't get to do things like smoke and drink and have sex anymore. So the sosyete banks favors by letting the spirits take over their bodies for a while."

"Wait, Peregrine and Pascal are going to have *sex*?"

Caleb shakes his head. "Not quite. But things get pretty . . . hot." Even in the dim lighting, I can tell he looks embarrassed. "It's the best way to gather power in the short term. If everything goes right and the spirits get what they want, they'll help us, and the Main de Lumière operative who killed the fraternity guy will be powerless again. He'll become immediately paralyzed the second he tries to use a weapon against any of us. We'll all be safe. This is something we have to do."

He squeezes my hand tighter just as Peregrine steps into the center of the circle beside Audowido. Chloe grabs my right hand and Justin's left to complete the ring.

Pascal breaks away from the group to strike a large triangle that hangs nearby. The sound reverberates throughout the room, and as Pascal rejoins the circle, Peregrine closes her eyes and looks skyward.

"Come to us now, Eloi Oke, and open the gate," Peregrine chants. "Come to us now, Eloi Oke, and open the gate. Come to us now, Eloi Oke, and open the gate."

She takes a small bundle of herbs, strikes a match, and lights them on fire. She drops them on the marble floor, and as soon as they're done smoldering, she says, "Ashes to ashes." She begins to dance, slowly at first, then more rapidly in the silence. I watch as Audowido uncurls and inches toward Peregrine. He begins to coil himself around her left leg just as she starts to chant again, but she doesn't seem to notice; she appears to be in a trance as she sways, moves her feet, and claps, while singing over and over in a high, sweet voice, "*Move lespri, pran kò mwen. Move lespri pran tèt mwen.*"

Caleb leans in to whisper to me, "She's asking the spirits to take her body and her mind. But in order for this to work, we all have to focus on the ceremony. I promise; I won't let anything happen to you."

His voice is deep and soothing, and I believe him entirely. I close my eyes and try to focus on Peregrine's words and on the melody. Then she abruptly stops chanting, and I open my eyes to see what's going on.

Peregrine is standing in the middle of the circle, completely still, with Audowido wrapped up her left leg and down her left arm. The snake looks like he's become a part of her. I can see him breathing, his skin expanding and contracting.

"Just follow along," Caleb whispers as Peregrine returns to chanting. This time, on her second verse, the whole room begins to hum along with her. Peregrine starts to dance again, and when she does, everyone else in the circle begins swaying to the music too. I do my best to join in as the movements get more and more frenzied. Audowido is slowly unwinding himself from Peregrine now, and he, too, appears to be moving in time to the beat.

Suddenly, Peregrine stops singing and cries out. Everyone else's eyes are closed, but I keep mine open a sliver to watch what's happening. The air in the room has changed, and my Stone of Carrefour is suddenly so hot it's burning me. My heart thuds as I watch Pascal step silently into the circle. But he doesn't look like himself anymore; his body moves fluidly, like a rubber doll's.

He bends to pick up a pale purple handkerchief from the ground, where Audowido is slowly slithering in a wide circle. Pascal takes one end of the handkerchief and puts it into his mouth. Peregrine steps closer, until she and Pascal are just inches apart. She slowly takes the other end of the handkerchief and puts it in her mouth too.

The second she does so, the others in the circle resume their dance. Chloe starts chanting the now-familiar *Move lespri, pran kò mwen. Move lespri pran tèt mwen.* As she begins singing faster and faster, Peregrine and Pascal move closer and closer to each other until their bodies are touching. Caleb's hand is warm and reassuring in mine, but as Peregrine and Pascal's dance grows more sensual, I feel uncomfortable. I continue moving my hips from side to side, but as I watch, Pascal begins to touch Peregrine. She responds by pulling him closer and grinding against him. It looks like they're about to start ripping each other's clothes off.

Suddenly, goose bumps prickle up and down my arms, and I can feel my hair standing on end. There's something different in the room now, a shift in the equilibrium, and once again everyone instantly stops chanting and dancing. We're plunged into silence, and for a moment, it's as if the room is entirely frozen.

Then, Pascal suddenly breaks away from Peregrine and grabs the bottle of bourbon from the floor beside Audowido.

He rips off the cap, tilts his head back, and drinks the entire bottle without taking a breath.

My jaw drops. "Did he just drink a *whole bottle* of alcohol?" I whisper to Caleb. But Caleb doesn't respond; his eyes are closed, and he looks just as out of it as the rest of the group. I begin to pull away—I want to get out of here—but Caleb's grip on me is like a vise. I'm feeling woozier by the moment, and my legs are unsteady beneath me. It's similar to the exhaustion that swept over me at Cristof's after Glory possessed me, but far worse.

My heart thuds even faster as Pascal begins mumbling what sounds like nonsense. Peregrine remains in a trance as Pascal approaches and begins peeling her clothes off, right there in the middle of the circle. First, he removes the shawl she has wrapped lightly around her shoulders, then he roughly pulls her dress over her head, so that she's standing there in only a shell-pink bra, matching panties, and her five-inch heels.

Pascal and Peregrine begin to kiss now, sloppily and aggressively. Pascal's hands tangle through Peregrine's ebony curls and I feel weaker and weaker as their movement grows more frantic. It's almost like my own energy is being sucked out of me and funneled into the center of the circle. I look at Caleb again, and when I see that his eyes are open now, I feel a surge of momentary hope. But my heart sinks when I realize he, too, is possessed by whatever spirit is filling this room. I look around and see that everyone else appears as blank and wide-eyed as he does. I seem to be the only one who hasn't succumbed to the magic.

I don't have time to think about it, though, because in that instant, Pascal lets go of Peregrine and swings in my direction. I'm frozen in place as his eyes rake me over. Then he grins, a big, sloppy grin that doesn't look a thing like the carefully controlled Pascal. *It's not him anymore*, I realize. *It's the spirit who's in him.*

In his eyes, I can read evil and foreboding. His grin melts into a sneer. "Eveny Cheval," he slurs in a deep Louisiana accent that doesn't sound at all like Pascal's aristocratic drawl. Then he begins to laugh. Suddenly, the sneer vanishes from his face, and I feel a chill run through me.

"They're coming for you," he says in a flat voice, staring directly into my eyes. "Bang bang, you're dead."

25

Terrified, I use the last of my strength to rip my hand out of Caleb's grip. My arms and legs feel like they're made of sand, but I manage to stumble away from the circle and toward the door. I land in a heap in the living room while behind me, Pascal is still cackling maniacally. I can hear him saying again and again in a singsong voice, "Bang bang, Eveny's dead! Bang bang, Eveny's dead!"

The moment I'm outside of the ceremonial room, my body feels more normal. My limbs aren't as heavy, and I can move again. I lurch toward the front door of Peregrine's mansion, pull it open, and land facedown on her front porch. The air outside is cool and crisp, and I drink it in hungrily as I try to gather the strength to run.

I struggle to my feet and head for the cemetery. It creeps me out to think about cutting across it in the dark of night, but it's the quickest way home. I'm still woozy and unsteady, but Peregrine's house doesn't have a wall separating it from the cemetery like mine does, so I only have to climb over a waist-high picket fence. I land on my feet and plunge into the darkness between a cluster of tombs. Far away, I can see my back porch light glowing like a beacon.

As I move down Peregrine's hill, deeper into the cemetery, the tree cover grows heavier overhead, and I begin to lose the moonlight. The farther I go, the heavier my feet feel. My brain is foggy, and I stumble over exposed roots that I can't see in the darkness. I wince in pain as I come down hard on my left knee, slicing it open. I smell blood in the air as I struggle to my feet, and I can no longer see the light from my house. The graveyard is swallowing me whole.

I pause to catch my breath, and when I do, I hear footsteps somewhere behind me, moving fast. I stifle a scream. I can't get Pascal's words out of my head: *Bang bang, Eveny's dead*.

But maybe it's Caleb. My heart soars for a second in relief. I begin to turn toward the sound, but my heel catches on another root, and my knees buckle beneath me, betraying me. I go down hard. The last thing I'm aware of is the sharp pain of hitting the back of my head on a grainy tombstone as the world goes black.

When I wake up, my head is pounding, and I'm not sure how much time has passed. I blink into the darkness, and the first thing I realize is that I'm still in the cemetery, lying in a patch of grass.

"Hello, Eveny," says a smooth voice just to my right, and I jump, startled. My neck aches and my head throbs anew as I turn. I scream and struggle to sit up when I realize there's a man in a dark jacket bent over me, peering at me like I'm a specimen in a jar.

It takes me a moment to recognize him.

"Blake Montoire," I whisper. His pale face seems to glow in the dappled moonlight, and his eyes, which had appeared to be a normal shade of brown at the party, are now a chilling shade of almost translucent ice blue. He must have been wearing contacts so that he didn't look so freakish.

"That was just the name I used at that silly little party of yours," he says. "Very frat-boy chic, if I do say so myself." His accent, I realize, is vaguely French.

"I wouldn't know," I mutter. "So I'm guessing you're the Main de Lumière soldier who killed the real Blake Montoire outside our gates." My pulse is pounding, but I'm trying to appear calm.

"Main de Lumière *soldier*?" he repeats. "Heavens, no. I'm a Main de Lumière *général*. In other words, I'm in charge of the Louisiana division of our little organization. And you, Eveny Cheval, are our biggest problem."

I begin to inch away, but he puts an ice-cold hand on my arm, and I find myself pinned to the spot.

"What do you think you're doing?" I demand, trying to sound brave.

He chuckles, and it reminds me for a moment of Pascal's evil laughter. "So impolite," he says. "That's no way to greet an old friend, Eveny."

"You're not my friend, you murderous asshole," I tell him. "Besides, I don't even know your real name."

His mirthless laughter chills me to the bone. I struggle again, but his viselike grip becomes tighter. "Of course. How terribly rude of me. I'm Aloysius Vauclain."

"No wonder you decided on an alias," I say under my breath.

He ignores me. "Now, before you waste any energy trying to get away or calling for help, understand this: I will not hesitate to strike down anyone who comes to your aid. Is that clear?"

I swallow hard, thinking of Caleb. I glare at Vauclain and say, "You're powerless now anyhow. We've restored the protection of the gates."

Concern flashes across his face for a split second but vanishes just as quickly, replaced by a smirk. "Oh, but you don't know that for sure, do you?" he asks. "You fled before your little ceremony was over."

He's right. For all I know, I disrupted the power of our circle by breaking away from it. I curse myself for being so stupid.

"Now, Eveny," he says smoothly, releasing my arm. "I was hoping we could speak for a moment like rational adults. Do you think you can handle that?"

Instinctively, I reach for my Stone of Carrefour, but

Vauclain's hand shoots out again at lightning speed, his cold fingers wrapping around my wrist.

"Ah ah ah," he chides. "Don't even think about it. Using magic right now would be a very, very bad idea. I'll have no choice but to end your life."

"Get it over with, then," I say. "If you're going to kill me, just do it."

He smiles. "But what's the rush, Eveny? The small talk is my very favorite part."

"Well, gee, don't let me stop you."

Vauclain laughs again, and the sound makes my blood run cold. "A sense of humor, I see. I like that. But then, I already knew you had wit. We've been watching you for years, and I must say, we've been very impressed with your aunt's resolve not to introduce you to zandara."

"I don't see how that's your concern."

"She's a wise woman, Eveny. She's kept you from magic because she finds it detestable. Yet you seem not to have inherited her intelligence, for here we sit in a cemetery, just after you've performed a serious zandara ceremony."

"It wasn't some magic joyride," I say. "It was a ceremony to fix what we screwed up last week when we opened the gates for that party. We were trying to get rid of *you*."

He chuckles again. "How very foolish and small-minded of you to assume that taking care of me would remove the threat to your town. You must know by now that there's someone on the inside who wishes you dead. After all, an attempt has already been made on your life."

"Drew's truck," I say softly. "That wasn't you?"

He looks offended. "I would never end your life in such an unimaginative way. Plus, of course, there are the far-too-obvious parallels with your mother's staged suicide. But this, conversing with you in the very cemetery where your ancestors lie just before I end your life, well, it's much more poetic. When I recall your death later, these are the moments I'll savor."

A chill runs through me. "So I suppose you've spent a lot of time savoring the details of Glory Jones's death too."

He laughs coldly. "I didn't do that myself, of course. I would never get my hands dirty with someone with no real power of her own. And to be honest, it wasn't part of the plan, but she was, how do I put it, *uncooperative*. Although I admit, the soldier who killed her has gone a bit rogue. It's rather amusing to watch the unraveling."

"Did one of your soldiers kill my mother too?" I ask. The words are thick and sour in my throat.

He looks surprised. "Of course not. It would be pointless to kill a queen without stabbing her through the heart," he says, as if it's the most logical thing in the world. "Her murder wasn't our style at all, although we're certainly grateful that someone else chose to do it."

He begins to explain that stabbing a queen through the heart prevents her from taking power on to the afterlife and seeking revenge, but I tune him out, realizing that as he's talking, his grip on my wrist is relaxing. I scan my brain for an herb I can channel if I'm able to touch my Stone of Carrefour.

The only thing that comes to mind is an image of wishing on dandelions with my mother when I was a little girl.

It's not perfect, but it will have to do.

I silently ask Eloi Oke to open the gate, and then, just as Vauclain is concluding his explanation of how a queen's heart is her greatest source of magic but also her greatest vulnerability, I twist my left hand away from him and punch him across the face with my right.

In the seconds it takes him to recover, I grab my Stone of Carrefour and say, "Dandelion, I draw your power. Spirits, please grant my wish and render Aloysius Vauclain incapable of following me. *Mesi, zanset.*"

He's already grabbing for me, and I have no idea if the charm worked, but I don't wait to find out. I begin to run back in the direction of Peregrine's house, my head throbbing and my mouth dry with fear. I trip over a root and scramble to my feet again.

Once I'm out of the clearing, I run for my life, branches scraping my face. Their gnarled fingers reach for me in the darkness as I stumble into the tombs that rise from the soft, decaying earth. The ground rolls beneath my feet, and I can't trust my own steps.

The only thing I do know is that Vauclain is somewhere behind me, his long jacket making him one with the black shadows of the cemetery. I can hear his footsteps in the darkness. The jagged edge of a broken tombstone appears just ahead, and I stumble, landing flat on my face. A buried rock slices into my cheek, and I feel blood as I scramble to my feet.

"Help!" I cry, hoarse with terror as the mansion on the edge of the graveyard comes into view. It glows in the blackness, but I fear I won't make it that far.

I just have to get out of the cemetery, I tell myself.

I struggle to my feet once again. I want to live. I have to live. I hold so many lives in my hands.

It feels like an eternity passes before I can see Peregrine's back fence. I turn to glance behind me and as I do, I collide hard with someone warm and solid who lets out a startled "Oof!"

I scream, sure that it's Vauclain, that he's somehow materialized in front of me to kill me within sight of salvation.

"Please don't!" I cry.

"Eveny?" says a deep voice, and that's when I realize it's not the Main de Lumière general. Relief floods through me as I look up to see Caleb's face creased with worry.

"Caleb," I breathe, collapsing into him.

He holds me for a moment, then pulls away, steadying me by putting his hands on my forearms. "Eveny, what is it?"

"The frat guy," I begin, but I'm barely able to get the rest of the words out. The ceremony-induced exhaustion I've been fighting for the last hour is overtaking me. "It was the Main de Lumière guy," I finally manage. "The one from the party."

He's already scooping me into his arms and carrying me

toward Peregrine's house. "I thought he was going to kill me," I say weakly, my voice muffled against the soft nub of his shirt.

"Eveny, I'm so sorry I wasn't there." Caleb's voice is rough with emotion, and it looks like he's about to cry. "I tried to follow you, but possession ceremonies take all the life out of you. By the time I got to the door, you were gone, and . . ."

"Caleb, if you'd been there, he could have killed you."

We've reached Peregrine's back door now, and Caleb gently sets me back on my feet. "Are you okay? Can you stand?"

I nod, but before I can say anything, he pulls me toward him, and I melt into his strong chest, already feeling safer. "How can I ever ask you to forgive me, Eveny?" he whispers into my hair.

"It's not your fault," I say softly, and Caleb makes a deep guttural sound in the back of his throat.

"Eveny—" he begins, but then he stops.

"What?" I whisper.

"It *is* my fault." He looks away from me and puts his hand on Peregrine's back door. "It's just like I said. My feelings for you . . . I didn't know you were in trouble until it was too late."

"But it wasn't too late," I say, and I pull him back toward me. "I'm here. I'm okay." I never want him to let me go.

But then the door flies open, and the moment is over as Peregrine and Chloe stumble out. Their eyes focus unsteadily on Caleb and me, and Peregrine's mouth opens into a little *o*.

"Eveny," she begins, her eyes flicking uncertainly between

Caleb and me. "I didn't mean for you . . ." Her voice is slurred and she trails off.

"We're sorry, Eveny." Chloe's voice is stronger and clearer, but she doesn't sound normal either; it's more like she's just run a marathon and is weak and out of breath. "We didn't expect the spirit to say what he did through Pascal," she says. "But whatever it is, we'll deal with it together."

It takes me a moment to realize that she and Peregrine think I'm shivering in fear because of what happened during the ceremony. "It's not that," I tell them. "I . . . I tried to run home, but in the cemetery, I was attacked by the guy from Main de Lumière." I add pointedly, "The one who was posing as Blake Montoire at *your* party."

I watch as their eyes widen into saucers, and I realize for the first time how dilated their pupils are. "Wait, what?" Peregrine whispers.

"Are you sure?" Chloe asks at the same time.

"Positive," I say and recap my encounter in the cemetery.

"Well, he was just bluffing," Peregrine says when I'm done, her eyes darting nervously to Chloe, who's chewing her lip. "The ceremony worked. He's powerless in Carrefour now."

"But he confirmed that there's already an operative here," I tell them. "Someone we trust. Someone who killed Glory. Someone who *isn't* powerless because they have a key to Carrefour. It's just like we thought."

Peregrine grabs my right hand and Chloe my left, and

before I know it, I'm being pulled away from Caleb. The moment I'm out of his arms, I feel cold and exposed.

"We'll call our mothers now," Peregrine says. "Let's get inside."

Caleb steps back into the darkness, and I hesitate. "Aren't you coming in?" I ask.

"There's something I have to do." His jaw is set, and I realize what he means.

"You can't go after him, Caleb," I say. "It's not safe."

"I'll be fine." He doesn't give me a chance to argue. He turns away and strides toward the cemetery, his fists clenched.

"Caleb!" I cry out. But Chloe and Peregrine hold me back as he vanishes into the darkness.

"He'll be okay," Peregrine says. "Don't worry."

"Don't worry?" I demand. "You just let him go after a Main de Lumière general!"

"A Main de Lumière general who's powerless now," Peregrine corrects. "Caleb can take care of himself."

I don't believe her. I call out once more for him, but the only answer is the cawing of a raven from somewhere beyond the cemetery wall.

26

"You performed a ceremony with Eveny without bothering to explain it to her first?" Peregrine's mother demands twenty minutes later once we're all gathered in her living room. She and Chloe's mother came right away from a cocktail party on the other side of town. Peregrine's mother has her black hair done in a thousand tiny braided extensions, and she looks impossibly slim in a shimmery silver dress. Chloe's mother's sleek blond hair is pulled into a chignon at the nape of her neck, and she's wearing a black cocktail dress that hugs her slender curves. They're both clutching flutes of champagne, which the maid handed to them as soon as they walked in the door.

"We thought it would make it easier on her if she didn't know what was going to happen," Peregrine whimpers, looking at the floor.

"Easier on her?" her mother asks, her eyes flashing. "Or easier on *you*?"

"I—" Peregrine begins, but her mother cuts her off.

"Enough," she says in a voice that's deadly calm. She looks at me. "Eveny, on behalf of my daughter, and of both sosyetes, yours and mine, I apologize. What Peregrine and Chloe did was inappropriate. You're one of us, and you deserve a full explanation from now on."

"Chloe knows better too," Chloe's mother pipes up, looking nervously at her daughter, who, like Peregrine, is staring at the floor like it's the most interesting thing she's ever seen.

I shrug uncomfortably. I don't need an apology—particularly not from the mothers, whose carelessness has nearly destroyed the town. "What about Caleb?" I ask. "He's out there all alone."

The mothers exchange looks. "He's not alone," Chloe's mother says. "Oscar and Patrick are with him."

"Besides, it's certainly not your job to feel such concern for him. Quite the opposite," Peregrine's mother says. "Now, on to the more pressing matter at hand. Main de Lumière. Eveny, what did you find out?"

As I tell them about the conversation with Aloysius Vauclain, everyone in the room stands completely still. There's a collective gasp when I tell them how easily he admitted to Main de Lumière's involvement in Glory's murder, and another gasp when I say that he disavowed any Main de Lumière involvement in my mother's death.

"We need to figure out who the Main de Lumière operative

in Carrefour is," I conclude. "If we find out who killed Glory, we can protect ourselves."

"You know," says Arelia, "the only new people in town in *years* have been Eveny herself and her aunt."

I open my mouth to defend Aunt Bea, but Peregrine's mother beats me to it. "Arelia, I don't care for Bea Cheval either," she says stiffly. "But to accuse her of being affiliated with Main de Lumière is taking things too far."

"And how do we know it wasn't you?" I hear myself say to Arelia. I hadn't meant to confront her, but her blind accusation of my aunt makes me furious.

"Eveny," Peregrine says in a warning tone.

"No," I say, turning to her. "Glory said she was meeting Arelia only hours before she died." I look back at Arelia. "Do *you* have an alibi for the night she was killed?"

I expect Arelia to have a retort ready, but instead, her face crumples, and she looks away. It's Margaux who steps forward and says, "She was with me. I swear it on our sosyete."

"Well, there you have it," Chloe's mother says, clapping her hands together enthusiastically. "I take it that will be the end of that discussion." She turns to me and adds in a lower voice, "In Carrefour, the women of the sosyetes stick together. They don't accuse each other of things."

I'm being chastised. I don't have a response, but I shoot a suspicious look at Arelia, who's glowering at me now.

Peregrine takes a step forward. "I say we hold a ceremony tomorrow night to cast as many protective charms over our sosyetes as we can."

"I disagree. I think we should stop practicing zandara for now, at least until the big Mardi Gras ceremony," I say immediately.

"This again?" Peregrine asks.

"I'm just suggesting we stop until we figure out what the situation is and who's after us," I say. "We're a target as long as we keep practicing magic."

"You're assuming that this Vauclain person was being truthful with you about Main de Lumière's motives," Peregrine says.

"I don't think he would have bothered lying if he thought he was about to kill me," I point out.

"I agree with Eveny," Chloe says. "It doesn't mean we won't be ready if there's an attack. But there's not much we can do without knowing the identity of the traitor."

"But we can't just stop doing zandara," Margaux protests. "That's who we are."

"Which is all well and good until another one of us winds up six feet under," Peregrine's mother says sharply.

"I agree," Chloe's mother says. "For now."

"There we have it," Peregrine's mother says crisply. "This means that for the next few days at least, no zandara in Carrefour. We must avoid calling attention to ourselves until we know what we're facing."

"But Mom—" Peregrine begins to protest.

Her mother cuts her off. "That means you girls."

"So what now?" asks Arelia.

"Now," says Peregrine's mother, "we attempt to make

contact with a few magical sects we trust in other parts of the country."

"And in the meantime," adds Chloe's mother, "we lie low and keep our eyes open for signs that something's not right."

"But—" Peregrine begins.

Her mother interrupts again. "This isn't open for discussion."

Peregrine seethes in silence as the meeting draws to a close.

After I say my good-byes, I head out the front door, thoroughly exhausted. I'm worried about the walk home, but Peregrine's mother hands me a sachet of protective herbs and promises that she'll cast a charm so that she'll know if I'm in any danger. "Besides, you'll be fine," she says. "Caleb and the boys are taking care of things."

I'm too tired to argue, plus I'm glad to get away from the sosyetes for the night. Still, I'm relieved when I hear Caleb calling my name. I turn to see him emerging from the cemetery, his shirt ripped on the right side and dirt streaked across his left cheek.

"Hey," he says, falling into step beside me.

"What happened?" I ask.

"We caught the guy who attacked you." Caleb hesitates. "He won't be bothering you anymore."

Something cold wraps itself around my heart. "You killed Vauclain," I say softly.

"We had to," Caleb says. His voice breaks, and he pauses

before continuing. "Patrick was the one who caught him, and Oscar was right behind him. He was already dead by the time I got there."

"He was their leader," I say. "They'll want revenge even more now."

"We didn't have a choice," he says. "If anything had happened to you . . ." He trails off, sending a shiver up my spine. "Eveny, I never would have forgiven myself."

He stops walking, and a few steps later, I stop too. I look up at him, and he puts a warm, rough hand on my cheek. We stare at each other for a long moment. He leans in, and I'm sure he's about to kiss me, so I close my eyes. But his lips never meet mine, and when I open my eyes a moment later, I feel like an idiot.

He's just staring at me. "Eveny. Have you made plans for the Mardi Gras Ball yet?"

"No." I hold my breath.

"Do you think . . . What I mean is . . . . Would you want to go with me?"

My heart leaps into my throat, but there's something about his expression that feels off. "You don't have to ask me if you don't want to, you know," I say.

"I know. It doesn't change anything between us, but," he says, looking into my eyes, "I want to. So is that a yes?"

"Of course it is."

"Good." He clears his throat and looks up at the moon. "Now come on. Let's get you home before we lose the light."

I walk inside to find Aunt Bea pacing the living room. "There'd better be a good explanation for what happened tonight," she asks, but before I can open my mouth, she adds, "Because this isn't the way I raised you, Eveny. You have no idea what you're dealing with here."

I open and close my mouth before I finally settle for, "Who called you?"

"Chloe's mother," she says. "I *told* you this was the sort of thing that could happen if you got involved in zandara, Eveny!" Aunt Bea slams her fist against the wall.

All of a sudden, a wave of calm rushes over me. "Aunt Bea," I say, "I can't run away from this."

"But *I* can. And I can make you come with me. We're going back to New York. I never should have brought you here."

They're the words I would have given anything to hear a few weeks ago. But now, everything's different. "No."

"*No?*" she repeats.

I shake my head. "It's not what Mom would have wanted. I know things are messed up here, Aunt Bea, but I think I'm the one who's supposed to fix them."

Her eyes are suddenly awash with sadness. "But Main de Lumière *killed* your mother," she says. "You want to wait around and have the same thing happen to you?"

"But Main de Lumière *didn't* kill her," I say, explaining what Vauclain told me in the cemetery. "I don't think he was lying. He had no problem admitting what they did to Glory."

"Well, if they didn't kill your mother, who did?"

"I was hoping you'd have some idea," I reply. "Vauclain

said I should be worried."

Aunt Bea looks down at the floor. "That doesn't make any sense."

"Maybe it was my dad," I venture after a pause.

Her head snaps up. "Where would you get an idea like that?"

"You despise him. You refuse to talk about him. And he's completely vanished."

Aunt Bea looks away. "Your father didn't kill your mother, Eveny. We are not living in an episode of *The Jerry Springer Show*."

"You hate him so much, though."

She gazes out the window. "Yes, because he left. Because your mother always believed he'd done the right thing, even when he abandoned you. Because he can't run from who he is, or who he was born to be."

Something inside me lurches. "What do you mean? Who was he born to be?" My pulse quickens; I have the feeling that whatever she's about to say is important.

But her face goes blank, and she looks away. "It's none of your concern, Eveny," she says tightly. "It has nothing to do with you."

"Of course it does," I reply, but Aunt Bea is already striding away, her heels echoing on the hardwood floors. "It has everything to do with me!"

But there's no reply. She's already gone.

27

A week passes and everyone in the sosyete is on edge. True to their word, Peregrine and Chloe stop practicing zandara, but in the meantime they're assembling a stockpile of herbs and furiously poring over charms from their mothers' notes. I stay up late and cram too, trying to memorize the uses of all the herbs my mother lists in her journal. "We have to be ready," Chloe keeps saying.

"I hate sitting around and waiting for some traitor to come get us," Peregrine whines on Thursday as we sit down on the cashmere blanket in the Hickories. "This feels like a ridiculous waste of our powers. I mean, have you seen my skin? I really need a refresher."

"We just have to figure out who the Main de Lumière person is, and then we can go back to normal," Chloe says, holding up the list we've been working on each day. There are already thirty-five names on it, everyone from Mrs. Perkins in the main office to the head cheerleader to Mrs. Potter at the library. Arelia forced us to put Bea's name on there, so I put hers on too, which has earned me countless snarls.

I glance toward the caf to see Drew, Liv, and Max coming our way. They've been eating with us all week, which Peregrine and Chloe accepted without complaint after I mentioned that if the Main de Lumière insider is a student or teacher, the presence of non-sosyete members will make it obvious we're backing off. I know I have to speak quickly before they arrive. "The ban on magic is temporary," I remind Peregrine. "Besides, it's about time you had a breakout. Welcome to the real world."

"I hate the real world," she moans. "How do people live like this?"

The conversation ends abruptly as Drew, Liv, and Max sit down on the opposite end of the blanket. Margaux, who looks like she's developed a beer belly in the last week, and Arelia, whose thighs seem to be expanding, just stare at them. "There's not enough to feed the three of you today," Arelia says sourly.

"Don't be rude, Arelia," Chloe chides halfheartedly. "They can have mine. And from the looks of it, you two shouldn't be going back for seconds either."

Arelia and Margaux glower at her, but they pile smoked salmon blinis onto plates without further complaint.

"What's up with all of you perfect people?" Drew asks as

he takes his meal. "Everyone's looking a little rough around the edges this week."

"Drew!" Liv says. But she appears delighted as she shoots Peregrine and Chloe a look of triumph. The Dolls just glare back.

"Perhaps your friends would be more comfortable eating in the cafeteria in the future," Peregrine says tightly, turning to me.

"Oh, he didn't mean it!" Max says eagerly. When Drew doesn't say anything, Max adds, "Seriously, man, apologize!"

Drew shrugs. "Sorry."

"Can't everyone just get along?" I ask. But from the dirty looks I get in reply, I'm guessing the answer is no.

By the next morning, though, something is different. Peregrine is keeping her head down in English class, and I can't help but notice that her curls are bouncy, and Chloe's hair looks like silk. When Peregrine finally looks up and meets my eye at the end of class, I know for sure by the guilty expression on her face.

"You used zandara!" I hiss as I catch up with them leaving the classroom.

"I don't know what you're talking about," Peregrine says haughtily. But her skin is clear, and the circles under her eyes have vanished.

"Chloe?" I ask.

She looks at me ruefully. "We should have called you, I guess."

"You *guess*?" I repeat. "How could you two do this after everything that happened? And after what your moms said?"

"Oh, get off your high horse, Eveny," Peregrine says. Two guys whistle at her as we pass. "This is who we are. I told you that. And we did it the old-fashioned way, with herbs. No harm to your precious Périphérie."

"But the danger—" I begin.

"The danger may not be real," Peregrine says sharply. "For all you know, Vauclain was bluffing. Not to mention that he's dead now."

"He wasn't bluffing," I say flatly. "And I'm sure there are a lot more Main de Lumière soldiers out there. His being dead doesn't mean we're safe."

Peregrine ignores me. "This town relies on us. We couldn't just turn our backs on it."

"Really? You're worried about the *town*? Not your pimples?"

Peregrine gives me a dirty look.

Chloe clears her throat. "Besides, our moms got back from New Orleans last night. They talked to a few voodoo priestesses there, who said the best way to get Main de Lumière to lose interest is to ignore them and go about our business. If we give in to their demands so easily, they'll know they have the upper hand."

"Did these priestesses have any firsthand experience with Main de Lumière?"

"Not that I know of," Chloe says.

"Then this situation is different!"

"Quiet down, Eveny," Peregrine says. "People are staring. This isn't the place."

I'm so angry I don't care. "So your mothers know you did this?"

"Yes," Chloe says.

"Our mothers feel, as do we, that we've been given this gift for a reason, and it's our right—our *duty*—to use it," Peregrine whispers.

"Just because you want better skin," I say. "And better grades. And better hair. And better boys."

"But now that you're back, we're not drawing our power from the Périphérie anymore," Peregrine says. "Things are in complete balance. I don't see what's so wrong about what we're doing."

"Everything's wrong with it, Peregrine. And I'm really afraid we're about to find that out." I walk away quickly before she can say anything else, but a moment later, I realize Chloe is following me.

"What?" I whirl to face her. "There's no way to justify what you've done. This was a decision we were supposed to make together, the three of us, and you and Peregrine just did what you wanted!"

That's when I realize she looks like she's about to cry. "It's not that," she says. "It's . . . it's Justin. I need some advice."

I realize with a surge of guilt that between the car accident with Drew and Main de Lumière, I'd forgotten to say something to Chloe about him. "I've been meaning to talk to you about him too. Want to go outside for a bit?"

She nods, and we head out the door as the bell rings to start second period. No one seems to notice, but then again, I'm getting accustomed to the rules being different for Dolls like us.

She looks at her hands once we're sitting on a bench facing the Hickories. "So I've been thinking a lot about what you said. About how maybe I should let Justin make up his own mind about me."

I wait for her to go on.

"The thing is, I'm scared. Do you think he'll want to keep dating me without a charm?"

I hesitate. "I think that's a chance you have to take."

"I'm scared he's in love with another girl," she mumbles.

"I'm sure he's not," I answer honestly. "But if there's someone else he's meant to be with, you're taking that possibility away. If he's supposed to be with you, he will be."

"It could mean losing him," she says almost inaudibly.

"But it could also mean opening the door to someone who's right for you. If you're in the wrong relationship, your eyes won't be open for the right one."

She's quiet for a moment. "Eveny," she says, "you're in love with Caleb, aren't you?"

I can feel myself turning red. "I don't know. Maybe. Why do you say that?"

"It's just the way you get when he's around. Like you're a

little nervous, but also happy. Like seeing him makes you feel better."

I consider this. "That's pretty much exactly how I feel."

"But you know you can't be with him. He's explained that to you."

"I keep hoping he'll change his mind."

She looks sad. "It's more complicated than that for him. I think he's trying to do the right thing." She hesitates and adds, "You know, you could cast a charm on him to make him see things your way."

"It's tempting," I reply. "But whatever would come of it, it wouldn't be real."

"I guess." After a moment, she stands up. "Wait, what were you going to say? You were going to tell me something about Justin."

I hesitate. "I just wanted to say I know you'll do the right thing."

"You too, Eveny." She walks away without another word.

In her wake, I'm left wondering exactly what that right thing is, though, and how I'll find my way there.

I spend the afternoon reading and rereading my mother's letter, studying her herb book, and trying to figure out what I'm supposed to do.

It takes me until late that night to come to the conclusion that although zandara has gotten terribly off track in Carrefour, it's still who we are. I've been so focused on making sure the Périphérie isn't harmed anymore and making sure Main de Lumière doesn't have a reason to attack us, that I'm losing sight of our gift.

Sure, zandara can be misused. But that's the case with everything. If I walk away now, the inevitable result is that the scales will one day be tipped too far, and who knows what could happen then? I can't fix anything by turning my back on it.

It's nearly midnight when I show up at Peregrine's house unannounced to tell her I'm not going to run from who I am anymore. I expect to find her alone, but instead, when she opens the door wearing a low-cut caftan that shows off her cleavage, I see Caleb standing in the shadows of her front hall.

"What are you doing here?" I ask, looking back and forth between them as my stomach drops.

Peregrine just rolls her eyes. "Don't you call first, Eveny? It's rude to drop by unannounced so late without a warning."

"It's not what you think," Caleb says quickly. "We were talking about you."

"You were?" I ask uncertainly.

"Oh for goodness' sake, don't be so melodramatic, Eveny," Peregrine says. "We're not *banging* each other, if that's what you're asking. Not yet, anyhow," she adds. "Stop being so theatrical and come in."

I close the door behind me and follow the two of them into the living room. Peregrine settles onto the sofa and folds her long legs under her. A moment later, Audowido slithers out from behind a pillow and slinks into her lap. She pets him absentmindedly like he's a cat.

"So why are you here?" Peregrine says, once Caleb has taken a seat in an armchair and I've perched uneasily on an ottoman. "More criticisms about how I'm horrible and selfish and superficial?"

"I came to tell you I'm in." I glance at Caleb, who looks troubled.

"Meaning . . . ?" she says.

"Meaning I know I have to embrace this. I have to be the queen I was born to be."

"I knew you'd come around," Peregrine says. "Chloe will be so thrilled. So what do you want to do first?"

"What do you mean?" I ask.

She gestures to me. "Well, we could fix your hair or make your legs look longer. Or maybe we should start with your boobs. I'm sure Caleb would prefer C cups to A cups on you."

I can feel my cheeks heating up. "I'm not here for a new body."

She stops petting Audowido and waits for me to continue.

"I'm here to say that I'll work zandara with you, but we've got to stop being so careless. Could you just hear me out for a second?"

Peregrine snorts. "Oh, this should be good."

"Look, I know you think I'm being a goody-goody. But we have to fix what's been done already, or it's only a matter of time until we're destroyed."

"I see you've appointed yourself queen of the queens now?"

I ignore her. "You've only been using your power to make your own lives easier. Maybe once we stop being selfish, we'll have a little more perspective on what to do about Main de Lumière."

Peregrine studies me for a moment, then she leans forward so that Audowido can slither up her arm. When she stands to look at me, she looks positively creepy with her violet eyes blazing and her snake wrapped around her shoulders. He hisses at me, and I look away. He's the one thing in this town I know I'll never get used to.

"You know, it occurred to me as you were speaking how little you really know," she says slowly. "And it seems to me that someone who's so ignorant about things isn't exactly qualified to give other people advice on how to run their lives."

"I know I'm new at this—"

She cuts me off. "No, not that. I'm not referring to your little do-gooder speech. I'm talking about how clueless you are about your own life and how horrendously underqualified that makes you to judge mine."

"Peregrine—" Caleb says, but this just makes her turn on him.

"Caleb, I know it's your job to protect her, but this is a little much, don't you think? You don't get to shield her feelings too." Peregrine smiles at me, her eyes glinting. "Like for example, it might hurt Eveny to know the real reason you're so fixated on the rules is that your father let her mother die, and now you have to salvage your family reputation."

A knot forms in the pit of my stomach. "Caleb?" I say softly. "That's not true, is it?"

But he merely hangs his head, and I realize in an instant that Peregrine must be right. I can't believe it didn't occur to me before: If my mother's dead, that means her protector— Caleb's dad—didn't do his job.

"So Caleb probably didn't tell you that when your mother was being stabbed to death, his father was at home having a good ol' time with his wife and son?" Peregrine says with a cold smile. "He sensed the danger, but by the time he got back to your house, your mom was already dead."

"Peregrine!" Caleb says, his voice choked.

Peregrine ignores him. "He also probably didn't mention that the guilt and shame drove his father out of town. And that his mother always blamed your family for destroying hers. So, you see, Caleb's not just torn about his responsibilities as your protector. He's torn because he was raised to hate everything Cheval. It all gets rather complicated, doesn't it?"

"Caleb—" I whisper, turning to him.

Caleb doesn't answer; he just stares. And so without another word, I turn to go. I've heard enough.

"Oh, Eveny, one more thing!" Peregrine calls out as I stride toward her front door.

I stop, because even though I can't stand to hear another word, I know I have to. I need to understand everything.

"The thing about our protectors is that if they let you die, they'll die within a year themselves. Our ancestors designed it that way to make sure they always stayed loyal."

My breath catches in my throat as she goes on.

"So if Caleb doesn't protect you, he's dead, which is exactly what happened to his dad," she says. "Now you can see why he's so motivated to hang out with you. He's confusing self-preservation with feelings. Or maybe it's just that he wants you to believe he likes you, so that you care about keeping him alive too."

"Eveny," Caleb says, "that's not true!" But I'm already walking away.

"Just let her go," I hear Peregrine coo in her syrupy smooth voice. "She'll be fine. Come here. I'll make you feel better."

I slam the door behind to shut their voices out. The whole way home, I try very hard not to think about the fact that the things I thought mattered were all in my head.

28

A lock myself in my room the next day and dodge five calls from Chloe and one from Caleb. Aunt Bea knocks on my door around seven to ask me to come down to dinner, but I tell her I'm not hungry. Finally, around eight she knocks again, and I open the door reluctantly.

"Did one of the Dolls do something to you?" she asks bluntly.

"Peregrine told me about Caleb Shaw and the fact that his survival is tied to mine."

Her expression shows me she already knew, which makes me feel even more betrayed. "Oh."

"Why didn't *you* tell me?" I demand.

"I don't like to talk about the Shaws."

"Because Caleb's father let Mom get killed," I guess in a flat voice.

Aunt Bea looks surprised. "No. I've never blamed him for that. Neither did Peregrine's mother or Chloe's mother. Whoever got to your mom got through every one of us." She shakes her head. "That poor man always blamed himself. He felt he'd failed to uphold his family's end of the pact. He left town soon after, and about a year later his body was found in Savannah."

My blood runs cold. "What happened to him?"

"The police never solved the case. Rumor is that he was stabbed over a gambling debt. But of course his death was tied to the original pact," she adds. "It was inevitable."

It takes me a second to realize what she means. "He died within a year of Mom because he failed to protect her," I say.

"I'm afraid so. I think Peregrine's and Chloe's moms felt guilty, like they'd driven him away. They gave Caleb and his mother some money to get back on their feet, and they continued paying Charles's salary until Caleb was old enough to take over."

I blink. "Charles's *salary*?"

"Part of the deal the Shaws made with your great-great-great-grandmother was that they'd be rewarded financially for protecting Cheval queens, plus they would always be members of the sosyete and be provided with whatever they needed to live comfortably. Caleb's mother should be a sosyete member too, but after her husband's death, she became a recluse. She didn't want anything to do with zandara."

"Poor Caleb. Having to carry on a tradition that destroyed his family . . ." I shake my head. "He should hate me."

"I think that's the last emotion he feels for you." She pauses and changes the subject. "I'll make you a plate and bring it up. I don't want you going to bed hungry."

But for the rest of the night, I can't stop thinking about Caleb's father. My mom's death was at the hands of a random murderer, but his dad's death would forever be tied to my mom—and to an obligation he never asked for.

I'm attempting to catch up on some homework Sunday afternoon when the doorbell rings. Aunt Bea pokes her head into my room a moment later to tell me that Peregrine and Chloe are here.

"I have nothing to say to them," I tell her without looking up.

She hesitates. "I think Peregrine's here to apologize. With things as dangerous as they are right now, maybe it can't hurt to hear her out."

"Fine," I grumble.

I follow her downstairs and find Peregrine and Chloe waiting in the front hall.

"I'll leave you girls alone," Aunt Bea says. She narrows her eyes at Peregrine before slipping away.

"What do you want?" I say once Aunt Bea is gone.

Chloe looks at Peregrine, who's still staring at the floor. After a pause, she nudges her.

Peregrine looks up and blinks at me a few times. "Look, I'm sorry, okay?" she says. It seems difficult for her to get the words out; I assume she's not used to contrition.

Chloe nudges her again. "Go ahead, tell her the rest."

Peregrine glares at Chloe for a moment, but then she looks up again and says, "Fine, I *might* have been a little jealous. Caleb's the only guy I've ever really liked, and he rejected me. Then you get to town, and he's all over you. And not only that, but our sosyete's supposed to bend over backward to do what's right now that you're here. It doesn't seem fair."

"You think this is what I want?" I demand. "Besides, it's not like anything's ever going to happen with me and Caleb anyhow." I wave my hand distractedly and try my hardest to pretend I don't care. "What matters is that we're in danger."

"Exactly my point. That's why we have no choice but to do the ceremony. Think you can get your panties out of a twist long enough for that?"

"The Mardi Gras ceremony?" I ask.

Peregrine's expression turns reverent. "The Mardi Gras *Possession*. The single most important ceremony we hold each year. If you do it with us, Eveny, it can protect us entirely and restore Carrefour's power, which has been chipping away for the last fourteen years. It'll even bank us enough power to start to fix the Périphérie."

I hesitate. "If it's the only way, I'm in." I don't like it, but I know I don't have a choice.

"Wonderful. We do it right after the Mardi Gras Ball next Tuesday," Chloe explains. "After the ball ends, our sosyete caravans to New Orleans."

"Mardi Gras is the craziest day of the year in New Orleans, so everyone will be out in the streets partying," Peregrine says. "We'll do a mass possession ceremony soon after we arrive, then join the party."

"It's like the ceremony that freaked you out at Peregrine's," Chloe cuts in, "but *everyone* gets possessed. It's the best way to draw power to us. Eloi Oke and the other spirits that possess us have free rein to party, drink, and be among real people for the first time in a year. It's the greatest gift we can give them, and in return they give us tremendous power."

"But leaving Carrefour means leaving the protection of the town," I point out.

"It's a chance we have to take," Peregrine says. "If we don't do this ceremony, we won't be able to fix anything that's gone wrong. And that could destroy us."

"The ceremony has to take place in New Orleans?" I ask.

"It's the only place the spirits are entirely free to revel in public without anyone blinking an eye," she says. "Our defenses might have been down before, but they're not anymore."

"Eveny," Chloe says, "I don't like this either. But I think we're out of options."

Caleb is gone from school Monday and Tuesday, which makes me feel sadder than it should. I know he's off training with Patrick and Oscar as the Mardi Gras Possession approaches, but I miss his presence. There are times I glance out the classroom windows and see flashes of someone in the woods that I'm sure is him, but I know I'm imagining things.

He does call twice, but he doesn't leave messages, and I don't bother calling back. What is there to say? There's undeniably something between us, but he simply wants those feelings to go away.

An eerie calm settles over Pointe Laveau the next several days, and even those who aren't in on the Secret of Carrefour seem to sense that something's wrong.

"The Dolls are being even weirder than usual," says Drew as we head up to the Hickories on Wednesday.

I try to appear nonchalant. "I hadn't noticed."

"Don't be so dramatic," Liv says, nudging him gently. They're flirting, and it's cute. More than that, though, I'm glad they're distracting each other. As long as they're sneaking adoring looks, they won't be thinking too hard about the peculiar behavior of the Dolls.

"What happened between Chloe and Justin?" Max whispers to me on the way back to class that day. "He hasn't been up here in the Hickories since last week."

"I don't know," I tell him honestly, but I'm hoping Chloe did what she said and released him from her charm.

"Do you think they broke up?" he asks.

"I hope so. It would be the right thing."

On Friday, Peregrine's not in school, but Chloe offers me a ride home in her little white BMW so I don't have to wait in the rain for Aunt Bea to pick me up.

"You know," she says as we pull out of the parking lot, "you still have to go to the ball with Caleb. It's safest that way. If Main de Lumière knows about the Mardi Gras Possession we do each year, that's going to be a dangerous night. You need Caleb to protect you, now more than ever."

"Great," I mutter. "So he's obligated to take me to the ball. How delightful for him." Thunder rolls outside, and lightning flashes across the sky, illuminating dark, hulking clouds.

"He *wants* to take you, Eveny."

I snort and look out the window. The rain is coming down in sheets, and the world has turned black.

"Things are different with you two," she adds after a minute. "Seeing you with him made me realize that I needed to let Justin go."

"Did you do it?"

"Yes," she says. "He's still part of the sosyete as long as he wants to be. And he'll still be my date to the ball, because he's coming with us to New Orleans. But after that, we're done." She pauses. "You know, it's true that Caleb had no choice about protecting you unless he wanted his family to lose everything. But he did have a choice about falling in love with you."

I look at her in disbelief. "You think Caleb is in *love* with me?"

But Chloe isn't laughing. "You're different from the rest of us. Maybe it's because you didn't grow up here. Maybe it's because you're just a different kind of person. But I think Caleb sees you for *you*."

I ponder this in silence for a moment. "It doesn't matter, though. He's making a choice, and the choice is to distance himself from me."

"You're not being fair to him," she says. "It's not like he's being a jerk. He's trying to do the right thing."

"Only because his life depends on it," I say.

"No!" Chloe exclaims, and I can tell she's getting frustrated with me. "It's because he's a good guy. It's because he understands that you're in danger. It's because he would do anything to protect you—including staying out of your life."

"He's just doing his duty," I say softly. "That's all."

"Look, never in the history of this town has there been an incident of a protector falling for one of the queens," Chloe says after a pause. "It's forbidden. This wasn't supposed to happen. But it did. That means something."

My heart thuds as I turn to look out the window again.

"Can he sever his obligation to me if he wants to?" I ask.

"Well, technically, he could stop protecting you at any time," she says. "But he'd instantly lose everything his family has ever had. He and his mom would be out on the street. And of course if something happened to you . . ."

"He'd die too," I fill in.

"Yes."

"But I can release him from the obligation," I say.

Chloe looks startled. "That wouldn't make any sense. You'd be putting yourself in serious danger."

"Humor me. Is it possible? If I did it, would it free him

from his fate being tied to mine?"

She hesitates. "I guess so. But it would be crazy to do that now, Eveny, with Main de Lumière after us. Caleb has been training his whole life to protect you. Besides, think about future generations. If you sever the protectorate, you leave your children, your grandchildren, and their children unprotected."

My stomach lurches at the thought, but there's no justification for protecting myself and my family at the expense of Caleb and his. "I need you to tell me how I'd do it," I say.

Chloe's grip tightens on the steering wheel, but after a long pause, she begins to explain. And by the time she drops me off at my front door, I'm beginning to have an idea of how I can change everything—if not for everyone, then at least for the future of the one person in my life who's willing to sacrifice everything for me.

29

That weekend, I ignore calls from everyone, including Liv, who seems to think she's done something to offend me. I shoot her a text telling her that I'm just worried about the ball, but the truth is, I don't have the energy to make up another story about why the Dolls are acting so strange.

I go to bed early Saturday night, hoping that I'll dream of my mom. The more alone I feel in this town, the more I long for her advice and comfort. But my sleep is annoyingly dreamless. I wake up frustrated, wondering what good my powers are if I can't call upon my mom—or at least someone helpful—when I need to.

Aunt Bea and I eat grilled cheese in silence on Sunday, and afterward, I shut myself in my room. I tell her I'm studying for a test, but in reality I'm leafing through my mother's herb book, hoping there's something there I've missed. Perhaps a "How to Save the Whole Town from Impending Disaster" charm? No such luck.

It's nearing twilight when I head out to the garden to think. It's the place where I most feel my mother's presence, and tonight I want to do everything I can to channel her wisdom, in hopes that I can find some answers.

But all I'm left with are the cryptic words of her letter. *In order to survive, you'll have to tap into everything inside of you. You have the chance to become the greatest queen the world has ever known.*

I keep searching my heart for the insights she seemed to think would be there, but all I can find are betrayal and loss. My mother is gone. My father is gone. The truth about Caleb has come to light. Everything is wrapped in secrets and lies.

I'm still sitting in the garden a few hours later, no closer to an answer, when a rustling from behind the rosebushes startles me. I turn and see Boniface approaching.

"Oh," I say, putting my hand over my heart. "It's you."

"Sorry, honey," he says gently. He gestures to the bench beside me. "Mind if I sit for a minute?"

I shake my head, and he settles down next to me. I haven't seen much of him since the incident in the garden where I nearly killed him, and although I feel like I should be freaked out by the realization that he's been alive for more than a century and a half, I'm not. This town is weird, and after a while, the weirdness becomes the norm.

"It seems like you have some decisions to make," he says.

I look at him in surprise. "How do you know?"

He chuckles. "Do you think I'm just here to care for the house? I'm here for you too, Eveny. You're my family, just like your mom was."

"I keep wondering what she'd do right now if she were in my shoes."

He puts a hand on my back. "You know right from wrong. You realize it's your job to stand up for the right thing. I don't think you have to expend so much energy wondering what decisions your mother would make. They're the choices that are in your heart already."

"So what do I do?" I ask. "How do I protect everyone? How do I do what's right?"

"Is your sosyete still planning to do the Mardi Gras Possession on Tuesday night?"

"That's the plan."

"Then go to New Orleans and work your magic. You must." He stands, and for a moment, I think the conversation is over and he's walking away, but then he gestures for me to follow him. "I have something I'd like to give you."

He leads me into his cottage, which is lit by a dozen squat, dripping candles. "Have a seat," he says, gesturing to two wooden chairs beside a small table. I settle into one of them while he disappears. He returns a moment later with something clutched in his hand.

"After your aunt moved you to New York, she asked me

to go through your mother's things," he begins. He sits down in the chair opposite me and leans forward. "Everything I held on to is stored in the attic for you. But this, I took down a few days ago." He unfolds his palm, and I peer at what he's holding.

"Lip gloss?" I ask.

He chuckles. "It belonged to your mother."

"Oh. Thanks." I force a polite smile. I'd hoped he was going to give me something that could help me, but I appreciate him trying to make me feel better. "It'll be nice to think of my mom when I wear it to the ball."

"No, you misunderstand," he says. "I'm not giving you this to remind you of your mother. I'm giving it to you because once upon a time, she imbued it with power."

I look at him and then back to the tube of gloss.

"She spent months working desperately to come up with the right combination of herbs," he explains. "This sort of thing is difficult, because in zandara herbs are used in the moment, in ceremonies, not to give inanimate objects power of their own. But just before she died, she told me she thought she'd done it; she added ground alder leaf to uncover someone's true motives, thyme to reveal a liar, and peony to bring the truth to light. She never had a chance to charm it, though."

He hands the tube to me. "It's meant to show you betrayal around you." I roll it over in my palm while he continues. "It will be clear on your lips, and it will be clear on people who are being honest with you. But if you charm it correctly, it will show up blood red on the face of the person who's lying to you about the night Glory Jones died. And only you will be able to see the mark of the traitor."

"Are you sure it will work?" I ask.

"No," he admits. "But it may be your best chance."

I consider this for a moment. "What made my mom so desperate to perfect this before she died?"

He frowns. "She had the feeling she was in danger, and she wanted to find out if there was someone here in Carrefour lying to her." He puts his hand on my shoulder. "Your mother's magic didn't save her. But it could be the thing that saves you."

Mardi Gras arrives crisp and clear in Carrefour, the first cloudless day we've had in a while. Pointe Laveau is closed in honor of the holiday, so I don't set my alarm, but I'm up before five thirty anyhow, my nerves on edge.

The first thing I do is cross to my window and look out at the garden. I'm startled to see Caleb sitting in the predawn darkness on the bench beneath my mom's favorite roses, staring up at me.

I open the window. "Come inside," I call down.

He shakes his head. "Thanks. But I'm okay."

"Caleb, you don't have to do this."

He looks down at the ground and then back up at me. "I'm fine, Eveny. Go on with your day."

I pause and say, "You've been avoiding me all week. What

are you doing here now?"

I'm hoping he'll say he's here because he wants to be. But instead he says, "It's Mardi Gras, Eveny. The most dangerous day of the year for our sosyete."

I stare at him for a long time before nodding and closing the window, a lump in my throat. He's here because he has to be; that's all. But that doesn't stop me from being touched. Or from making him a cup of coffee once I'm dressed and bringing it out to the garden. I hand it to him and sit down on the bench next to him with a mug of my own. I try not to notice as he scoots away.

"You know, you don't have to take me to the ball tonight," I say.

He turns to look at me as the steam rises from his coffee mug, blurring his face for a moment. "I want to," he says bluntly.

"Of course you do," I say, trying not to sound bitter. "It's your job."

He seems to choose his words carefully before speaking. "I'm obligated to protect you, not to take you to the ball. I *want* to take you to the ball." He doesn't look at me, but he takes a sip of his coffee, which feels a bit like an acceptance of my olive branch. "That's why I asked you," he adds a moment later.

We sit in silence for a long time. Finally, he says, "I'm sorry," in such a low voice that I almost don't hear him.

"For what?" I ask in disbelief.

"For everything. For all of this. You didn't ask for any of it."

"Neither did you," I say.

He nods and takes another sip of his coffee, and I take a sip of mine. Around us, the world comes to life as the sun rises, turning the sky a million beautiful shades of watercolor blue.

I lock myself in my room that afternoon and, after poring over my mother's herb journal and thinking a lot about what Boniface said, I take a deep breath, hope my mother was right about the lip gloss, and call on Eloi Oke.

"Alder leaf, thyme, and peony, I draw your power," I say. "Spirits, please imbue this gloss with the truth that could save our lives tonight. Let it show up blood red on the face of the person who's lying about the night Glory Jones died." The air pressure shifts, and I feel a breeze as I murmur, "*Mesi, zanset. Mesi, zanset. Mesi, zanset.*"

I call Peregrine when I'm done and ask if she can conference Chloe in. When they're both on the line, I hastily explain my mother's lip gloss and the charm I just cast over it.

"How do you know it will work?" Peregrine asks.

"I don't," I say. "But do you have a better idea?"

"No," she admits. "But you're the only one who will see the mark of the traitor?"

"That's what Boniface said," I tell her.

"Can't hurt to try," Chloe says. "Let us know the second you see anything, okay?"

"Of course," I say. "Don't tell anyone, though. I know you two aren't the ones who betrayed Glory, but it could be someone else we trust."

"Like one of your unfortunate little friends from the Périphérie?" Peregrine asks sweetly.

Chloe surprises me by saying, "Lay off, Peregrine. It could be anyone. And Eveny, I agree. We don't know who to trust. Your secret's safe."

"Peregrine?" I ask.

"Whatever," she says. I hear a doorbell ring in the background and Peregrine says, "Cristof is here. I'm getting my hair done. See you tonight."

I hear a click, then Chloe's voice. "You still there?" she asks.

"I'm here." I pause. "Will you call Caleb and tell him about this too? I don't think I can handle talking to him right now."

"I'll do it." She pauses and adds, "Good luck, Eveny. I hope this works."

"Me too."

Liv comes over late that afternoon so we can get ready for the ball together. She's so excited about her dress—a slinky purple satin sheath—and her date with Drew that she doesn't seem to notice how quiet I'm being.

"Do you think Drew'll try anything tonight?" she asks as she curls her hair in my bathroom mirror. I'm standing beside her, putting on my eye makeup. "I think he likes me, but this will be our first date-date. We've been talking on the phone every night, though, and our chemistry is pretty insane. Am I being totally lame?"

She's talking so quickly I can barely keep up with her, but her enthusiasm is just what I need to keep my mind off of what might happen later.

"You're not being lame at all. And I bet he'll try to kiss you," I say.

Liv laughs. "Maybe." She fluffs her curls in satisfaction, turns to look at herself from both the left and the right in the mirror, then unplugs the curling iron. "How do I look?"

"Gorgeous."

"You okay, Eveny?" she asks, watching my reflection in the mirror closely.

"Me? I'm fine!" I overenthuse.

"You're nervous about Caleb." Her expression is sympathetic and concerned. "I know I keep saying this, but I don't think you have anything to worry about," she says. "Just kiss him!"

I look down at the tube of charmed lip gloss, which lies on the bathroom counter. "I will."

I finish putting on mascara, then add a dusting of peach blush, which makes my skin look luminous. My hair falls around my shoulders in gentle, rippling waves, and the beautiful champagne-colored dress I've pulled from my mother's closet complements my coloring perfectly.

The last thing I do before leaving the bathroom is to uncap

the charmed gloss, slick it over my lips, and glance once more at the mirror. *Thanks, Mom*, I think as I set the gloss down on the bathroom counter.

I take a deep breath, pray that Liv isn't the one I need to worry about, and give her a kiss on the cheek. I sigh in relief when no mark appears. "I'm so glad we're friends," I tell her.

"Me too, Eveny." She looks at me more closely. "Ooh, let me grab some of that gloss," she says, reaching for the tube. She runs it over her own lips before I can stop her.

Liv hands me back the tube, and I shove it into the little beige purse she loaned me for the evening, hoping she didn't affect the potency of the magic.

"You okay?" I ask uncertainly.

"Of course. Why wouldn't I be?"

The doorbell rings before I can answer, and Liv's eyes widen. "They're here!"

She's already barreling out of the bathroom before I have a chance to reply. I say a little prayer that nothing bad will happen to her tonight, and follow her downstairs.

Liv blows me a kiss then pulls the door open. Drew and Caleb are standing there side by side, each of them clutching small, clear boxes with corsages inside.

"We pulled up at the same time," Drew says, gesturing to Caleb. "Although now I'm thinking we should have coordinated." He refocuses on Liv and holds out the corsage, which is white with little green ribbons. "You look really pretty, Liv."

Caleb looks at me with sad, almost desperate eyes while

Drew slips the corsage onto Liv's left wrist. When Drew is done, Caleb holds up his little box. "For you," he says, handing it to me.

It's a beautiful cluster of white roses, a white lily, and a sprig of baby's breath, wrapped with a deep green ribbon trimmed in gold. "It's gorgeous," I say.

"Well, put it on her!" Liv urges with a laugh.

Caleb clears his throat and steps forward.

"Roses for strength, a lily for peace, and baby's breath for hope," he whispers. As his fingers touch my wrist, I feel a jolt of electricity shoot through me. From the way he looks at me, I know he feels it too.

"Thank you," I say once he slips the corsage onto my wrist and looks away. I take a deep breath and lean in to kiss him on the cheek. I exhale in relief when nothing shows up on his face.

He offers me his arm and I lock the front door behind us. I feel like I'm floating down the driveway as we head toward his Jeep.

"I'll let them pull out first," Caleb says, after he shuts the passenger door behind me and climbs into the driver's seat. We watch as Drew helps Liv into the old Nissan he's borrowed from his mother. Liv giggles and blushes, and Drew almost trips over his own two feet as he hurries to the driver's seat to get in. "They're kind of cute together," Caleb says.

Drew starts his car up, and the two of them head out without looking back. I look over at Caleb, expecting that he'll turn the key in the ignition too, but he just sits there staring straight ahead.

"Caleb?" I ask after a moment.

He turns to look at me. "Eveny," he says after a pause. "You really do look beautiful." He stares at me for another long moment, then he leans across and touches my cheek so gently I can barely feel it.

"I wish things were different," he says. He doesn't wait for me to respond before starting the car. We drive into town in silence.

30

The ball is even more spectacular than I imagined. I attended Homecoming my sophomore year in Brooklyn—Mer and I went stag together—and I suppose I'd expected an upgraded, Carrefour-ized version of that: a punch bowl, streamers hanging from the rafters, maybe a deejay. But the Lietz Theater on Main Street has been transformed into a wonderland of cascading gold sheets, deep purple uplighting, and a million twinkling lights overhead. The oval dance floor is a deep ebony, and instead of a deejay, there's a small orchestra in the corner. Tuxedoed waiters circulate with trays full of champagne flutes and appetizers.

"This is amazing," I say. The whole town seems to be here. I even recognize a bunch of Drew's friends from the Périphérie, and I assume that many of the adults clustered near them are their parents or their parents' friends. The men are all wearing tuxes or dark suits, and the women around the room are all in elaborate ball gowns. It's decadent, outlandish, ritzy, and over the top.

Peregrine's and Chloe's mothers both make a beeline for Caleb and me as we walk through the door.

"Your aunt isn't here, is she?" Peregrine's mother asks once they've both hugged and air-kissed us.

I shake my head. "I don't think she's coming."

Peregrine's mom makes a tsk-tsk sound. "I wish she had even a little of your mother's courage."

I feel a surge of annoyance in defense of my aunt. "Maybe she doesn't feel like it's her duty to fight your battles."

Peregrine's mother looks at me. "Honey, this is your battle as much as it is ours. And she's your blood. You'd think she'd want to help you."

Chloe's mother cuts in. "Or perhaps she just knows things are in your hands now and there's nothing more she can do."

I bite my tongue and resist the urge to tell them that maybe if they and their daughters had practiced even a little self-control, we wouldn't be in this mess. Instead I kiss both of them on their cheeks, just in case. When no lipstick mark shows up, I excuse myself and hurry away.

I spend the next hour greeting everyone with cheek kisses and reapplying my lip gloss every few minutes. I'm sure I look like a crazy person, and I'm beginning to wonder if maybe I am. Maybe it's madness to have put my faith in an old tube of gloss, but I know Boniface cares as much about the fate of this town as I do, and that has to mean something. Plus, I trust my mom. If she believed this would work, then I do too.

It's not until nine o'clock that it occurs to me for the first time that the traitor might not even be here, rendering the whole issue of the charmed gloss moot.

"I love that you're finally loosening up tonight and kissing everyone. It's very sexy." Pascal interrupts my thought process by sidling up behind me and putting a hand on my waist. I turn to find him leering at me. "If you're looking for someone to make out with, look no further." He puckers up as I roll my eyes.

"I'm here with Caleb," I say.

"Who, might I point out, is nowhere to be found," he replies.

"He went to the bathroom ten seconds ago. He'll be right back."

"And in the meantime, if you want to make out with me . . . ," Pascal says.

I grit my teeth and dive in to kiss him on the cheek, which seems to shock him. I'm relieved when I don't see any red mark develop.

"Seriously, Eveny, if you're into it, we could slip outside for a few minutes," Pascal says, his eyes darting around like pinballs.

"Pascal," I say calmly, "I wouldn't slip outside with you if you were the last guy on earth."

"That's just because you haven't had any of this body yet,"

he says, gesturing proudly to himself.

"That must be it." I turn to walk away before he has a chance to say anything else. My shoulders sag in relief as I see Caleb coming toward me from across the dance floor.

"How you doing?" he asks, his forehead creased with concern. He puts his right hand gently on the small of my back, and for a moment, it feels like everything is okay. Then, he quickly pulls away like he's done something wrong.

"I'm fine," I say, looking at the floor. "Just confused."

Caleb clears his throat. "About me?"

"About everything."

"I'm right here," he says after a minute.

"I know."

Caleb stays protectively by my side all evening. To anyone who doesn't know us, who doesn't understand what's happening, I'm sure we look like the perfect couple. He keeps a hand gently on my waist or my back all night; he dances with me to the slow songs; he even pushes my hair out of my face when it tumbles over my shoulders.

He's so close, so *mine*. But none of it's real.

This year's Carrefour Mardi Gras king and queen are supposed to be crowned at ten, and just a few minutes before that, I ask Caleb if he'll step outside with me for a minute.

He hesitates. "Sure."

We duck out a side door, and as we do, I catch Liv's eye. She's slow dancing with Drew, her head resting on his shoulder. She waves, and I force a smile back. Drew turns to look at me too. Liv says something to him, and he gives me a thumbs-up. I'm sure they both think we're heading into the alley to make out.

"Before you say anything, I need to tell you how sorry I am," Caleb says once the door has shut behind us and we're alone. "I know I should have told you everything sooner. But I was afraid you wouldn't understand. I guess selfishly, I didn't want anything to change between us. . . ."

"I understand perfectly, Caleb," I say. "I just hope you can forgive me too."

His face clouds. "Forgive you for what?"

Instead of answering, I place my right hand on his cheek. It's warm, and the stubble on his jaw tickles my hand. I look at him for a moment, then I touch the Stone of Carrefour hanging from my neck and ask Eloi Oke to open the gate.

"Lemon balm to release you, saltpeter to change your fate, rue to reverse a charm," I say quickly, before he has a chance to stop me. "Spirits, please grant the Shaw family a return of their free will."

"Eveny, what are you—" Caleb begins to say.

But I cut him off by continuing with the brief incantation Chloe taught me. "*M'lage ou. M'lage ou. M'lage ou*," I say quickly, the Creole version of *I release you*.

There's a brief swirling wind in the alley, and then everything goes still.

Caleb pulls away. "What did you just do, Eveny?"

"I let you go," I tell him. "Officially. So you're not obligated to protect me anymore. You and your family have your life back. And if I die, you still live."

His eyes get even bigger. "Eveny, no, you don't know what you're doing!"

"I know exactly what I'm doing."

"But you just broke the bond between us! That means I won't know where you are if you're in trouble and you need me!"

I take a deep breath. "I know that. So you're free now. Get on with your life."

"Eveny!" he begins again, but I shake my head.

"It's all taken care of," I say quickly. "Chloe told you about the lip gloss, right? We'll find the killer tonight, and then you'll have nothing to worry about anymore."

"What if it doesn't work?" Caleb asks. "And what about the future? The threat to you won't end tonight."

"But your responsibility to me is over," I say firmly. Then I steel myself for the lie I'm about to tell. "I don't need you anymore, Caleb."

He begins to protest, but I don't stay to listen.

I run back inside and stand in the doorway for a moment, expecting him to come after me. Although I fully intend to push him away if he does, I'm still disappointed when the door behind me doesn't open at all.

But there's no time to think about it, because they're announcing this year's Mardi Gras king and queen, and the crowd is going wild. Pascal is already on stage, wearing a crown and a sash that says KING OF CARREFOUR. I'm not surprised; apparently he won last year too, and if I were a betting woman, I'd say that he probably asked the spirits for some favors during a possession ceremony.

"And now, it's time to announce this year's Mardi Gras queen!" says the announcer, a silver-haired, faux-tanned man in a tux. Someone hands him an envelope, and as he opens it, his expression changes. He looks back at the crowd and says, "Well, this is unusual! For the first time in the history of this town's Mardi Gras Ball, we have a dead tie for queen. We've split the winner's bouquet in half, but we only have one crown and one sash, though, ladies, so you'll have to share!"

The crowd laughs lightly and then quiets down again in anticipation.

"This year's first Mardi Gras queen should be no surprise to any of you, since she was last year's queen too," the man says in his booming voice. "Let's welcome Peregrine Marceau!"

The crowd erupts in applause as Peregrine glides toward the stage in a slinky black dress and red-soled Christian Louboutin heels. She accepts the small cluster of roses handed to her, as well as a kiss on the cheek from the host.

"So, queen number one, would you prefer the sash or the crown?" The host holds up a sparkly tiara in one hand and a pretty purple sash in the other.

"The crown," Peregrine coos into the microphone without missing a beat. "I've brought my own sash."

The crowd gasps as Chloe appears at the foot of the stage and hands over Audowido. He wraps himself around Peregrine and hisses at the audience while the host nervously holds out her crown. She laughs and puts it on as Audowido slithers around her shoulders.

"And now, for the announcement of the second queen," the host says, inching away from Peregrine. I glance at Chloe, because who else could it be? I know the voting is fixed by the sosyete. She's lingering near the front of the stage, smiling up at the host.

"Drumroll, please!" the host says, and the drummer in the small orchestra acquiesces with a slow snare roll. "Tonight's second queen is . . . Eveny Cheval!"

For a moment, I'm sure I've heard him wrong, but when I look up at Peregrine, she's smiling at me knowingly, and I realize this is her version of making peace with me. She's somehow fixed it so that I get to be her co-queen, which she's expecting will mean a lot more to me than it actually does. As applause echoes around the room, Margaux appears from somewhere behind me and gives me a not-so-gentle shove toward the stage. "What are you waiting for?" she hisses. "Go on!"

My feet carry me through the cheering crowd toward the stage. The announcer squints at me as I walk up. "Are you Eveny Cheval?" he asks.

"Yes," I say, glancing at Peregrine, who looks triumphant, as if this moment is the answer to all our problems.

The announcer offers his hand to help me on stage, and after ascertaining that I don't have a reptile concealed anywhere on me, he drops the sash over my head and hands me a bouquet of roses before retreating. Peregrine squeezes my hand and leans toward my ear. I expect her to say something sarcastic, but instead, she whispers, "If I've got to share this with anyone, it might as well be you."

I look at her in surprise just as Pascal slides between us. "Looks like we're a threesome tonight, ladies," he says in a Barry White voice as he drapes his arms around our waists.

"You're truly disgusting," Peregrine says cheerfully, wriggling out of his grip. I do the same, smacking his roving hand away.

"Well, folks," the host cuts back in. "Thanks for coming tonight. Please get home safely!"

The band launches into a slow version of "New York, New York," which makes me homesick, and above us, the houselights come on. "It's only ten thirty," I say, puzzled.

Peregrine shakes her head at me. "The ball always ends early so that the controlling sosyete has plenty of time to make it to New Orleans. The rest of the town just thinks it's because the Main Street district has an eleven o'clock noise ordinance curfew.

"Meet us outside in ten minutes," Peregrine adds before disappearing into the crowd.

I'm escorted off stage, and I head over to find Liv, who's been dancing with Drew all night. She's smiling in disbelief as I approach.

"Congratulations, girl!" she exclaims.

She hugs me, and I hug tightly back. "Thanks," I say, a little embarrassed. "It's no big deal."

"I beg to differ," she says. "Dude, you just got crowned queen of the biggest ball of the year!"

"Co-queen," I say.

"A mere technicality," she replies.

I change the subject. "So where'd Drew go? I wanted to say good-bye to him too."

"He just went to the bathroom. He'll be right back. Where's Caleb?"

I frown. "I don't know."

"Did you two have a fight?"

"Something like that," I mumble.

"Do you need a ride home?"

"Peregrine and Chloe can drive me," I promise. "But enough about me. So has Drew kissed you yet?"

She looks so excited that I can't help but smile as she exclaims, "Yes! Totally! And Eveny, he is *such* a good kisser! I think there's really a future in this."

I pull her into a fierce hug. "I'm so happy for you," I murmur. I hold on just a moment longer than I have to, because who knows what will happen tonight? "Thanks for being my friend," I say.

She pulls away and looks at me with concern. "What's wrong, Eveny?"

I shake my head. "Nothing."

I turn to walk away and collide with Arelia, who's hurrying

in the opposite direction. "What, now that you've been voted the queen of the ball, you're too good to watch where you're going?" she demands.

I realize that she looks like she's been crying. "What's wrong?" I ask. "Are you okay?"

"What do you care?" she asks, sniffling.

That's when I realize that she's one of the few people at the ball I haven't kissed yet. Knowing she'll think I'm completely nuts since I've already seen and ignored her several times tonight, I dive in and give her a quick peck on the cheek. "What the hell?" she demands, her hand flying to her face like I've burned her.

But I'm too frozen to reply. That's because a raspberry-red mark has bloomed on her cheek, exactly where my lips met her skin.

"It's you," I breathe.

She narrows her eyes. "*What's* me?"

"You're the one who killed Glory," I say, my voice hollow with disbelief.

Her gaze slides away from me. "Oh, honestly, Eveny, haven't we been through this already? Just because Glory mentioned my name doesn't mean anything."

"No," I say. "But the red stain on your cheek does. You've been lying about what happened that night."

She reaches up and touches her face in confusion just as I spot Caleb across the room. "Caleb!" I cry, gesturing wildly. He looks confused, but he hurries over.

"You okay?" he asks.

"It was Arelia," I tell him tersely.

He looks at her, and she winds her finger in a circle around her ear to indicate that I'm crazy. "What are you talking about, Eveny?" he asks.

"The red mark from my lip gloss," is all I need to say to make him understand.

"She's obviously losing her mind," Arelia begins to protest.

But Caleb interrupts her, his eyes blazing. "You're absolutely sure?" he asks me.

"Positive," I say.

"Okay, I'll take care of it," he says, already grabbing her arm. She's struggling and trying to tell us something, but we both ignore her. The red mark speaks for itself. "Hurry. Go join the others and explain. I'll be along as soon as I can," he says.

I hesitate. "Will you be okay?"

"I'm fine, Eveny. Just go. Tell Peregrine and Chloe what's going on."

I pause and look Arelia in the eye. "I don't know what your game is, or what you hoped to accomplish here," I say. "But it's over. You're done."

"Eveny, you have to let me explain!" she cries, but Caleb is already dragging her away.

He looks back once, and as our eyes lock, he mouths, *Go*.

I run outside, where Peregrine's Aston Martin is idling at the curb.

"What took you so long?" Peregrine calls out the driver's-side window. Chloe, Oscar, and Patrick are wedged in the backseat.

"It's Arelia," I say quickly. I cross in front of the car and get into the passenger seat quickly as they all stare at me. "She's the traitor," I say as I buckle my seat belt. "She's from Main de Lumière."

"The lip gloss?" Chloe asks.

I nod as Peregrine guns the engine. "I can't believe it," she says in a tight voice as she roars away from the curb. "Damn it!"

"Where's Caleb?" Chloe asks after a minute. "He should be here with us, protecting you."

"He's not my protector anymore," I tell them. Peregrine gasps and Chloe sighs in realization.

"What?" Oscar asks.

"She let him go," Chloe answers sadly for me. "Eveny, do you realize what you've done?"

"Yes. I've given him his life back," I say.

"Or you've doomed us all," Peregrine whispers after a moment.

She floors the accelerator, and as the speedometer creeps past ninety, we all stop talking.

We roar through the bayou toward New Orleans and our date with destiny.

31

We're all mostly quiet on the way to New Orleans as we digest the revelation about Arelia. "I just can't believe she'd betray us like that," Peregrine says four times before falling silent again.

It's not until we get to the edge of the city that Oscar speaks up. "You know, Patrick and I were suspicious of her all along. I mean, the way she was always lurking around and glaring at everyone . . ."

"You never thought to mention that?" Peregrine asks.

"You never listen to us," Oscar says. "You act like we don't have brains."

Chloe jumps in before Peregrine makes the situation worse. "Oscar, Patrick, we're very grateful for your protection. Peregrine's just on edge."

"Of course I am," Peregrine says sharply. "This girl who's

been acting like our friend for years has just been lying in wait to murder us. It's a lot to digest."

"I just can't understand her motives," I say. "She had everything she wanted."

"Not everything," Peregrine says. "We were always going to be more powerful, more beautiful, and more privileged than her. We're queens, and she's not. Some people can't handle coming in second."

I think about my first day in the Hickories, when Arelia snapped at me that it had taken her years to become a Doll, and I had no right to assume that doors would open for me just because of my family name. "She did seem jealous," I admit. "It's just a long leap from envy to joining Main de Lumière and murdering innocent people."

"You said yourself that Glory mentioned Arelia's name the night she died," Peregrine says.

"I know," I reply. "I guess I should have listened to my gut all along, but it seemed so farfetched. I'm an idiot."

"You're not an idiot," Chloe says as Peregrine begins to weave her Aston Martin swiftly through the city streets toward the heart of the French Quarter. "If anything, we're the ones who talked you out of suspecting her. But let's try to forget about Arelia for the time being and focus on what we have to do, okay? Tonight's important, and our minds have to be clear."

"Fine," Peregrine says.

I look out the window and feel a little dazed as I try to turn my thoughts to the task at hand. The streets of New Orleans are heaving with people, many of them wearing hundreds of strings of beads as well as elaborate masks and, in some cases, feather headdresses. The city itself is saturated in bright colors, its soundtrack a cacophony of blaring trumpets, banging drums, and laughing revelers. People swig huge beers and bright red drinks, trip over each other, fall on the pavement, and sing off-key as we inch past on some of the side streets that aren't closed to traffic. Peregrine's jaw is set, and her lips are pressed together in a fine line as she drives.

"I've never seen anything like this," I say as a woman near our car screams up at several men hanging off an ornate balcony, pulls up her tank top to flash them, and receives a shower of beads and catcalls in reply.

Peregrine finally makes a right turn on a side street and pulls the car into a disabled parking spot along the curb. As we get out and head toward the back door of a big mansion, Chloe explains, "We were here last year to take part in the ceremony with our mothers' sosyete—that always happens when a sosyete is a year away from inheriting its power—but this year, we're the ones with the control." The words make me shudder. Control seems like the wrong way to put it when we're really just players in a game set up long before we were born.

Peregrine unlocks the mansion's back door and flips on the lights inside. A huge, opulent parlor, all done in black and white marble, is illuminated before us.

"Beautiful place," I say.

"It's ours, you know," Chloe says, turning to me. "This mansion."

"Ours?" I ask.

"Yours, mine, and Peregrine's," she responds. "The great-great-great-grandmothers willed it to us. It's our haven for practicing magic in New Orleans."

"And," Peregrine says, "our occasional place to get hammered and hook up."

Chloe nudges me. "You and Caleb should come here some weekend. It's really romantic."

I swallow hard. "I'm pretty sure Caleb and I are done."

Chloe pats my back. "Don't give up on him yet. What you two have . . ." She doesn't finish her sentence.

"We don't have anything," I say after a pause.

"You're wrong," she says. "And now that it's not his responsibility to protect you anymore . . ."

Peregrine gives me a sour look over her shoulder as she leads us into the kitchen, which has beige marble countertops and state-of-the-art stainless steel appliances. In the corner sits a teak bar with several bottles of liquor on top. "Chloe," she says, "I think it's pretty clear Eveny has ended things forever with Caleb." My heart lurches, and I feel ill as she turns and says sweetly, "Champagne, guys? We're fully stocked, and hello, we've just escaped a murderer! Shouldn't we be celebrating?"

I look into the fridge, where the top shelf is lined with

at least a dozen bottles of champagne with bright yellow foil wrappers.

"I'll have a glass," Patrick says.

"Me too," Oscar adds.

"Me three," Chloe says quickly. "Eveny'll have one too. Right?"

"Um," I say weakly. I should be feeling relieved, but instead, I just feel oddly unsettled. Knowing that Arelia was acting like our friend while she planned our murders unsettles me. It also reminds me that the deepest threats can come from the people you trust the most. I wonder if the person who betrayed my mom was someone she trusted too.

Peregrine plugs her iPhone into a pair of silver speakers and pulls up a playlist. A moment later, there's music blasting, and Chloe, Patrick, and Oscar head into the kitchen to do shots.

"For one night, Eveny, do you think you could stop being so lame?" Peregrine asks, handing me a flute of champagne. "Let loose. Have fun. We deserve this."

Margaux, Pascal, and Justin arrive ten minutes later, just as Peregrine is joining Chloe, Oscar, and Patrick for another round of tequila shots in the kitchen.

"The traffic was killer," Pascal reports as he strolls in and tosses his keys on a coffee table.

"Maybe if you hadn't stopped and leered at every topless girl we passed, we would have gotten here faster," Margaux says. She pauses and looks around. "Hey, where's Arelia? I thought she was with you guys."

Chloe and Peregrine emerge from the kitchen, looking uneasy. I turn the music down, and for a moment, we just stand in uncomfortable silence.

"What?" Margaux demands. "What happened? Is she okay?"

"Margaux," Chloe says gently. "Arelia's the one who killed Glory."

"That's impossible," Margaux says instantly. "This is some kind of a joke, right?"

"I'm afraid not," Peregrine says. She quickly recaps the story about the lip gloss and the crimson stain on Arelia's cheek. Before she finishes speaking, Margaux is already shaking her head vigorously.

"No, no, no, no," she says. "This is all wrong." She turns to me, her eyes blazing. "What did you say in your charm? Tell me the *exact* words!"

Startled, I explain that I asked that the gloss turn blood red on the face of the person who was lying about the night Glory died.

Margaux puts her hand over her mouth, and for a moment, she's silent. "She *was* lying about that night," she says finally. "But it's not what you think. She didn't kill Glory. She *loved* Glory." When we all stare at her blankly, she exclaims, "She and Glory were dating, you morons! They thought you guys would ban them from the sosyete if you found out." She turns to Peregrine and adds, "You're not exactly the most tolerant people in the world."

We gape at her. "Are you sure?" It's Chloe who finally speaks. "Maybe she and Glory got into some kind of fight—"

Margaux cuts her off. "Just like I've already said, she was with me at the time Glory was killed. I swear on the graves of my ancestors." She turns to me. "You kissed my cheek too, didn't you? You know I'm not lying!"

"She's right," I say uneasily.

"Kiss her again," Peregrine demands. When I hesitate, she says, "Do it!"

I give Margaux a quick peck on the cheek, and nothing happens. A knot of dread is forming in the pit of my stomach. Margaux's telling the truth; it wasn't Arelia, which means the real killer is still out there.

"I told you so," Margaux says, her face pink with anger.

"We have to let Caleb know we screwed up," I say.

"*You* screwed up," Peregrine corrects, turning to glare at me.

"I'll call him now," I mutter. But I dial his number three times, and each time, it goes directly to voice mail.

"We just have to wait for him to get here," Chloe says.

"I'm so sorry," I whisper.

"You should be," Peregrine says. "Not only is the Main de Lumière traitor still out there, but now we're down one sosyete member for our ceremony at a time we could use all the help we can get. Excellent work, Eveny."

Caleb arrives forty-five minutes later, just after twelve thirty, his suit rumpled, his eyes wild.

"I was wrong about Arelia," I blurt out as soon as he walks through the door.

He glances at me as he greets Peregrine and Chloe. "Yeah," he says, running his hand distractedly over the top of his head. "I know. She told me everything."

"What happened to her?" I ask in a small voice, my heart hammering.

"She's fine. She's with Boniface. She was too shaken up to come along."

"She must hate my guts," I say.

"You were only doing what you thought was right," Caleb says after a minute. "I don't think she blames you. She knows she lied."

"But that was her secret to keep if she wanted to," I say.

"The bigger problem," he says, "is that the killer is still out there."

Peregrine comes over and whispers something to him, and he disappears for a few minutes with her. I'm sitting by myself in the corner of the room, nursing the same glass of champagne I was handed an hour ago, when he gets back, a tall glass of what I assume is gin and tonic in his hand. He doesn't look at me once as he joins the group.

"Loosen up, baby," Pascal purrs at me as he makes his way to the kitchen for another cocktail. He's slightly unsteady on his feet. "This is supposed to be fun."

"Don't you understand?" I shoot back. "We could die tonight. We don't know who's trying to hurt us."

He snorts. "Nothing's going to happen here. Geez, Eveny, could you just give the let's-save-the-world crap a rest for once?"

When the clock strikes one, the whole group moves upstairs and out to the huge balcony overlooking Chartres Street, two blocks away from the famous Bourbon Street. The road below us is still throbbing with people, and I back against the wall, my whole body tense, as Peregrine and Chloe lean over the rail and flirt with guys, and as Pascal throws beads out to the dozens of girls who seem all too happy to show him their breasts.

"I love Mardi Gras!" he shouts, laughing, as a pair of twins flash him enthusiastically. I catch Caleb's eye for a millisecond and am heartened to see him looking as uneasy as I feel. I brace myself and head over to him.

"Hey," I say. "Are you mad at me about Arelia?"

"No, of course not," he says. "But why did you release me from being your protector?"

I'm startled at the anger in his eyes. "I was trying to help you."

"I didn't ask for your help."

"You didn't have to. It wasn't fair to you, Caleb. The whole system of you having to put your life on the line for me? I can't ask you to do that."

"That wasn't your decision to make." He walks away before I can say anything else.

I turn to see Peregrine staring at me with an indecipherable expression on her face. She looks away after a moment and claps her hands. "People!" she yells, and then when everyone just goes right on reveling, she whistles loudly, and the conversation on the balcony comes to a halt. "It's time," she says.

The world below us on Chartres suddenly seems far away and disconnected as she leads the group into the house and into a huge chamber that looks like a much larger and more ornate version of my parlor. Several crystal chandeliers hang in the shadows on the ceiling, and blood-red candles flicker everywhere.

Peregrine asks us to join hands, and Caleb winds up on my right side. His grasp is so warm and comforting, it makes my heart hurt.

Pascal grabs my other hand and says, "Just go with it. Open yourself. There's nothing in the world like being possessed. On Mardi Gras, it's supposed to be positively *orgasmic*."

I play along as Peregrine moves to the center of the circle, lights a cluster of dandelion and anise seed and calls to Eloi Oke. Chloe steps into the middle of the circle as she and Peregrine raise their hands to the sky and begin to dance in the center of the room. They're chanting softly, and as the tempo picks up, the rest of the group begins chanting too.

"Open yourself, Eveny," Margaux hisses at me across the circle just before her eyes turn empty. "Don't be so selfish as to think you're above all this. It's your fault Arelia's not here to help us."

I glance at Caleb, but his eyes are already glazed over; he seems to have slipped into another level of consciousness along with everyone else.

One by one, around the circle, I see people's expressions go blank. Everyone's still singing the same phrase over and over—something like, "*Esprits du passé, entre en moi.*"

I search my rudimentary French knowledge; they're saying something along the lines of *Spirits, enter into me.*

As a breeze picks up inside the room, I feel something pushing at the corner of my mind. I know without asking that it's a spirit trying to get in; it feels like the pressure just before Glory's spirit slipped into my body at Cristof's. I push the presence away; I have to keep my wits about me tonight.

Move aside, girl, a hissing voice in my head says suddenly. *I want to use you.*

"No," I say aloud. Caleb glances quickly at me and then goes back to looking blank. Everyone else in the circle seems lost in his or her own world; they're all stumbling around now. They're all possessed.

Move aside, I said! The voice in my head is more insistent now, and I mentally push back. The spirit trying to get in is stronger than I expected. *Do you really think you can stop me?*

I summon all my energy and push back. "Yes," I say aloud.

"I do." There's a sharp pain on the left side of my head, and then, all is quiet, and the pressure is gone. The spirit has moved on.

Soon, the rest of the Dolls begin acting like they've gone crazy. I watch, my breath caught in my throat, as Margaux flings herself to the ground, wailing and rolling around. Peregrine's eyes are wide and her limbs rubbery as she contorts into Gumby-like positions that no human body should be able to move into. Justin is lying on his back, languidly making snow angels on the marble floor, while Pascal and Chloe are draped all over each other, their hands roaming each other's bodies. Even Patrick and Oscar are dancing in the corner with blank expressions, and Caleb is leaning against the wall, moaning softly with his eyes closed.

I take a deep breath and pretend that I'm possessed too, so that the other spirits won't get suspicious.

I cringe as Oscar begins to rub up against me. I take a deep breath and let it happen for a moment, playing the part. Then I begin to dance, as if the spirit inside of me would rather do that than be groped. Oscar follows, grunting at me, but then he loses interest and moves over to Margaux, who's rubbing herself against a chair now.

Peregrine finally writhes over to the giant triangle in the corner of the room, picks up the wand that lies beside it, and strikes it. The sound reverberates through the house, and everyone stops what they're doing instantly and heads in a single file line toward a door in the corner of the room.

Peregrine opens it, revealing a big walk-in closet containing at least a hundred silk robes in varying shades of gold, green, and purple. One wall is filled entirely with elaborate feathered masks propped on long, wooden shelves.

Without speaking, the others begin shedding their clothes with a complete lack of self-consciousness. Margaux simply steps out of her dress, bra-less, and casually grabs a robe from the wall, cinching it around her waist. Chloe and Peregrine are both wearing elaborate, lacy lingerie sets, but they don't seem worried about anyone seeing them as they shed their dresses too and step into robes. Everyone is still possessed, as evidenced by the completely empty looks on their faces, and my heart thuds faster as I realize I'll need to take off my clothes too.

For an instant, I could swear Caleb's hesitating. But then his face goes blank, and he begins taking his suit off slowly. *At least he's not really in there*, I tell myself as I unzip my dress.

I try not to look as he peels off his jacket then his shirt, revealing abs that look like they've been chiseled from stone and arms that ripple with strength. I bite my lower lip as he unbuckles his belt, unzips his pants and takes them off, revealing a pair of charcoal gray boxer briefs. I hurry to shrug off my own dress as he throws on a green robe from the closet. It feels like Caleb is watching me, but he goes back to swaying languidly as soon as I look in his direction. I swallow hard, slip into a rich emerald robe that matches Caleb's, and cinch the belt tightly.

Once everyone is done donning robes, Peregrine grabs a mask—an elaborate white one with gold swirls and black feathers—and pulls it on. Everyone quickly follows suit, so I take a deep breath, pick up a gold mask with long white and green feathers, pull it over my face, and watch as Caleb puts on a black mask trimmed in gold.

Peregrine makes a grunting sound, then she emerges from the closet and strikes the triangle again. Everyone instantly lines up and follows her down the stairs and toward the front door of the mansion. I fall into line, just in front of Caleb, and when I feel his hand on my hips through the cool silk of my robe, I have to remind myself that it's not really him, that he's not really there. Still, his touch sears me.

The front door opens ahead of us, and as it does, the sounds of the outside world pour in. The street is still over-flowing with drunken revelers, and many of them turn to stare as we move out of the house and into the crowd.

"I told you this is the place with the sluts in robes," I hear a rough-looking bearded guy in a stained T-shirt slur to his friend. "I call the hot black chick with the crazy hair."

"I'll take the blonde," his friend growls back.

I watch in horror as the two men move toward Peregrine and Chloe and begin trying to talk to them. When Peregrine and Chloe don't respond and instead just continue swaying their way down the street, the rougher-looking one who'd called dibs on Peregrine reaches for her, his hand roughly grazing her breasts. She doesn't react at all. *They're not really in there*, I tell myself. *They don't know this is happening.* But then Caleb comes out of nowhere and barrels into the guy groping Peregrine.

"What the f—?" the guy growls, turning to Caleb. But Caleb is flailing wildly now and catches the bearded guy square in the jaw with his elbow. An instant later, his knee connects with the other guy's crotch, sending him sprawling and wincing in pain.

"Dude, he's just as effed up as they are," says the guy on the ground, clutching his crotch protectively and rolling away from Caleb. "Maybe he's their boyfriend or something."

Caleb sways unsteadily away from the men, and if I didn't know better, I'd think he was herding an oblivious Peregrine and Chloe in the other direction.

"Caleb?" I call out, suddenly sure that he's faking it too. But then he goes back to writhing strangely, and my heart sinks.

The group stays loosely together as we turn left, heading toward the bigger crowd on Bourbon. One by one, members of our group begin drifting off, and I resist the urge to try to protect them from the crowd. I remind myself that they've all come here willingly. I cringe as strangers reach out from the crowd to grope me, and I cinch my belt tighter.

The closer we get to Bourbon Street, the wilder the crowd is. I'm losing sight of more of the members of our group, and I feel a sense of panic setting in. The only Dolls in my eyesight are Pascal and Margaux, and both of them are up ahead, getting swallowed in the sea of people.

"Wait!" I cry out before clamping a hand over my mouth. I'm supposed to look possessed. I take a deep breath, heart thudding, and continue to play along, although I dance through the crowd more quickly now, trying to catch up to the others.

I feel a pair of hands grab my waist, and as I try to wriggle away, the grip grows tighter. I feel a lump of fear in my throat as I pull harder and the hands begin pulling me back.

"Let me go!" I cry, dropping the possessed act. When I feel myself being dragged forcefully away from the street, I begin to scream.

All around me, people are too caught up in their own drinking, partying, singing, and making out to notice me. I grab a man's hand as I'm dragged past, but he merely shakes me off. "Help!" I scream, clutching at a group of guys with bloodshot eyes, who are swaying on their feet as they discuss what to do next. The only one I make contact with brushes away the spot I'd grabbed like he's swatting a fly. I cry out once more, struggling against the person behind me, who's dressed all in black. He's pulling me toward a darkened alley.

"Just come quietly," he says suddenly in my ear. "I have a knife, Eveny, and I'm more than happy to use it on anyone who tries to save you."

"Who are you?" I struggle to turn around in the shadows and see his face, the top half of which is totally covered with an elaborate silver mask. Just then, we pass beneath a streetlight and I gasp. His mouth is completely covered in crimson stains, just like the single one that showed up on Arelia's cheek. But how? I haven't kissed anyone on the lips tonight.

I realize suddenly, though, that Liv did. While wearing my gloss. "Drew," I breathe.

The pieces tumble into place quickly. The way Drew happened to show up at my door right after I arrived back in town. The eagerness with which he kept hanging around even after he realized I was interested in Caleb. The way he moved on seamlessly to Liv, which still kept him in my immediate circle of trusted friends. The truck crash that would have most likely killed me if I hadn't reached for my stone.

He's the Main de Lumière soldier, the one Aloysius Vauclain said had gone rogue.

There's only one question left. "Why the hell are you doing this?"

"What, did you think we were friends?" His laughter is coarse and cruel. "I know all about you and your slutty sister queens. I know how you've been making yourselves richer at our expense. You're everything that's wrong with this society, but it stops tonight."

"You don't understand, Drew," I protest as he drags me farther into the alley. "You're making a mistake."

"Shut up, Eveny," he sneers. "And try to relax. It'll only hurt for a minute when I stop your heart."

32

*D*rew pulls me toward the end of a long, closed passageway between two dilapidated buildings, and as he does, the sounds of Bourbon Street become more and more muted behind us. As Drew jerks me closer, he presses the knife deeper into my side in warning. He's already sliced through my robe, and I can feel the blade cutting into my skin.

"I've been training for this moment for a long time," he says as we move deeper into the blackness. He shoves me against a wall. "Nothing's getting in my way tonight."

Hands shaking, I reach up and rip his mask off. I'm unprepared for the wide range of emotions I see playing across his face. His features are twisted in anger, but I also see sadness and regret.

"How long have you been part of Main de Lumière?" I ask.

He tears off my mask too and pins me against the wall. "They came to me when I was thirteen and told me everything: the way you zandara whores destroy the balance of the universe; the way you keep getting richer while people like me suffer; the way every little thing in your pathetic lives is fake."

"They're just using you, Drew. Don't you realize that?"

This earns me a slap across the face. "You don't know a damned thing. We're not in Carrefour anymore. This is my game now." He calms down after a pause and resumes his story. "They told me that ending your life was the only way to fix things. All I had to do was learn Main de Lumière's tactics and wait for you to come home."

Something in his eyes flickers, and he looks away.

"But you didn't even know I'd be back," I say.

"Of course I did. Main de Lumière knew. It was only a matter of time until your aunt decided you'd be safer in Carrefour. And I was paid handsomely to train in methods of murdering zandara practitioners while we waited for your return."

I reach for my Stone of Carrefour, but Drew sees me and grabs my hand before I can get to it. He pins both of my arms against the wall above my head and sneers at me. "Really, Eveny? You really thought I'd let you use your evil magic on me?"

I struggle to get away, but he holds me tighter. Finally, I relax my arms. "I don't understand how you could hate me so much."

"It's not really about you," he says. "It's about the bigger picture."

I take a deep breath. "You were my friend when we were kids—my mom was friends with your mom—and you threw that all away because they fed you some lies about zandara and promised to pay you?"

He glares at me. "You're stupider than I thought. Of course it's not just for money. Once they told me about who you really were, I began to understand how much you queens are screwing with fate and the lives of my friends and family. I saw the good Main de Lumière was doing by eliminating people like you from the world. And you know what? I wanted to be a part of it."

"How can you say that?"

"There's a balance to the universe," he says flatly, almost as if he's reciting something he's memorized. "And you and your slutty, greedy friends have been violating that balance. We're restoring the world to its natural order."

"Murdering people isn't the answer."

He casually twirls his knife, studying it as it catches the light of a streetlamp. "I don't see another way, and neither did Général Vauclain. My orders have always been to kill you as soon as you started using your powers. And if I let you go back to Carrefour, I won't have another chance."

"Why me?" I demand. "Why wouldn't Main de Lumière just have you go after one of the other queens years ago?"

For the first time, he looks genuinely surprised. "Because of how powerful you are, of course."

"But Peregrine and Chloe are way more powerful than I

am," I protest in confusion. "I'm only just beginning to learn."

He studies me for a moment, then laughs in disbelief. "You don't know?"

"Know *what*?"

He grabs a handful of my hair and pulls, jerking my head to the side so hard that I wince in pain. He holds the knife to my throat. "It's because of your father, stupid." I can see him searching my face to discern whether I know what he's talking about.

"Drew, I don't know my dad," I say desperately. "You know that."

"I thought you were lying," he says, almost to himself. "Well, you may as well hear the truth since you're about to die anyhow. Your deadbeat father is a very powerful king in the world of dark magic."

My heart thumps against my chest as I wait for him to say more.

"He's the leader of a sosyete in Georgia that practices andaba, which is like zandara, except they use bones instead of flowers to commune with spirits, and men have the power instead of women."

"That can't be true. My aunt would have told me. *Someone* would have told me."

"Apparently not. Your dad fell in love with your mom, married her, and boom, you were conceived. Her sister queens didn't trust him, though, and he didn't trust them. He thought they were irresponsible with how they practiced magic, the way they were so generous with themselves and so inconsiderate of those less fortunate."

"Less fortunate people like you and your mom," I whisper.

Drew steps closer and his expression grows more menacing. He presses me against the wall and draws a small line across my chest with his knife. I gasp in pain as my own blood streams, hot and wet, down my robe.

"You know *nothing* about my mother," he growls. "Let's just get that straight."

I'm already feeling light-headed. I struggle to maintain my composure. "Go on," I manage.

"The three queens—your mom, Peregrine's mom, and Chloe's mom—were actually close to listening to your dad and changing their selfish little ways," Drew continues. "And then one day, he just up and left. He left your mom; he left you. And they realized he was using them, drawing on their power to enhance his."

"That can't be true," I say. "My mother loved him until the day she died."

"Then your mother was a pretty stupid woman. Face it, Eveny, you and your mom didn't mean anything to your dad."

The words cut deep. "But he came back," I protest. "He promised to look after me."

Drew guffaws. "Well, he's doing a superb job of that right now, isn't he?" He presses me against the wall and holds the knife just below my collarbone. "You see this?" he asks, nicking the skin of my chest with the tip of his blade. He pulls the knife against my skin, and I watch dully as he opens up a large wound. A thick trail of blood begins a steady descent down my body.

"This blood," he continues, staring at the wash of crimson sliding down my chest, "makes you the most powerful queen in the *world*. You're the only one we've ever known who has a king for a father and a queen for a mother. There's no telling how powerful you could be if properly trained. But right now? I have *all* the power, and you have none. And when I kill you, I'll be restoring balance to the world. I'll be a hero."

"Don't you understand that I agree with you? We made some mistakes, but now I'm trying to make things right."

Drew snorts. "By performing your most powerful ceremony of the year?"

"It wasn't to gain anything for ourselves! It was only to protect Carrefour against Main de Lumière! And to restore the Périphérie!"

"You really think I'm that stupid? Eveny, it was to gather favors so your sosyete could continue to make themselves richer and us poorer."

"That's not true." My voice is growing weaker. The world around me is starting to swim. "Was it you who killed Glory?" I whisper.

He looks down instead of meeting my gaze. "She figured out who I was. I was trying to turn her to our side, and it went wrong."

"But she was your friend," I say.

"So are you, supposedly. But unfortunately that doesn't change a thing," he says casually. He looks at his watch and sighs heavily. "I'm afraid we're nearly out of time. It's been nice knowing you, Eveny, it really has. But you're an abomination of nature. You're of the devil. And I'm afraid I'm going to have to kill you now."

His words are smooth and determined, but something flickers in his eyes as he says them, something like regret, and I use his moment of indecision to muster the last of my strength and pull away. The blood covering my body makes me slippery enough that he loses his grip, but I only manage to stumble a few feet down the alley before he's on top of me. His knife glints angry in the light again as it slices through the air toward my heart, but I twist at the last minute and it lodges deeply in my upper left shoulder instead.

I cry out in agony. This cut finds muscle, and the pain is excruciating as he removes the knife and prepares to bring it down again.

Once again, I roll out of the way just in time, so that his knife clatters against the pavement instead of cutting through to my heart. But this only makes him more furious, and he's far stronger than me. I try to touch my Stone of Carrefour, my only hope, but he sees me going for it and grabs my wrists.

"You're not using that damned thing again," he growls. "Not like you did when I tried to kill you in the truck crash." He pins my arms above me against the ground using his left hand, and with his right, he raises the knife again.

I can no longer move. The blood is flowing out of me too quickly. My eyelids are growing heavy. My whole body throbs. And as Drew holds the knife over me, mumbling something about my heartbeat being silenced so that evil can be stricken from the world, I close my eyes and prepare to die.

But suddenly, out of nowhere, something springs from the darkness and pounces on Drew, knocking him off me. My eyelids are fluttering, and I'm finding it hard to breathe. I can hardly see. In fact, it's not until I hear the shape mutter a curse that I realize it's a man. All I can see are shadows, blurs.

"It's going to be okay, Eveny," he says, and for the first time, I realize that it's Caleb. Caleb has come back for me.

"Watch out," I croak. "Drew has . . . knife . . ."

My voice is fading with my consciousness, but I'm aware of Caleb grunting, "I know."

The shadows rise and fall around me, and I can hear fists connecting with faces, heads hitting pavement, grunts of pain. I muster all my strength and reach for my Stone of Carrefour.

My heart is full of only one thing: a fierce desire to protect Caleb. And when my fingers brush the stone, that's enough to invoke some kind of magic, even without words or herbs. I watch in frozen surprise as a bubble with a faint greenish tint surrounds Caleb. Drew attempts to stab him, but the knife just bounces off like the bubble is made of iron, not air. Both guys look momentarily confused; I know I'm the only one who can see the protection surrounding Caleb.

"Caleb," I say, and what I'm trying to tell him is that the

magic isn't strong enough, the bubble is already starting to fade. But he seems to realize it too, and this time, as Drew slices toward him again, the knife gets through and gashes through Caleb's upper arm. I hear him cry out, but just as quickly, he spins away and grabs the knife.

Drew rolls over and tries to come after him. He cries out as he lunges forward, his features twisted in anger.

And that's when his chest meets the tip of the knife Caleb is holding unsteadily in his hand. Later, when I try to reconstruct it all in my mind, I'll remember Caleb's eyes widening, his hand going slack, the knife remaining wedged in Drew's chest as he staggers backward and falls.

But right now, the world is still growing dim, and all I know is that Drew has stopped moving and is lying on his back, his eyes wide, the knife lodged deep in the left side of his chest. He makes a gurgling sound, gasps for air, and then goes still.

"Caleb?" I whisper into the nothingness. The noise of Bourbon Street is still very far away. I feel like we're surrounded by overwhelming silence.

"Come on, Eveny," Caleb says, struggling to his feet. "We have to get out of here before someone else from Main de Lumière arrives."

He scoops me up in his arms, wincing, and I'm vaguely aware of the blood flowing from the gaping wound on his shoulder. He begins stumbling back toward Bourbon Street, and as I strain to see behind him, the world begins to fade.

"We just have to find Peregrine or Chloe, and they'll heal you," Caleb says, his voice sounding very far away, although I know I'm still nestled against his blood-soaked chest. "You just have to hold on. . . ."

His voice disappears as I lose consciousness.

I come to for a moment, long enough to register that we're back in the mansion on Chartres Street, and that Caleb is leaning over me on the couch.

"Thank God you're awake," he sighs.

It's only then that I realize Caleb is crying. "Caleb," I say weakly, reaching up to touch his face, which only makes his tears fall faster. He wipes them away.

"I didn't mean to kill him," he says.

"Caleb." I struggle to sit up. He puts his strong arm on my back to support me, and I gaze into his eyes.

"He was coming at me with that knife, Eveny," he says. "I knew he'd come for you next. . . ."

Before I can think what I'm doing, I silence him with a kiss, pressing my lips to his with as much force as I can muster. I feel a sob escape his mouth, and then he's kissing back, passionately, hungrily. "Eveny," he breathes.

He pulls me closer, and I wince, suddenly all too aware of the knife wounds that have shredded my neck and chest.

"I'm so sorry," he gasps, lowering me slowly back down to the couch.

"You came back for me," I murmur.

I look at him in awe as his eyes fill with tears again.

"Of course." He pushes a tendril of my hair out of my face and leans down to kiss me gently on the lips. "I came back because I love you."

It's the last thing I remember before the world once again fades to black.

33

Drew's funeral is the following Wednesday in the Carrefour cemetery.

Peregrine and Chloe had healed me the night of Mardi Gras, and once I was conscious again, the three of us had joined hands and mended Caleb's wounds. Physically, we're no worse for the wear today as we stand beside Drew's grave and watch two cemetery workers from the Périphérie slide his simple oak casket into his family's mausoleum. Our whole sosyete is there, mourning him publicly.

I'm surprised to realize that the tears I'm crying are real. Even though Drew tried to kill me, I still feel a sense of loss over his death. He wasn't all evil.

"He made his own choices, Eveny," Peregrine whispers in my ear as if she knows what I'm thinking.

I nod and dry my eyes, but I'm wondering whether that's

really true. Yes, we all have free will, but in a way, our fates have chosen us already. I've been given power and riches beyond my wildest dreams, and although I don't want either, I know I no longer have a choice. This is my destiny.

The official story of Drew's death—the conclusion the police have come to, anyhow—is that he was murdered by a random stranger during Mardi Gras. Probably someone drunk and confused, everyone is saying.

Aunt Bea, who sat stone-faced while I filled her in on the details of what happened in New Orleans last week, is at the funeral too, sitting beside Drew's mother, who's either entirely uninvolved in her son's deception or is a terribly good actress. Arelia is on Aunt Bea's other side, her eyes red from crying. She'd called me yesterday to apologize for not being truthful from the start about Glory. "I thought everyone would judge me," she said miserably.

Aunt Bea turns and locks eyes with me as the cemetery workers walk away from the gravesite. I force a smile to let her know I'm okay. She's been buzzing around me since I returned from Mardi Gras, apologizing profusely for keeping me in the dark for so long and therefore putting me in danger.

"There's no excuse for how removed and distant I've been these last few weeks," she'd said this morning as we walked to the funeral together. "I couldn't stand to feel like I'd lost another person I loved because I was complicit in all of this. I just wanted to forget that zandara existed. But that means I wasn't there for you. I'm so sorry."

"You don't owe me an apology," I'd told her honestly. "You've always done your best with me. It's up to me from here."

But although the words seemed to make her feel better, I knew they were a lie. Because while the threat of Drew is gone, I have the feeling Main de Lumière isn't going to stop. If anything, they'll be angrier. We've killed two of their own now, and I expect them to come after us with a vengeance. What if there's another sleeper in our midst, someone who's been here as long as—or longer than—Drew? And I still don't know who killed my mother. I don't trust anyone anymore. Except Caleb.

I'd told him, two days after Mardi Gras, the truths Drew had revealed about my father and how powerful my lineage makes me. He'd listened somberly while I spoke, then promised he hadn't known about any of it. "This means you may be in grave danger all the time," he'd said.

"Not if I learn how to use my powers to protect myself," I had replied. "Not if I use them to protect Carrefour."

"It's not up to you," Caleb had said. "It doesn't have to be."

"I don't have a choice," I had replied.

Now, as we begin to shuffle away from Drew's grave and into the pale morning light of the cemetery, I try to catch Caleb's eye across the gravesite, but he doesn't look at me. I know he's still carrying the burden of being the one who killed Drew. I know no one can take that pain away from him.

Liv, who hasn't taken any of my calls in the last week, brushes up against me on the way out of the cemetery.

"Liv," I say. "I'm so, so sorry about what happened to Drew."

I'm unprepared for the anger I see in her eyes as she looks up at me. "I know it's crazy," she says, her voice tight and controlled. "But I have to ask. Did you have anything to do with Drew's death?"

"What?"

Liv frowns. "I know you were in New Orleans too. Drew told me that night, before he left the ball, that he was coming to find you. He said he had to warn you about something. Did you see him?"

"No," I lie. "I didn't."

"Well, then, did something happen between the two of you that I should know about?" she demands. "Because he was talking about you after you said you'd had that fight with Caleb. Like he was obsessed."

"That's crazy," I say without meeting her eye. "He was totally into you."

Liv looks at me suspiciously and presses her lips tightly together. I know she's trying not to cry. "I don't believe you," she says.

My heart breaks a little as she walks away. I'll do what I can to make it up to her in the future, but right now I know she needs some time alone.

Peregrine and Chloe hurry over and flank me as we head back toward our mansions on the cemetery edge.

"How are you feeling?" Chloe asks, putting a hand on my arm.

"Physically, better," I say. I lower my voice and add, "Emotionally? I'm feeling terrible."

"You can't blame yourself," Peregrine says.

"I know. But that doesn't make it any easier."

I'm still mad at them for not telling me about my father. They swore up and down that their mothers had only told them the basics: that my father was involved with some sort of magical sect in Georgia, and that they weren't sure whether to trust him. But they've told me several times that it never occurred to them that his blood might have made Main de Lumière more interested in me.

"We don't actually know that you're any more powerful than we are," Peregrine had said snippily.

But as they walk across the cemetery now, Chloe nudges me gently and says, "When this blows over, we'll get everyone together and talk to your aunt and our mothers. You deserve to know everything they know about your dad and what it means for you. We'll figure out what to do."

They walk away to join Margaux and Arelia, who have already reached the sunshine near Peregrine's back fence.

A few minutes later, I feel someone fall into step beside me, and I know without looking up that it's Caleb. We walk a few steps in silence, and then he gently takes my hand.

"Are you okay?" I ask him.

"Getting there. So, can I take my job back?" he asks. "Officially? I want to be your protector again, Eveny. I almost missed the chance to save you in New Orleans because you broke the link between us. If I hadn't been faking being possessed so I could try to keep an eye on you . . ." He trails off and adds, "I don't want to think what could have happened. As it was, I was almost too late."

"I don't want to put you in a position where you're under any obligation to me. Or where your life is tied to mine."

He stops walking, and when I stop too and look at him, I read frustration across his perfect face. "It has nothing to do with obligation anymore," he says. "Have you thought of the fact that maybe I *want* my life tied to yours?"

We look at each other for a long time, then we begin walking again.

"What if I was just a normal girl?" I ask. "Instead of the most powerful zandara queen in Louisiana?"

"I'd still want to protect you," he says right away. He pauses. "What if I was just a normal guy?"

"I'd still want you around all the time," I say.

We continue to walk in silence, our fingers threaded together, our breath heavy, until we reach my back wall. Caleb helps me over and follows a second later, landing with a soft thud beside me.

He moves closer and pulls me toward him. "If you were just a normal girl, and I was just a normal guy, I'd probably do this"—he kisses me softly—"all the time."

I kiss him back, hungrily, and after a pause, he responds with a hunger of his own. The garden, the woods, Carrefour itself all disappear as I fade into him. He holds me, caresses me, drinks me in like I'm the only thing anchoring him to earth.

When the kiss ends and we finally pull away, there are tears in his eyes. "But I let my guard down once. I let my feelings, my pride get in the way. And you almost died."

"I *didn't* die, though," I whisper. "You saved me."

He shakes his head. "Next time, we might not be so lucky." He takes a deep breath. "Eveny, I love you. But this is why protectors are forbidden from having a relationship with their queens; I can't think straight and protect you when I feel like this."

"But—" I begin.

"I'm sorry," he says. "I'm so sorry. I can't do this. But I'll always be nearby, watching over you if you need me."

"Caleb," I say desperately. "I *do* need you. I need you now. I need you to be with me. I need you to forget all the things we're supposed to do and just follow your heart."

He smiles sadly. "I'm sorry, Eveny. But you know as well as I do that's not how this town works."

And then he's gone, back over the cemetery wall, before I can say anything else. I stare in the direction he disappeared for a very long time, tears streaming down my face, before I whisper, "I love you too."

I turn and walk slowly toward the back door of my house. The world feels like it's been upended again. I want to go after him, to beg him to stay, to plead with him to reconsider. But I saw the resolution in his eyes. I'll have to find another way.

I open the door. The first thing I realize once I'm standing inside is that something feels different. There's a heaviness in the air that puts me instantly on edge.

Before I can say anything, Boniface steps out from the living room, his face creased with concern. "Honey, I didn't know—" he begins, but a voice behind him cuts him off.

"I'll take it from here," says the tall, handsome man who rounds the corner behind Boniface. His hair is sandy, his eyes a brilliant green. I recognize him instantly.

"Dad?" I ask in disbelief.

"Eveny," he says. He crosses the space between us swiftly and pulls me into a tight hug. I'm so shocked, I can barely hug back.

"What are you . . . ?" My brain is suddenly a jumble of questions, and I can't find the words to ask him why he's here. "You left us," I finally manage to say, my voice breaking.

"I had to," he says. "I had to keep you safe. Staying would have put you in terrible danger."

"But . . ." I can hardly believe what I'm seeing. "You came back."

"You needed my help." He touches my cheek gently, and for a second, I'm not thinking about the present; I'm thinking about the moments like this that we missed, the times he should have been there to hold my hand, the instances I felt so abandoned by both of my parents when one of them was out there all along.

"But why now?" I manage. "After all this time?"

"What happened with Main de Lumière is only the beginning, Eveny. You're going to be in danger until we figure out how to stop them for good."

I nod. He's right, of course.

"So the way I see it," he continues gravely, "we have two choices: You and I can run tonight, go somewhere they'll never be able to find us. Or we can stay and do our best to protect this town. It's up to you, Eveny. I'll stand by you, whatever decision you make."

My heart hammers, and my Stone of Carrefour grows hot against my chest. Magic is in my blood—it's who I'm destined to be. My mom believed I'd become the greatest queen the world has ever known, and I won't let her down. I take a deep breath and steel myself. "We'll stay."

"You're sure?" His eyes bore into mine. "You could die trying. You realize that's a risk, don't you? I'll do everything I can to protect you, but there's always a chance. . . ."

"Mom lost her life trying to make things right," I say. "I have to stay—for her. Carrefour was her home. It's *my* home. Everything about this place, it's who I am. I can't run from that anymore."

He stares at me for a minute. "Your mother would be so proud of the young woman you've grown up to be." He smiles sadly. "I'm with you. So let's win back Carrefour and avenge your mom's death. Whatever it takes."

"*Whatever* it takes," I agree, my heart hammering. I don't quite know what to make of my father's return after all these years, but my gut tells me the emotion in his eyes is real. So I push aside thoughts of Caleb, the Dolls, and everything else

I'm responsible for, and for just a second, I let myself believe in a future that isn't fraught with complications and lies.

Outside, a mist begins to rise over the cemetery as the setting sun paints the sky a burning red. By the time morning comes, news of my father's return will have begun to spread. There will be no going back from the decision we're making tonight, the decision to stay and defend what's ours. We've chosen our path.

The only way through the fire is forward. I know that now. And I'm ready to fight.

Acknowledgments

This book was the result of some pretty incredible teamwork, so I'd love to say a huge "thank you" to Holly Root (the world's best literary agent), Nick Harris (who provided the seed from which this book grew and who has been a huge advocate for the story), and Sara Sargent (whose patience, vision, keen editorial eye, and witty emails kept me sane—and made this book a thousand times better). Novelist Wendy Toliver—my longtime friend and the closest thing I have to a writing partner—also supported me every step of the way and speed-read drafts for me in record time. She's a rock star.

Thanks to Jerry Gandolfo of the New Orleans Historic Voodoo Museum for welcoming me into his world and helping me to understand the intricacies of a fascinating spiritual system in which herbs, dolls, spirits, and magic intersect. And of course thanks to the people of New Orleans: your city's beautiful blend of history, culture, food, drink, architecture, excess, faith, and *bon temps* inspires me to no end.

Thanks to the other great folks of Waxman Leavell Literary Agency, The Story Foundation, and Balzer + Bray, especially Sam Howard, Taylor Haggerty, Julianna Wojcik, Alessandra Balzer, Donna Bray, Caroline Sun, Emilie Polster, Stefanie Hoffman, Alison Klapthor, Viana Siniscalchi, and Veronica Ambrose. A special thank-you to literary agent Farley Chase (a foreign rights superhero) and the lovely Kate McLennan in London.

And thanks to all my family and friends whose patience I certainly tried while writing this novel! Special thanks to my very own Prince Charming, who listened to me babble endlessly about magic, brought me flowers when I was under tight deadlines, and took me out for Louisiana-style crawfish to celebrate the completion of drafts. I love you, Jas!